since you've been gone

Keep up with Anouska Knight at

www.Facebook.com/AnouskaKnightAuthor

www.Twitter.com/AnouskaKnight

And watch for more exciting books by Anouska, coming soon!

ANOUSKA KNIGHT

since you've been gone

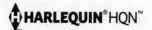

Recycling programs
for this product may
not exist in your area.

ISBN-13: 978-0-373-77928-4

SINCE YOU'VE BEEN GONE

Copyright © 2013 by Anouska Knight

This edition published by arrangement with Harlequin Books S.A.

For questions and comments about the quality of this book, please contact us
at CustomerService@Harlequin.com.

Printed in U.S.A.

For my boys, who I love more than snow.

chapter 1

It was supposed to be a day off. He'd promised me he wouldn't be gone long. He just needed to check that the lads were behaving themselves, staying safe; he didn't want to be writing up any more incidents of severed anythings for a while, and that meant keeping on top of them. I'd promised to make his favourite—lemon-and-basil linguine—and he'd promised to be home on time, before it had chance to spoil.

It didn't look appetizing now anyway. I looked down at the cool congealed mess of pasta I'd been pushing around the plate in front of me and tried not to feel abandoned. I automatically set my knife and fork neatly on top, handles parallel in the four o'clock position as was appropriate for a meal finished, and wondered again why the hell I bothered.

Table manners were one of those ironies, superfluous to those who for the most part ate with company who really didn't care whether elbows were on the table or not.

My mother, Pattie, had drilled them into us when we were kids, and would be less than impressed to see her little girl roughing it out over the breakfast bar instead of using any one of the twelve redundant dining chairs. Catching wind of how often I ate over the sink would be enough to trigger her mouth to twitch.

The tick of disapproval—I'd seen that a few times.

We all knew that my mother had endured a life of discomfiture, not *quite* able to keep up with her friends on my father's average income. She loved him, we knew that, too—how could she not?—but my mother hadn't resisted overcompensating by raising Martha and me as though we were enrolled in some sort of finishing school, prepping us for the best chances of bagging ourselves a lawyer or doctor—anyone, in fact, with means. She thought little girls should be ladylike, grow up to find husbands who could provide them with a good standard of living, therefore guaranteeing their happy ever after.

But I know all about those.

With my sister, Mum's strategy had largely stuck, although Martha had been deft enough to find a lawyer with a big heart. But when I'd first seen Charlie, loading logs onto his boss's truck, sun-kissed forearms flexing from underneath his forest-issue jacket, and absolutely no concept of how attractive he was, I knew right then who my table manners were for.

Mum had warned me that Charlie was rough around the edges; *unrefined*, she'd said, with too much charm for his own good. That twenty-five was too young to get married—to a forester at least—and that it would all end in tears.

She'd been right. Charlie had a lot to be sorry for these days.

I watched as flecks of basil cemented themselves to the plate in front of me.

I needed to call my parents.

I hadn't spoken to them for nearly three weeks and I was supposed to keep them updated on the size of Martha's ankles. Being twenty-seven didn't afford me much respite from my mother's rightness, but thankfully the three-hour flight between the UK and their retirement home on Minorca did.

The stool wobbled from under me as I slid from it and rounded the breakfast bar, plonking my things into the left of two adjacent Belfast sinks. We'd gone for his-and-hers, Mr Jefferson and I. Largely because I couldn't stand it when Charlie barged into the kitchen with an armful of muddy veg, and partly—quietly—because there was an element of charm having two sinks sat side by side in front of the best view in the house. Those are the kinds of uncharacteristic decisions you make when you're love-drunk. That blissful time before the tears arrived.

I looked for more washing up on the worktops while water thrashed into the sink over the handful of items I'd deposited there. It was six forty-five.

Where is he? I wondered, squirting a generous dose of washing liquid into the steaming bowl. I'd called dinner already.

There was still no sign of him outside as I plunged my hands into the hot suds. The skin between my fingers was starting to get a little sore. I could invest in a pair of Marigolds but my hands were washed so many times at the cake shop it seemed pointless to bother with gloves at home.

Martha said I'm the only person she knows who actively opts to use the sink over the dishwasher. Martha's the only person I know who actively opts to teeter precariously on heels at eight months pregnant, indifferent to the fact her ankles are now as wide as her knees. She's tried to convince me of the benefits of heels—elongation of the leg, posture, femininity in general—just as I've tried explaining to her that unless we're having guests for dinner it would take me a week to fill the dishwasher. Besides, this view across the valley is more than worthy of the occasional chapped hand.

When we'd first bought our half of the farmhouse from

Mrs Hedley next door, we widened this window for just that reason. A stunning view through the side face of the cottage, out across the gentle fall of our lawns to the blue-black waters of the reservoir.

You can see every colour nature has to offer through that window, helped no end by Charlie's weakness for planting the foreground with every bulb, shrub and tree he could get away with. When we'd started renovating the cottage he'd concentrated on planting the grounds, so that while the two of us battled it out over room colours, the gardens would all the while be growing.

Eventually, I had to start hiding his wallet during the garden centre's opening hours. It lives in my dresser now with other important, useless things.

I realised now, I'd nagged him too much.

I snatched my hand free as scalding water I hadn't anticipated stung at the back of it, then resumed my surveillance through the glass. The lawns needed cutting. Long grass growing tall against legs of rusting garden furniture.

Where is he? I asked myself again.

I had a straight view down onto half of the reservoir, the rest obscured by the small copse of trees and bushes Charlie had lobbed the tops from after our last big row. Chainsaws were an unusual way to relieve tension, but it had worked for him and the trees were already nearly back to the same height. If I had to bet on it, I'd say my wayward company was over there somewhere.

He couldn't be far but he'd obviously found something far more interesting than my chicken and pasta. Maybe he was sore at me; I'd shouted at him this morning. It was the second time he'd left me to eat alone this week, but I wasn't going to let my meal go cold while I stood on the doorstep hollering like a fishwife. If he wanted to eat his later, fine, but if he kept this up he'd be eating out of tins.

I'd been less than three minutes at the sink and the dishes were done. Martha would never be convinced, but we'd always been different. The picture sat on the sink windowsill testified to that.

My hair had been longer when the photo was taken, but the panic attacks had been easier to manage once I'd hacked off my loose straggly curls. Long hair was an avoidable hindrance when struggling for breath in bed at night.

Further down the kitchen the air was warmer where the earlier light had streamed into the room; Charlie had created a sun-trap here between the two cream bookcases he'd built perpendicular to the window seat. This was where he chose to eat breakfast every morning, with the sun on his back and the dog somewhere near his feet.

Charlie's mum had said that the one-hundred-and-eighty-degree views from the kitchen across all of the gardens would come in very handy when her grandchildren started to arrive. Particularly if they were anywhere near as naughty as their father. Naughty children weren't the problem here.

The side doors clicked open and I stepped out into the garden. "Dave? *Dave?* Last call, big guy." A handful of birds skittered from the tops of the trees Charlie had attacked. He was coming. I could see him now, galumphing his way up the hill.

He was one ugly creature. A blundering spectacle of pale brown fur as he ran up the embankment towards me, his whole face flying in every direction as the black of his dewlap momentarily defied gravity.

He reached my feet and lolloped back onto his haunches, tail thumping against the ground.

"Hi, Dave." Dave huffed a response. "You're late for dinner." I scowled.

He didn't seem repentant as I followed him into the house.

I kicked my boots off in the hall to the sounds of him inhaling the chicken I'd left for him, making it halfway up the stairs before the phone rang below me.

I knew it would be Martha, calling to check which roast she should make for us Sunday. I didn't want to stay for lunch, but so far I hadn't worked out what my excuse was going to be.

The phone rang on, pricking my conscience. It might not be lunch. It could be the baby. My hand made a play for the handset when the answerphone cut in.

"Hi, you've reached the Jeffersons' money pit. We can't get to the phone right now—I'll be hanging from a stepladder somewhere, and Holly will be out begging our friends to come help us. Leave a message."

"Hol? It's me. I was just wondering if you'd like lamb on Sunday? Or chicken? I think we have chicken, too. If you prefer? Why aren't you home yet? Call me when you get home. Okay, love you. 'Bye."

Dave joined me at the foot of the stairs. "Now you want to keep me company? Stand me up for dinner but happy to watch me take a shower?" Dave didn't answer.

The bare timber treads were hard underfoot as I made my way back upstairs, but there were benefits of having no carpets or wallpaper yet, like not having to worry when two hundred pounds of mastiff shadowed you around the house.

Dave made himself comfortable on the bathroom tiles while I hopped under the steaming jets of the shower. Clouds of icing-sugar dust had left their usual residue all over me. Sugar seemed to cling to skin as it did to teeth.

Bugger.

I'd forgotten to buy a new toothbrush today. Mine had become steadily more and more feathered next to its neighbour over at the sink, which I'd told my sister was a spare. I could buy one before work in the morning, or I could bring mine back from Martha's after the weekend. If I remembered. I'd been so tired lately. I'd be sleepwalking again by November.

Dave was snoozing peacefully when I stepped from the steam. The air was cool on my damp shoulders when I crossed the landing to my bedroom. I quickly dried off and wriggled into my favourite baseball tee and sweats. It was too early to go to bed yet—just looking at it reminded me of the trouble I was having in that department, if *trouble* was the right word for it. It came in waves, I'd realised, and while I could do without the tiredness I was desperate to enjoy another visit from him tonight. I didn't want to jinx anything so I'd stick with the formula that had seemed to work lately and slip into bed around ten.

Killing time had become a compulsion. Minutes, weeks… now years. I could find something to do for a couple of *hours*, the meagre pile of ironing that had been sat on my dresser would do. I fished out a few hangers from the wardrobe and began squeezing more clothes in there. A second wardrobe was one of the things we'd never got around to. I straightened up the garments I'd disrupted and scanned the perfect uniformity of Charlie's side of the hanging rail. How did dust even get into wardrobes? Was it some sort of domestic phenomenon? I pulled a few items out for closer inspection. Charlie's summer jacket, Charlie's winter coat, Charlie's shirt, Charlie's shirt, Charlie's shirt. I blew the unloved items in my arms free of their dustings, trying not to let the resentment bubble up in me so close to bedtime. But it was always there, lurking just under the surface, waiting for its chance of escape.

Yes, Charlie Jefferson. You have a lot to be sorry for.

chapter 2

I didn't want it to stop.

It was perfect. The perfect choreography of his need pulsing with my own, grinding in against my hungering body. I'd missed this. I'd missed this so much. Somewhere in the distance, I knew we were against the clock, but it was a warning I pushed away. We were here now and that's all that mattered.

He'd come.

Everything I had, every thirsty nerve ending desperate for his touch, I could feel him with, taste him with, but it wasn't enough. I needed more, more of this delicious euphoria. Goose bumps raged over me every time his breath chilled the thin film of sweat on my skin, the sweet earthy scent of him swelling around me with every delectable thrust, the saltiness of his neck inviting me to taste him again—I wanted to drink it all down, to gorge myself with everything of him I was being allowed.

Charlie found his rhythm and locked in on me. I let him. The slick covering of sweat we had each bestowed upon the other the only relief in what would otherwise be a crushing frenzy of need. I didn't care. I wanted it to reign over me like an insatiable creature, to devour me, to gorge itself on us both and force us harder into one another until the lines between our writhing bodies were no more.

I used the hard press of the wall behind me to defy him, to remain unyielding to all that strength as he forced himself into me, again and again. I managed to pull my head away from him, away from all that reward my senses so wanted, so that I could better see the face that had changed my world.

I couldn't hold myself away for long. My hands were already reaching up to slide desperate fingers through the short ruffle of his hair, to grab what I could and take hold of all that dark splendor before pulling his head far enough away to reveal those arresting blue eyes.

He was so beautiful, a perfect combination of light and dark, in all things. From his character to his features, he was the best of both extremes. His pale eyes were staggering against the near-black chestnut of his hair and depending on his mood could hold all the warmth of a Bahamian lagoon or the foreboding of a frozen lake.

He looked back to me now, those eyes the colour of ice water as they burned voraciously at me. He made my breath catch in my throat as though it wasn't supposed to be there— not looking at me but into me, to the promise of the gratification I would give him. I knew from those eyes that only dark thoughts were governing Charlie now, and it excited me.

The first wave of warmth began to build in me, deep and low. It chased all threads of cohesiveness away and I broke eye contact, searching the air around him for any sign of the next moment my pleasure would find me out again. He responded to the shift in my breathlessness as though he could smell the change creeping its way through me.

Another roll, building and building below…warm between my legs, spreading outwards through that part of me and up through my core, towards my breasts, to my neck, where Charlie's hands chased it. It was coming to claim me. The thought of it overpowering me, sweeping me away on a torrent of pleasure, was enough to send me spiralling into its grasp. I struggled to keep rhythm with him now. The choreography was gone as we neared the final act that would see us both explode into our sweet trembling crescendo. I wanted to share it with him, for him to see in my eyes what he did to me, but Charlie was in his own fight, his broad shoulders tense around me as he thundered fiercely through me harder and faster and—

I lost my hold on his hair and felt my body being yanked away from him, away into my ocean of pleasure. I wanted to drown in all that sensation, again and again and again, but not without him. *He has to come, too!* Desperately I raked my fingers along the centre of his back, down the tanned musculature he'd unintentionally honed through years of working in the forest, and finally, I succumbed to all that he'd offered me.

The last thing, the only thing, I heard besides the frantic labouring of our lungs, was my name on his lips.

Holly…

Cold realisation.

Morning is the cruellest time of the day. Between the hours of 5:00 and 8:00 a.m., grief and remembrance live.

Cruelty's not confined to those hours. If only that were the case I could just engineer my sleep pattern to skip the daily ordeal, but the truth is any part of the day can be as crushing when you wake on the battle line between dreams and reality, only to find you're always standing on the wrong side.

I clamped my eyes shut before they tried to find the clock

on the dresser, burying myself back beneath my duvet to savour the last echoes of my dream. *Sleep, Holly…get him back.*
But even thinking pulled him away.

Charlie had died two days after his twenty-seventh birthday.
It had been twenty-two months since I'd last felt his touch,
and five minutes since I'd last heard his voice.

chapter 3

The cake sitting downstairs was not the sort of thing an eighty-year-old lady should be looking at. I needed it out of the house and in the van, before Mrs Hedley, our neighbour, could poke her head out of her front door.

It took minutes to throw my clothes on and run a brush through my hair before loosely pinning it back in a scruffy bun. I liked scruffy buns. I liked anything that began with *scruffy*. Easier, quicker, done. Dave watched me as I applied a touch of powder in the mirror of the dresser, disguising the signs under my eyes of my recent sleepless nights. I'd savoured last night, every precious second I'd had with Charlie, but I still looked washed out.

I slipped on a pair of navy ballerina pumps, shut Dave up in the kitchen, grabbed my things and the cake and crept out over the gravelled path. I shouldn't really be wearing jeans to deliver to a stately home, but they were indigo and it had got dark as I'd changed. If I was lucky I'd just be in and out and my clothing would remain irrelevant. I was also delivering outside of shop hours, and at nearly eight o'clock on a Friday night, they were lucky I wasn't in pyjamas.

The darkness of the yard made avoiding Mrs Hedley a little easier, and getting the cake safely into the back of the van a little more perilous. Peril was the name of the game when it came to delivering cakes and a van as old as my dad didn't help that.

I'd just clicked my belt into place when Mrs Hedley opened her door and waved to me across the yard.

As soon as I wound down the driver's window, I instantly regretted it. You could roll the thing down all right—it was getting it to slide back up again that was the trick.

"I'm just popping out, Mrs Hedley. I'll only be an hour or so. Don't worry when you see the lights coming back up the track," I called. As if. We were secluded here but Mrs Hedley was the scariest thing in these parts.

She continued waving, so I started driving, steadily over the dirt track towards the main road, fighting all the way with the jammed handle.

It had never worked. We had Charlie's truck to use between us, but I needed something for deliveries. I had my eye on a nice clean little utility van, but Charlie said I needed something to help my business stand out from the crowd. Those innocent blue eyes of his had made easy work of convincing me that a Morris Minor was the best van for me. It was a cartoon of a vehicle, in deep burgundy with *CAKE!* emblazoned on both sides in bold gold lettering. I must have been mental. Cakes needed suspension. This van did not have suspension.

After five minutes of crawling my way steadily over the stones and divots of the track, I finally made it onto the smooth of the road. It was a straight run to Hawkeswood Manor Hall, about half an hour's drive from the cottage, less if I didn't detour around the forest. Which I would. I didn't use that road anymore, not since flowers had appeared tied to the trees.

Once out on the road, I relaxed, as the ride became a much easier one. Smoother, but definitely not much faster. Charlie had said that not managing more than fifty before the engine started screaming in protest was all part of the van's charm. Charm had a lot to answer for around these parts. The van was just one more in a long line of Charlie's daft ideas, like adopting a dog who ate more than we did, and driving into work on his day off when he should have been eating breakfast with his wife.

A car approached from the other direction, giving me a chance to check the cake when the headlights fell across the van. There were no streetlights here as the forest began to thicken out along the roadside.

All good so far, Hawkeswood was about another fifteen minutes away.

At the week's start, Jesse and I had just begun the Monday-morning ritual of divvying up jobs for the days ahead when the first customer of the week, a Mrs Ludlow-Burns, had walked into Cake.

"Testicles," she'd said tartly from the other side of the counter, "on a plate. If you're up to the job?" Her cool grey eyes had deviated then, first inspecting the displays around her, then giving all of Jesse's six-foot-something a considered once-over. Jess, wide and athletic, had towered over the woman, but despite the pearls and tweed she was by far the more intimidating of the two. Outside, a chauffeur had stood waiting dutifully beside a Bentley, which shone more violently than the sun. "And I'd like for them to be large," she'd added, holding up two gloved hands to make her point.

"Human?" I'd asked. It was all I could think to say.

She'd gone on to produce a pristine shoebox, *Dior* set in

gold against the crisp white of the lid, inside a pair of brand-new black patent-leather peep-toe heels, as shiny and new as the Bentley.

Jesse's sister was as shoe-crazy as mine, and knowing what the shoes had probably cost, he'd made the mistake of complimenting the customer on them.

"They're not mine," she'd snapped at him. "I've *never* worn an open-toe heel. Open-toes are for sluts."

A cake in the shape of a delicate male region wasn't the weirdest request we'd had in Cake, but customers weren't usually so...*aggressive.*

We were instructed to put one of the shoes, specifically the heel, right through the thick of a testicle. She said she wanted the cake to look painful. *Like marriage.*

She'd been a particular woman, used to things a certain way, no doubt. Even the delivery had its own set instruction— the cake had to be at Hawkeswood Hall, eight-thirty sharp, where a Mr Fergal Argyll was to sign for it personally. *Not* a member of the house staff, but Mr Argyll himself. I'd had the distinct impression Mr Argyll wasn't a very popular man; this cake didn't exactly look celebratory.

I felt into the top of my bag for the delivery sheet. No signature from Fergal Argyll would mean I forfeit the remaining half of the money, a condition Jess had told me I shouldn't have let her bully me into. I'd reminded him that with the summer wedding season drawing to a close we could do with more cash in the till.

"Don't worry, Fergal will like you," she'd said, looking us both over. "But I wouldn't send your friend here. They'll eat *him* alive."

I looked at Jess and wondered what she had meant by that. From the cornrows peeping out from under his beanie to his size-twelve high-tops, he didn't look like someone who couldn't take care of himself. But then, he'd certainly look out of place at Hawkeswood—we both would.

"Madam…your shoes!" I'd called after her as she'd strode out through the door.

"Keep them." She'd smiled coldly. "The slut will have to source her footwear elsewhere from now on."

The van growled as I tried to shift from third to fourth again. It stuck sometimes, and you had to double-pump the clutch. There was no place for heeled shoes in my life. I'd got married in wellies, the one day of the year, Martha had vehemently told me, I was *traditionally obliged* to make an effort with my footwear. So I did, and bought myself a brand-new pair of Hunters to match Charlie's. Mum's lip had twitched at least twice over their appearance in the wedding photos.

Between the glow of burning lanterns Hawkeswood Manor Hall was regally announced with a sweeping gated entrance off the main road. It wasn't usually all lit up like this. There must be some kind of function on tonight. Figured. Where there's a cake there was usually a function to go with it. I took the bend slowly so as not to jostle the delicate consignment in the back. I'd modelled the Dior shoe, a near enough perfect likeness for the real deals left behind in the shop. Jesse had made the main body of the cake, seeing as he had more physiological understanding of that area.

The van began to judder violently and I felt a flush of momentary panic. As if this van needed cattle grids to negotiate.

Finally, smoothly, the approach led me through opposing stone pillars and into Hawkeswood's courtyard. The intricate detailing of the Gothic priory before me was stunning, set in the warm glow of numerous uplights nestled in grassed borders. There was something special about Hawkeswood, something more than just its beauty. It wasn't the grandest place I'd seen, although it was certainly grand, but it differed from other stately homes I'd visited. It was lived-in, and there was something about a home that a venue simply couldn't emulate. Life maybe. Not just in its Sunday best.

I parked at the end of a row of cars, and pulled my phone from my bag. I had a little while yet—it was only a quarter past—so I sat wrestling the window back into place.

There was movement underneath the archway of the main entrance vestibule, where a young guy appeared leaning casually against the wall beside him. He looked over at me sat in the front of the van, and it was enough to make me leave the window until he looked away again. I went back to watching the time on my phone until a shock of red drew my eye back to him.

The woman looked as though she'd just stepped from a movie screen, a Nordic goddess dripping in elegance and a blood-red evening gown Martha would die for. She was stunning. No one would be looking at my clothes with women like her here; I could easily have gone with the PJs.

Her almost white-blonde hair was tied back from her neck in a bun, too, but it was far from scruffy. It was perfect. *She* was perfect. So striking, in fact, I was finding it hard not to look at her. If the man thought so, too, he was playing it very cool. The blonde lit herself a cigarette and leaned in towards him. I watched as he repositioned himself. A lovers' tiff maybe? Ah, well, we all had those, even the beautiful people it seemed. Hopefully they would move back inside before I had to haul the cake in past them both.

Eight-twenty. I'd just sit here quietly, then, minding my own business for a few more minutes.

Eight-twenty-three and they were *still* there, her still drawn to him, him still reluctant.

An absurdly loud and rigorous ringing cut through the hush in the courtyard. It made me jump out of my skin and the dream couple both snapped their heads around to stare at the source of the racket, blaring from my open window. "Damn it, Martha," I hissed, frantically trying to hit the right button, any button, to shut the noise off.

"Hello?"

"Hol, where are you? I've been ringing," she said, relief in her voice.

"I'm working, Martha. Where's the fire?" I glanced over at the couple under the archway. The goddess threw her cigarette and stalked back inside. The boyfriend was still looking on.

"No fire. I was just worried when you weren't at home."

"I'm not always at home, Martha. I do have other things to fill my days, you know." We both knew that was a skinny truth. "Look, I'll call you when I'm home. I'll be about an hour? Don't freak out until at least ten o'clock, okay?"

"Okay," she said, and already I felt guilty.

"Okay, love you."

"Love you, 'bye."

The call ended and, thankfully, the boyfriend had gone.

The doors into the lobby were left open, revealing a grand welcome to the manor with timber panelling to the walls and a huge staircase climbing at least two floors above me. An attractive brunette somewhere around fifty approached me with a smile. Her smart white blouse and black pencil skirt suggested she was staff of some sort.

"Hello, may I help you?" she said.

"Hi, yes. I have a delivery for Mr Argyll."

The cake was too tall to use the box lid, and her smile faltered when she caught sight of the cake.

"Oh!" she exclaimed. "And which Mr Argyll is expecting *this*?"

"I was asked to deliver it at eight-thirty sharp to a Mr Fergal Argyll." I smiled.

The lady nodded. That made sense to her.

"Well, Mr Argyll's in the games room, just through the double doors at the end of this corridor if you'd like to go through. Let me take your bag for you, dear. You have enough to carry."

I wasn't sure why I'd brought the bag in with me. It was unlikely anyone here would want to break into the van for it.

"Thank you. I just need to get the delivery sheet for Mr Argyll," I said, rummaging through my bag.

"Well, I can sign that for you," she offered.

"Oh, that's okay. Mr Argyll needs to sign for it in person."

The hallway was long, giving me more time to fathom how I was going to open the heavy double doors when I reached them. A nervous-looking gentleman in a dull suit stepped through one of the doors, hurriedly stepping into the hallway.

"Could you hold the door, please?" I asked, before he could scurry off. The gentleman obliged, allowing me and my armful of cake to slip through unobstructed into the hubbub of the voices on the other side.

"Good luck," he declared in an educated voice as the door closed between us.

Inside, I found myself standing in a room every bit as impressive as any I'd been in, bedecked with richly illustrated tapestries and wallpapers hanging against the warm tones of even more antique panelling. At the far end of the room a huge stone fireplace took up most of the wall there, others occupied by row upon row of books. It was a library-cum-games room, and smelled as it looked: cozy, old and vibrant. Charlie would have gone nuts for a room like this.

None of the twenty or thirty men, most in formal dress, slowed from their card games as I fumbled the cake onto the nearest surface. Laughter throbbed around me, along with cigar smoke and general merrymaking. This was very definitely a boys' club, not a place for girls.

Which one is Fergal Argyll? I wondered, scanning the room for a face to match the name, or maybe the cake. Over at the fireplace, the colour of danger caught my attention again. The only other woman in the room, the goddess's presence put me at ease instantly. I looked at her across the smoke and laughter, and smiled that smile of sisterhood women have for one another. She lifted her chin and looked away, and like that I was on my own. I watched as she waltzed past her admirers to the loudest gentleman in the room.

He was raucously shouting at his fellow card players, rising to his feet when the goddess–cum–ice maiden approached his table.

"Watch out, boys, here's ma lucky charm," he declared in a gentle Scottish accent. His hand rested where her gown dipped at the small of her back. He was handsome, in his jacket and kilt, and suited the vibrancy of his surroundings. I'd put him somewhere around the fifty mark, although something about him seemed both younger and older.

The ice maiden accommodated him with a smile and then looked over at me, her gaze leading his.

"What do we have here?" he asked. "Another gift from the dragon, perhaps?"

It was him. It had to be. "Mr Argyll?" I said.

"At your service, sweetheart. What can I do for ye?" His short, neatly cropped greying beard gave him the look of a laird, whilst darker hair falling forward over serious eyes were more the edge of a backstreet boxer.

"I have a delivery for you. Could you sign here, please?"

Argyll approached the table and peered down at his cake.

The boom of his laughter made me jump for the second time tonight.

"I take it this is te celebrate ma divorce papers?" he asked, a look of contentment in his dark eyes. "I have te hand it te her," he said. "She's got a streak, all right, that woman. Have a look at this, boys," he growled heartily, grabbing the cake from its box and spinning it around to show his company. "She always told me I got by not on the size of ma brain, gentlemen, but on the size of ma balls!"

He turned from his audience of dinner jackets and rested serious eyes heavily on me. He was a handsome man, if not flamboyant, and smelled of a heady mix of cigar smoke and brandy.

"You, miss, have got the size of me about right." He grinned, looking to the pair of testicles in his hands.

"Glad you like them, Mr Argyll. Would you mind signing for them?"

He put the cake back down on the table next to us and I held my pen out for him. His eyes still hadn't left mine.

"Ye don't look convinced, darlin'. Here…let me prove it to ye." I watched him cock his head, smiling, before my brain could register what was coming next. The ice maiden disappeared from view as Argyll's kilt rose high into the air between us. His beard wasn't the only thing greying. My eyes darted upwards, focusing on his huge hands. He had worker's hands, years of hard graft ingrained in the set of his knuckles, like Charlie's and my dad's.

It was time for me to leave.

I left the delivery sheet alongside the cake and calmly turned for the way out. I didn't need Mrs Ludlow-Ballbreaker's money that badly. Jesse would have to lump it.

The ice maiden's boyfriend stood watching, his eyes following as I crossed the room towards him. I hadn't felt enough embarrassment to blush until I saw him watching me closely. It was no wonder Fergal Argyll was so sure of himself—judging by his son, he must have had a youth full of women clamouring for his attention.

A Scottish accent followed me out through the doors, slipping from the mouthful of cake Argyll was chomping on. "No wonder the ladies love me, boys. I never knew I tasted so good!" It was safe to smile here. I was nearly out.

Charlie would have laughed his ass off. He gravitated towards men like Argyll, Jack-the-lads with big personalities.

The entrance lobby was deserted when I made it there. I should have just left my bag in the van. I peeked around the staircase, listening for signs of life. Nothing. Behind me, I heard the doors to the games room open and close again. I didn't look, not even when heavy certain steps grew slowly closer.

Daintier taps of a woman's feet came at me from the opposite side.

"Did you find him?" she asked. You had to love house staff—they were just so efficient.

"Hi, again. Yes, thanks. Could I get my bag, please?"

"Ah, of course. Just a minute, dear." And the friendly lady disappeared again.

Argyll junior had moved casually along the hallway and settled himself against one of the decorative pillars near the foot of the staircase. He was sharply dressed in a well-cut dark grey suit, his ice-white shirt unbuttoned at the neck. He was sharp, all right, but less formally so than his father, and every bit as certain it seemed.

I tried not to fidget as I waited for my bag's return.

"Working late?" He was being polite. I hadn't expected it.

"Yes." I smiled, knowing that it didn't quite reach my eyes. I let them fall away to the intricate tile work of the floor.

"I'm sorry if Fergal embarrassed you," he said in a smooth and certain voice that held only a fraction of his father's Celtic lilt. I smiled again. I used to feel more awkward about uncomfortable silences, but I'd survived a lot of them and I didn't feel the need to fill them the way others did.

"He gets carried away with cake." His eyes narrowed with the quip.

"He didn't mean any harm," I offered, looking off to the doors the lady had disappeared through.

"You're right—he doesn't," he said, pulling my eyes back to him again. His hair was a little longer on top than his father's, but fell forward slightly in nearly the same place.

Out here, without the clouds of cigar smoke, there was nothing to compete with the scent of the rich wooden panelling, the preparation of savoury foods somewhere off in the house and, over that, the subtle sweetness of the more polite Argyll's cologne. It wasn't like the bottle I slipped under Charlie's pillow every Christmas Eve, not quite so familiar. This had a sweeter edge to it, the difference between flowers and berries.

"Nice cake, by the way," he said, trying again for polite exchange. "I haven't seen one like that before." He smiled then— it was a good smile, but his didn't reach the eyes, either.

"Ciaran, your father's ready," the ice maiden purred, sashaying along the corridor to us. I hadn't heard the doors that time. This close I could see she'd made her blue eyes colder with smoky make-up.

"Here you go, dear." The friendly lady smiled, approaching us again.

"Thank you…. Good night." I smiled, taking my bag from her.

"Good night," Ciaran Argyll called as I reached the cool of the evening air outside.

I looked back over my shoulder to the perfect couple and gave him an acknowledging smile.

Moving into him, to mark her territory, the ice maiden gave me nothing.

chapter 4

I couldn't feel the bite of the freezing waters around me, only the urgency to swim further out into them. He was here—I knew that—waiting for me to find him. To bring him home.

Behind me on the jetty, the life ring hung idly against the timber post. Why hadn't I brought it with me? A sensation of unease deep in my chest tried to dig a foothold.

"Come on, Hol! Catch up, it's warmer here!" Charlie laughed, water sloshing against his face. The unease disappeared.

"I'm coming! Hang on!" I laughed, trying not to splutter. It wasn't easy swimming and laughing at the same time, but Charlie managed.

Over the sounds of water, slipping in and out of my ears, another voice found its way to me.

"Holly! Holly, come back!" Martha and Dave were on the jetty. She'd thrown the ring into the reservoir but it bobbed around without validation. I threw my hands above myself and waved at her.

"It's okay, Martha! We're just swimming! Look, I found

him! I found Charlie!" I turned back to see if Charlie had waited for me, but he was twice the distance away now. Still laughing.

"Charlie! Wait!" I called, the unease digging down again.

"Holly!" Martha called worriedly. *Can't she see? I'm with Charlie.*

"Charlie? *Charlie?*" The unease became heavier, like lead in my chest. *"I can't see you. I can't see you, Charlie!"*

"Holly?" Martha called, but I was swimming away from her.

"Come on, Hol," Charlie called, "catch me up!" I'd found him but he was further away again.

"Wait for me, Charlie. You're too fast!" I called, but still he swam. *Why won't he give me a chance?*

Martha's voice grew nearer.

"Holly? Holly?"

Swim harder, Holly. You can get there.

"Holly? Holly honey, wake up."

Martha was gently rocking me, concern etched into her face. My heart was still thudding, not realising the trickery yet.

"I'm awake," I whispered. *Please go now.* I could still get to him. He was still there, still within reach. I wasn't ready to give him up yet, not ready to accept the day.

"Are you okay, honey?"

Already I could feel him slipping. Now I'd never get him back.

I'd expected more dreams; it was coming up to that time. But not those ones. Not like the dreams that had plagued me last year.

That was when I'd stopped drinking with the girls. So that I wasn't spending my weekends waking up after midday not only with a hangover, but fewer hours to pull myself together again. It's hard enough nursing an aching heart; an aching head helps nothing.

Don't cry. You'll upset Martha. Be grateful.

"Hol? Were you having a nightmare?" I didn't think she would go, stationed eternally on the jetty.

In place of my self-imposed ban on girly nights, Martha instigated a nonnegotiable scaled-down version. For the two years since the accident, Saturday nights had been dedicated to the emotional well-being of her kid sister. She didn't realise that staying here every week, eating with her and Rob, sleeping in their guest room—it didn't take the edge off my loneliness as she hoped it would. It defined it.

"Hey. No, I'm good." I sent her the lie with a smile. It worked and she sent one back. I preferred Martha with her dishevelled morning look. Before she perfected her make-up for the day and set her hair flawlessly in place, she was the most beautiful girl I knew I'd see all day. But it was pointless telling her. I'd heard Dad try when Mum was out of earshot. Gilding a lily, he'd called it.

Really, she didn't need to gild anything. Martha had inherited all the good stuff, which was probably for the best as it would have been wasted on me. She had a respectable inch on my five-foot-six—that was without the heels—her eyes were more decisive as to the shade of hazel they wanted to be and she was bestowed our mother's rich blonde waves. I, on the other hand, had taken after our lovely dad—less polished and less blonde, with that not-quite-brown, not-quite-blonde colouring that could have been either had I'd ever decided which way to go with it.

But despite our differences, and the things I kept hidden from her, there was no question that we were tight.

Martha was a good sister, the best even. But this staying over every Saturday night was really about her emotional well-being more than it was mine. She needed to feel that she was doing some good, and I loved her enough to go each week as a spectator in her blossoming family life. It was the least I could do for her, since she lost Charlie, too.

"Rob's making breakfast," she chirped. "He's breaking the big guns out. Full English?" I wasn't a breakfast person, but Martha was hell-bent on taking care of me for the entirety of the time she was allocated each week. She was weeks away from giving birth to their first child and, happy as I was for them, I couldn't help but think of my impending niece or nephew as a welcome distraction. Maybe then I could have breakfastless Sunday mornings in my own home again.

"Sure."

Downstairs at the breakfast table Rob had spared no efforts in his quest to fatten me up. He was just shovelling the last of the scrambled eggs onto an already mountainous pile when I bypassed him for the coffeepot.

"Morning, gorgeous," he said, busying himself with the next bubbling saucepan. "Beans or tomatoes? Or both? I'm having both."

"You are not. You've got enough on your plate already," Martha warned him.

Rob leaned into me and whispered, "She's got that right." I stifled a smile while Martha scowled at him. "What? I'm a growing boy. I need my energy," he protested.

"Rob, we aren't going to fit in the bed if you carry on."

Rob looked at his beautifully rotund wife and then threw me a collusive look.

"Sorry, my love. I'll tell you what. I'll have half a grape-fruit next Sunday morning instead. Hol will hold me to it, right, Hol?"

"You got it." I grinned into my mug. Martha made good coffee. "Anyone else have a headache this morning?" I asked, sitting down to survey the man-sized portion waiting for me. It smelled good, actually.

"Only from Rob's snoring. You two were the only ones drinking last night."

"Was that you snoring, Rob?" I asked, biting into a triangle of toast. "I thought someone was firing up a Harley outside."

Martha smiled over the top of her *Sunday Journal*.

"Do you want some ibuprofen?" she asked, already setting the paper down. It was pointless stopping her; she'd only fuss until I'd swallowed a few painkillers. "Didn't you sleep too well last night?"

"No, I slept fine." Memories of my dream made me wonder what Martha might have heard through the night while Rob snored on. *Change the subject.* "It's been a grueller in the shop this week. I'm probably just a bit highly strung. You know what it's like—as soon as you stop, it all piles on top of you." One of the reasons I kept myself busy.

"Yes, Martha was flapping when she couldn't get hold of you Friday night. How come you were working so late?" Rob said as he chewed his way through a sausage. It was difficult to look at Rob without smiling. He reminded me in some ways of Dave, a little obedient maybe, but loyal to the core and utterly dependable. They were the gentle giants in my life, but whilst Martha's tolerance flexed for her husband, it didn't stretch to Dave. I guess Rob slobbered less. Just.

"I had to deliver to a *gentlemen's* evening, over at Hawkeswood."

"Oh, yeah?" Rob mumbled, a forkful of hash browns meeting its doom.

"I use the term *gentlemen* loosely. Dave has better manners."

"Hawkeswood's the property tycoon's place now, isn't it, Martha?"

Martha settled back behind paper. "Hmm?"

"Hawkeswood. Didn't you do something there years ago with Parry and Fitch?"

Martha loved to talk about her work. It was a shame Parry & Fitch Interiors had to scale back, but the UK property market had taken a big hit over the last few years and most people we knew had been affected in one way or another.

"Did you, Marth? What did you do there? I only got as far as the games room and that was impressive."

Martha had taken voluntary redundancy, slipping into her new life as a domestic goddess with ease. But all that extra time meant she'd stepped up her attempts at finishing the decorating at my place.

"The games room was original while we were there. Did you see the orangery at the back of the main house? The views over the countryside are a-ma-zing. Who are the current owners?" she asked.

"The property tycoon, like I said. What's his name? Martha, what's his name? Andrews or—"

"Argyll," I helped, trying to reduce the stack of mushrooms.

"That's him—Argyll. He's been in some scrapes the last few years. I work with a chap who used to be with Scargill's. They represent his company... That's them, Argyll Inc. He keeps Scargill's in a steady stream of work." Rob shook his head and carried on his assault on the food.

Why did that not surprise me? "Is Fergal Argyll the head of the company?" I asked, reaching for more coffee.

"That's him. Fergal Argyll. He's the big dog. Worked the whole empire up from scratch and then nearly lost the lot. Do you remember, Martha?"

"He seems to be doing okay now," I said. "What *does* he do exactly?" I asked, struggling to understand how a man like Fergal Argyll would have built anything but a dodgy reputation.

Rob finally took a breather between mouthfuls. "They're a property company. I'm not sure, but I think he started out in construction. Small scale, extensions, that sort of thing, and then I think he got lucky and bought a bit of land while the prices were good. If I remember correctly, these days Argyll Inc. shoot for large-scale property investment, developments, that sort of thing. But as with most of the construction industry, they've had their pain over the last few years. Didn't he marry into the aristocracy for good measure, Martha?"

Martha lifted her nose from the paper, and gave Rob a considered look.

"The hunky playboy!" Martha yelped. "You mean this guy?" she said, shuffling through her paper. Martha split the paper open, revealing a small thumbnail of the young Argyll and the ice maiden.

"Yeah, that's him," I said, examining the picture. He was a handsome man, but there was a melancholy about him, and melancholy knew its own reflection. On the page opposite, computer-generated images of starter homes, soon to be built on recently sold forestland, made my stomach flip over.

"Hel-*lo*, Ciaran Argyll. He's *utterly* gorgeous, Hol, don't you think? A womanizer, but gorgeous. I can't believe that *they* live around *here*!"

Charlie had worked tirelessly to protect the forests from sale.

"Keep your knickers on, my love. I think your hormones are playing up."

Martha swatted Rob with her paper.

"Rob? I can't eat any more. Please may I be excused?" I asked wryly.

"Sure," he replied. "You're washing up."

"Er, you're washing up, Rob. You made the mess, you ate it, you're cleaning it. Hol and I are going to talk colour swatches." Martha lifted a handful of binders onto the table in front of her. Inwardly, I groaned. "So I was thinking, and feel free to say no, but—"

"No."

"You don't know what I'm going to say yet," she countered.

"I do…. You're going to say, 'Holly, it's nearly October, and then it will be Christmas, and before you know it, your lounge and hall and wherever will have been left whitewashed for nearly three years, and—'" The look on Martha's face was enough to stop me mid-flow. *Damn it, why can't you just leave this alone?*

Six months after the accident, she'd talked me into letting her finish the bedroom for me. She'd made a beautiful job of it, all soft greys and dusky blues against the deep stain of our antique furniture. She'd made my bedroom look as though it belonged to a boutique hotel. The problem was, Charlie had never been in that boutique hotel with me, and so I couldn't picture him in it. It wasn't our bedroom anymore; it was just mine. I couldn't tell Martha that was the reason for fobbing off her offers to decorate the rest of the house for me when she was so desperate to. It would have devastated her that I felt that way about the room she'd already finished for me.

"Look, Martha. I'd love you to come help me, but I'm absolutely rushed off my feet in the shop and—"

"Well, that's what I was going to say!" A smile filling her eyes again. "Rob has some time off before the baby's due, but I've already sorted everything out. I've decorated the nursery, put the crib together, packed my hospital bag, written my birth plan, A and B actually. I've even vetted both of the nurseries we're thinking of using."

"You're thinking of nurseries?" I said. "Already? When will the baby start nursery?"

"When they're three."

"Months? Are you going back to work?"

"No, years. Well, I want to be prepared, Hol."

I knew it. I'd always known it. My sister was a domestic android. "So, Rob can come and do some DIY-ing for you." I looked at Rob, who looked about as enthused as I was.

Lie, lie, lie.

"You know what, Martha, I would really love that. But I kinda have a more pressing problem, if you guys wouldn't mind helping me out?" I knew how to reel Martha in. I had a childhood's worth of practice under my belt. "The shop's due an inspection sometime in the new year, and it could really do with some TLC." Rob's face dropped. He thought we were a team. "Nothing drastic, just a few maintenance issues, maybe a little painting. It's just too big a job on my own. If you could spend a few days in the shop, Rob, I'd appreciate it."

Martha didn't look convinced—but then, Martha's sole wish was to do what she could for me and I was at least offering her an inch in place of her mile.

"Um, okay. But what about the house? I have some ideas I think you'll like, Hol."

The guilt twisted in my stomach.

"Well, let's see them, then! If Rob moves his ass quickly enough, we might get started on the back bedroom before Junior arrives." I could keep Rob busy at the shop for as long as I needed to. All I had to do was keep Martha sweet until the baby was born, then she wouldn't have the energy, or the inclination, to pimp my house anymore. That was my grand plan.

Martha, instantly gripped with excitement that I was showing interest in her ideas, left the kitchen for yet more magazines. Rob fixed beady knowing eyes on me.

"Don't worry, big guy. You can eat cake all day and we'll just splash a little paint on your face before we send you home."

chapter 5

Things were only going to get quieter until Christmas fever kicked in.

It was Monday, I was tired, and thanks to Dave's eating habits, I was late.

Jesse, reliable wingman that he was, had opened up and made a start on the freshly baked cupcakes and cookies we offered alongside the bespoke services. It wasn't big money but it was consistent, and when the brides thinned out the lowly cupcake paid Jesse's wages and kept us going. We didn't open to the public until ten each day, largely because few people wanted to munch on cupcakes much before noon, but it also gave us a good three hours to get the fresh bakes out and on display, ready for the lunchtime rush.

There were only a handful of people milling around on the cobbled high street when I parked up and walked the hundred yards or so to Cake. I didn't like to park directly outside unless I needed to load up, preferring for passers-by to see the fantastical cakes Jesse and I had on display in the two huge windows. This morning, someone had already parked there anyway.

Hunterstone was a nice town. Too expensive to buy a house in, unless you were like Martha and Rob, but nestled halfway between the big city and the national park everything you could want was in reach. The castle pulled in a reasonable flow of tourists and the clean leafy Georgian streets housed a nice selection of eateries, galleries and shops to keep the tourists there a little longer.

We'd put a lot of effort into fixing up the shop, but the architecture of the building had helped make us the perfect place for a visit by beautiful brides between champagne dress fittings and floral consultations. Charlie had painstakingly finished painting cream all the fiddly nooks and crannies of the typically Georgian decorative facade after I'd got fed up with it. He'd also added the topiary outside, making our little shopfront every bit as tempting as the cakes inside. A swinging vintage sign was the only thing to throw off the symmetry of the frontage, declaring in burgundy and gold the nature of our business. Cake.

I skipped up the two stone steps to the doors and pushed my way in with a jingle overhead. It was already nearly eleven and Jesse would be about ready for a refuel. He ate more than Rob and never gained an ounce.

"Hey! I've got bagels and posh coffee," I called from the showroom as I threw a few new bridal magazines next to the sofa. I reached the counter and could already hear the drone of the mixers in the bakery out back. He wouldn't have heard me probably.

I took Jesse's breakfast through to where he was busily piping several trays of cupcakes in pale lilac butter cream, before finishing each one off with a sugar-frosted violet.

"They look great," I called, wiggling the warm paper bag

in my hand. Jess left the island worktop and moved over to shut off the mixer.

"Hey, Hol, how's Dave?" Jesse took the bag from me as I set the coffees down and hung my things in the far corner.

"He's okay—he has a bad tooth. I've left him moping in the garden. Mrs Hedley will throw him treats over the fence all day, no doubt." I wondered if that was part of the problem. She'd been the same with Charlie, making him second lunches when they thought I wasn't looking.

Jesse came over and started digging into the bagels as I slipped an apron over my head and started the first of a hundred hand-washes. I dried off and went to grab a bagel for myself but he pulled the bag away.

"You can't. You have a customer," he said, grinning at me.

"What customer? No one's booked in, are they?" I said, scanning the counters for the cake diary. We did the occasional wedding consultation in the mornings, but they were nearly always booked in for weekends when the mother of the bride was in town and the fiancé had no excuses not to attend.

"They are now. He's been here since I flipped the sign over."

"Oh, no, Jess, have I forgotten an appointment?" I said, with the first prickles of panic.

"No. He hasn't got an appointment," Jess said, still grinning.

"Why are you being weird?" I asked him, trying not to laugh at his ridiculous expression. "Where is he, then?"

I followed Jess as he walked from the bakery through the short corridor and out into the area behind the shop counter.

"He's over there, waiting for you to show up to work," Jesse said, looking out front.

I looked out through one of the windows over to the café across the street, glancing at the bistro tables outside for anyone I recognised. There were a couple of women in coats and shades enjoying the morning, but other than that no one. I was still watching when two business types, a man and woman, left the café together, followed by another sharply dressed guy in suit and shades. As he turned to check the road before crossing, I recognised the statuesque line of his jaw, passed down from one generation to the next.

"How *was* your weekend, Holly?" Jesse asked as it dawned on me who was heading this way.

I watched Ciaran Argyll draw closer as I tried to figure out what he was doing here.

"There must have been a problem with the cake," I thought aloud, readying myself for what might be. "I bet the old bugger wants to make a complaint because I didn't compliment him on his wedding tackle."

"Wedding tackle? What did you get up to this weekend, Hol?"

"Nothing," I answered, still pondering.

The door set the bell tingling and Ciaran Argyll walked assuredly into my shop. Jesse stopped munching on his bagel.

"Morning. Again," Argyll said, nodding at Jess standing over me. I got a gentle nod. "Hello."

"All right, mate? Enjoy your wait with the golden girls?" Jesse asked.

"Actually, the coffee was surprisingly good," Mr Argyll said, taking his sunglasses off. He didn't look so melancholy today; his smile was more relaxed than I'd remembered it. "But you were right. They did take care of me." He laughed, flashing a glimpse of perfect white teeth. I'd bet he was used to being taken care of.

"Ah, they love a gent over there, don't they, Hol? Hol stopped buying lunch from the café when she realised the old girls give better service to the fellas than the women. It's sexist, isn't it, Hol?" It sounded silly when I heard it that way, but yes, I was boycotting the place.

I flashed a full smile of my own at Jess.

"I'll just go and finish my brekkie, then. See you, mate," he said, leaving for the back. "Nice Vanquish."

Argyll turned to check the car sat outside the shop and nodded to himself.

"What can I do for you, Mr Argyll?" I asked, noting his cologne again. His hand dipped into the inside pocket of his jacket as he approached the counter between us.

"You left in a hurry Friday, understandably. You forgot this. I thought we at least owed you the courtesy of returning it," he said softly, pulling open a folded sheet of paper and handing it to me. I recognised the information immediately.

Two times ten-inch vanilla testicles gored with stiletto, deliver to Fergal Argyll, Hawkeswood Manor Friday 20th September 8.30 p.m. EXACTLY.

"Can I sign it for you? My father was a touch worse for wear over the weekend or I'd have asked him."

He'd brought the delivery note all this way?

"No, that's okay. It's not important, really," I said, realising too late that the delivery note had travelled some thirty miles back to the shop with this man. "But thank you for returning it."

His eyes were an intense brown, narrowing slightly as he tilted his head to watch me. He was a very attractive man, too good-looking all for just one person. My attention was snagged by the light flooding into the shop catching on the edges of his choppy hair, sending brown to blond in places. There was a hint of neatly cropped stubble I hadn't noticed on Friday.

I couldn't explain it, but I felt the beginnings of warmth creeping over my neck. Was I so out of practice interacting with the opposite sex that I blushed like a naive schoolgirl around them? How excruciatingly embarrassing.

"Are you sure?" he pressed, those eyes that didn't belong with the tones in his hair still watching me closely. "My step-mother can be quite the pedant when it comes to paperwork. And my father's anatomy."

Oh, dear, we were back onto Fergal's testicles. Yep. Definitely had a pink neck.

"Um, not really. She didn't hang around long," I said, trying to get off the subject of the vivacious Mr Argyll senior and any conversation that might lead me onto it.

"I believe Elsa offered you an additional sum for proof of delivery to Fergal in person?"

"She did. But it wasn't compulsory," I answered.

"Then you're out of pocket?" he asked, his eyes narrowing again. "Let me take care of that. It's not your fault my father was misbehaving. You shouldn't get into any trouble for it." He pulled a chequebook from the same inner pocket, laying it alongside his sunglasses on the counter.

"Would five hundred cover it?" he asked, clicking the cap of his pen. "I understand you were offered double the cost of the cake if you procured the signature? The cake was two-thirty, right? Consider the difference by way of an apology. Fergal can get...*excited*, sometimes," he said as his pen scratched against the chequebook.

"How do you kn—?"

"Toby's an old friend of mine. He helped me find you. Do you know there's no address on your delivery sheet?" he said, pausing to look at me again.

"The delivery sheets are just for our records...." I shrugged. "Toby?"

"Elsa's driver. He paid you for the cake. So shall we say five hundred, then?" Ciaran asked, waiting to scribble a final figure. These people… It was obscene how they threw their money around.

"Really, there's no need. It was all paid for."

He looked up at me from where he'd leaned in towards the oak surface Charlie had waxed five times before achieving the shade I liked. His left hand was flat against the wood as he stood poised over his chequebook. He didn't have worker's hands like his father. They looked softer than mine, with impeccably clean fingernails. No wedding band, either, but then, I didn't wear mine. The icing was always getting stuck underneath it, so I wore it instead on a chain around my neck, alongside Charlie's.

"That's very gracious of you," he said, "but don't you think you should run it past your boss first? Money's money, after all." I knew I was younger than the average for setting up on my own, but it always irked me when someone thought I was the run-around girl. Okay, so I was still doing a lot of running around, just not for anyone else. I'd done those jobs all through college and university. I may not have been sat on an empire, but I'd still earned my place on my own hillock.

"Is your boss around?" he asked.

Martha had filled me in on what had been written of the Argylls. Of Ciaran's fast living while his father footed the bill.

"Yes," I returned. "And that's very gracious of *you*, but don't you think you should run it past *your* boss first?"

Something in his face changed and I sensed that I'd hit a nerve. The chequebook slipped back into his pocket. For him, the son of a rich pest, it must have been like reholstering his weapon.

The smile was back again but I'd already seen the genuine version. This one was for show.

"So this is your business?" he asked, moving over to the glass display shelves nearest the counter.

"Sure is," I answered, knowing that I'd offended him.

I watched him as he looked over our array of summer designs. "And these are all real?" he asked, perambulating around the perimeter of the room.

"They're dummies," I said, watching him move as though wandering an art gallery. "We call them dummy cakes. They have a polystyrene core, and then we ice and decorate them for the displays."

"So then they're just for show?" he said, stopping and looking back to me.

"Just for show," I said.

He continued on his way over to the first window and crouched to look through the streets of the gingerbread village there.

"Did you make this?" he asked, not taking his attention from the miniature street scene. The intricately piped clock tower, and railway complete with train carriages and station house was the one thing that drew the interest of every boy, young and old, dragged in here by their mums, daughters and wives. Ciaran Argyll seemed no exception.

"Jesse and I, it's kind of a two-man job. One sticks, while the other holds in place."

He stood then, hovering by the door, as though unsure if he were leaving or not. "You're very talented." He had one hand on the brass handle. His eyes were strikingly dark, even from here.

"Thank you," I said, the warmth building again. I wished that I hadn't offended him. "And thanks for the sheet. I appreciate you bringing it back." I smiled as he pulled the door open. The bells jingled again.

"'Bye," he said softly.

"'Bye," I said, turning for the bakery.

Stepping out through the back, I heard the bells ring out again before the door clicked shut behind him. Jesse was hovering next to another batch of ninety-six cupcakes, which were waiting to be frosted. "If you've finished playing with Handsome, you've got some catching up to do," he teased.

"I was not playing with anybody." I pouted.

"But you don't deny that he's one handsome sucka."

"Did you just say *handsome sucka*? Is that the lingo these days, Jess?"

"Call it what you like. Did you see the man's motor?"

"No, Jess, I didn't see his car. What is it with you and shiny things? You're like a magpie," I teased, loading up another nozzled bag with butter cream.

"There's nothing wrong with appreciating the finer things in life, Hol, and that dude has got some fine things. His suit was sharp, too. Nice cut." I had noticed the suit. "So...who is he?"

"Are these ginger or treacle?" I asked, squeezing the lemon frosting to the end of the bag before twisting the top securely.

"Ginger and whisky. Well? Who's James Bond?"

I started to pipe a tangy lemony swirl onto a sticky ginger cupcake.

"Last Monday, the cake with the heel... Well, that was cake-man's son."

"Yeah? Well, he seemed a bit more chilled than the old girl was."

"I don't think it was him the cake depicted, Jess. His dad wasn't so calm."

"So what, was she James Bond's mum?"

"Stepmum. She wasn't there when I met his dad," I said, piping the next row of cakes.

"And what was Dad like? Loaded, I bet. Women like that don't marry outside their class."

I stopped swirling and tried to think of the word I'd use

to describe Fergal Argyll, a man very clearly in a class completely of his own.

"He was…*lively*. But harmless enough, I think," I said.

"So what was Junior doing here? *Was* there a problem with his old man's taters?"

I felt a smile eke across my face as I remembered how close I'd come to seeing the real thing. Yikes.

"I'm not sure, really. I think he came to smooth over any rucks."

"What kind of rucks?"

"The kind people with money are used to making go away with a chequebook." I finished the last row of gingers and set what was left in the piping bag down on the worktop. "I'm running out of room. I'm going to start getting these under the counters."

"I keep telling you, we need two more stainless workbenches, at least."

"After the oven, Jess. New oven takes priority over workbenches."

"So when are we getting the new oven?" he called after me.

"Soon! When we can afford to order it!"

I picked up the tray of cupcakes I'd just finished and carried them towards the shop. Before I reached the last doorway out of the bakery, I called back to Jess.

"You are right, though, Jess…. He is one *hell* of a handsome sucka." I was only playing, but it was nice to remind Jesse that even I could appreciate the finer-looking things in life. Just because I wasn't hungry didn't mean I'd forgotten how good food tasted.

Manoeuvring wide trays of cupcakes through the narrow doorway into the shop could be tricky, but that wasn't the reason I nearly dropped the entire batch.

"I forgot my sunglasses," Ciaran Argyll said, standing there watching me. The flush was back with a vengeance, raging up my neck and instantly taking up residence in my cheeks.

How is he standing here? The door didn't go!

"Er…" I stammered, realising to my horror that I hadn't actually seen him leave. Panic started rising as I ran through the conversation he might have just heard. The harder I tried, the less I could think of anything to say, so I settled for trying to cover my shell-shock with something resembling a smile. I thought I'd already experienced the embarrassment of blushing in Ciaran Argyll's presence, but this was an excruciating new level.

He carefully avoided looking at me; I was sure he was fighting a smile. "Actually, I have an event coming up. I was wondering what your thoughts might be on providing a cake?"

Please don't let him have heard, please don't let him have heard!

"Umm, yes. We can do that." I swallowed. "When for?" I asked, trying to salvage some sort of composure.

"October twenty-sixth," he said. "It's a Saturday."

As I slid the tray of cupcakes under the adjacent serving counter I could feel the beginnings of perspiration over the back of my neck. I didn't *sweat*. Clammy hands said I did.

The diary I'd been looking for was sat by the phone, on the side next to the till. In its place, for a change. I flicked through to the following month, hoping to find a week too full to take on another Argyll job.

"I know it's short notice," he said, also looking at the open diary as I checked over the bookings we had for that week. They were more than thin on the ground. Friday the twenty-fifth had been encircled in bright green ink, though, with *Martha's due date!* scrawled inside. Other than that, it would mostly be a week of passing trade. He surveyed the days, largely blank on the page, and watched me carefully.

"Sure. What were you looking for?" I asked, admitting defeat.

"Well, the event is themed, so would that be a good place to start?" he asked, cocking his head slightly again. He cut a relaxed figure, but I wasn't there yet. I could still feel the burn in my cheeks.

"Sure. What's the theme?" I asked, concentrating on my pen and the sketch pad I'd reached for.

"Hollywood heroes and villains," he replied with the beginnings of a playful grin. Well, of course it was. "It's a friend's thirtieth, so the cake should be fun, unique. Delicious."

I held off looking at him, as that seemed to trigger the blush response.

"*Hollywood heroes and villains?* As in Jaws and Brody?" I stole a look then; the smile had widened.

"If you like. Maybe mix it up, though. I don't think there will be many there dressed as great white sharks." He checked the watch on his wrist. "Look, I have to get to work. I'm not sure how these things are arranged?"

Thank goodness for that. He'd be out of here in minutes. He hadn't heard us larking around—it was all good. I just needed to wind things up.

"Well, you've given me a theme to run with. I just need an idea of flavours, how many people you'd like the cake to feed. An idea of budget, if you have one. Then we can sketch something up for you and take it from there." Jesse was so going to be handling this order.

"Okay," he said, tapping the arm of his sunglasses to his lip. "Make it to feed three hundred, budget…whatever you think is fine. Don't worry with the sketch. I know I'm in safe hands." He smiled and it softened the seriousness of his eyes, just as his father's face had been affected the same way.

"Okay. And will you need it delivered?"

"Yes, definitely," he said. "I'll get someone to call you with the details, payment, et cetera. Or I can pay you now?"

"No, no, I need to price it all up for you first. So…I just need flavours."

He tapped his lip a few more times before locking richly brown eyes firmly back on mine.

"The ginger and whisky sounded perfect."

chapter 6

A heavy haze of mist had been hanging over the reservoir when I left for work the following morning, but I knew that freezing though it was in a tin van spluttering against the sharp air, such mornings deceitfully heralded what would inevitably turn out to be a glorious day. It was only six-thirty, plenty of time for things to warm up and justify the aqua ballerina pumps now proving pitifully inadequate against the temperature in the footwell.

This was one of the summer's dying breaths—there wouldn't be many more of them—a last and valiant stand against the unstoppable autumn, advancing once more to mark another year without Charlie.

But today at least, things would get sunnier and sunny days were good for business. The golden girls in the café across the street would be enjoying a surge in alfresco diners, who'd all gaze over longingly at the goodies they knew we had waiting for them once they'd finished lunch. Grandmothers would pop in for iced cookies to take back to the kids, career girls would take advantage of their last chances to justify nibbling on something seasonally pretty and the odd eager male co-worker would follow them in.

The *pick 'n' mix girls*, Jess called them. Because they always got a couple of boxes between them, so they could all try a taste of everything.

Thanks to the wonders of dreamless sleep, I felt refreshed as I made my way into Hunterstone. It wasn't until I saw the shop that I found myself thinking of him again.

It was still cold as I opened up and let myself in. I collected a few scraps of mail then headed straight through for the kettle. Charlie couldn't abide junk mail, and had the irritating habit of giving out the shop address instead of home, he said because the businesses here had bigger recycling bins out back and I guess he had a point.

I flicked through the mail in my hand as the kettle bubbled to life: something from the electricity provider, two flyers for a local takeaway, and *ah*—a thank-you card. *That's nice.* I slipped the card from its envelope and walked back over to the far end of the bakery, where a battered plum sofa sat within the brick alcove. This was where we power-napped on those crazy days at the height of busy season. I plonked down onto the sofa and read the note inside the card.

Dear Holly and Jesse,

Thanks so much for our brilliant cake! It was absolutely stunning, everything we were hoping for. Even Ben's mum couldn't find a fault. (Which is saying something.)

We'll definitely be coming back for our first anniversary cake, and our tenth and our golden! Hopefully a christening cake, too!

Can't chat, I'm posting this on the way to the airport. Thailand, here we come!

Thanks again, you've been fab.

Very best wishes

Mr and Mrs Benjamin Day xx

I pinned the card with the others and looked at the last piece of post in my hand. It was an unusual pamphlet shaped like a teepee with an invitation to *Glamp it up in Wales*. On the reverse, a string of bunting joyfully held aloft an address panel marked for the attention of Charlie Jefferson. Charlie had fancied us as the glamping types, suggesting we give it a whirl for our first anniversary. We never made it.

Tea, ovens on, recycling bin, work.

Within twenty minutes the bakery was in full swing, filled with the happy beat of whatever was playing out on the radio and the wafts of warm vanilla and chocolate. I had four batches in before restocking my mug and switching the laptop on.

We'd chosen the right name for the shop—we were easy to find online and the email was simple enough. That also meant a reliable pile of virtual junk mail from suppliers. I clicked my way down the screen. Delete. Delete. Delete. Penny Richardson Re. Argyll Hollywood cake.

I clicked over the email feeling a trill of the awkwardness. And something else.

Miss Jefferson

We require you to provide a birthday cake for an upcoming event.

Mr Argyll has said that you've already discussed flavours with him, recommending the whisky & ginger option.

Minimum of 300 portions, delivery between 8 and 8.30 p.m.

Saturday October 26th. Venue details attached. Forward details of costs and payment will be arranged.
   Penny Richardson
   PA to CEO, Argyll Inc.

Great. Another evening delivery. And at that time most likely in full eyeshot of already present guests. I hated that, people watching, waiting for something terrible to go wrong so they could upload the blooper.

I opened the attachment. The Gold Rooms were not somewhere I'd ever been.

I'd overheard mention of the city's most exclusive venue when customers had chatted of beautiful people in the gossip mags out front, where some celebrity had been snapped necking with the wrong supermodel, but gatherings at the highly sought-after lounge were not usually toasted with cake, not when Moët and Glenlivet flowed so freely. And, let's face it, at three thousand pounds a booth I was not visiting a place like the Gold Rooms without a cake to get me in. Jesse was going to pee his pants when he knew. Groan.

I closed the document, leaving the whole thing for him to sort out when he got in. Other than the delivery it was his baby now, nothing more to do with me.

By the time he got to the shop, the bakes were out on display, I'd replaced the depleted shelves in the bakery with cake cards and drums and had taken delivery of the new, larger tubs of colourants we'd been waiting on.

All I had to do now was figure out where the fifteen tubs of edible paste colours were going to live. Nowhere up high, that was for sure. I'd knocked one of the old small tubs over once without realising. The viscosity of the pastes meant they didn't spill immediately, but rather leached out at a slow but steady pace. By the next morning, the bakery had looked like a crime scene, with blood-red goo dripping everywhere. I swear I half expected some psycho to spring from behind the storeroom when I first saw all the mess. That was years ago, and the stain on the worktop was just as angry now as it ever was.

"The king has returned," Jesse shouted from out front, barging in through the front door.

"I hope you have food!" I yelled back.

"I got you an almond croissant, but it is from the golden girls if you wanna pass?"

I took the bag from Jesse's hand and inhaled the delights of freshly baked pastries. "Damn, they do make good croissants."

Jess smiled, watching me take the treat as he knew I would. "How are you feeling this morning? After your rocky start to the week?"

I knew it wouldn't be long before he started ribbing me again about yesterday.

"Shut up, Jess, and get to work. Speaking of which, you have a job. Email from a Penny Richardson."

"What is it?" he asked.

"A headache in the making. And it's all yours, homeboy."

Jess dropped the backpack from his shoulders and slipped out of his hoody before grabbing an apron and going for the bunker corner.

He sat down with the laptop and started clicking through the screens. I busied myself clearing space for the new supplies. *Wait for it....*

"The mutha-funkin' Gold Rooms!"

I was grinning as Jess read every detail of the digital flyer, knowing he'd go back over it a few more times to drink in every last bit of it. This cake was going to be obscene.

"Like I said, headache."

"Headache! You're kidding me? Wait till I tell the lads that I've been in the Gold Rooms! Ah, man! They're gonna be bummed. I said he was a flash sucka… D'you know, I think he might actually be James Bond."

Technically, that wasn't what Jess had called him, but I wasn't about to point it out. Those words were never going to leave my mouth again.

"Yeah, well…we're only delivering, Jess. I'm sorry. I know it's an ask on a Saturday night but I can't do it alone."

"Hol, we're going to the Gold Rooms! I don't care what night of the week it is, once we're in, we're in, girl!"

I shot Jess a look.

"Hol, come on. You're not gonna make me leave as soon as the cake's in, are you? That would be like taking a kid to Disneyland, letting him catch sight of Mickey then taking him home again."

"Jess, we're not crashing this party. We don't know these people. We're not invited. And to be honest, it's not exactly my scene. People with more money than sense, all dressed up in designer gear talking about Daddy's yacht," I said, batting at Jesse's intentions hanging heavy in the air.

"Speak for yourself—it's totally my scene! I scrub up well, and I *love* yachts!" Jess was trying his best to will a change in me he knew he had no chance of uncovering.

"Don't look at me like that. If we were invited, it would be different. But I am no way crashing," I said. "We don't even know whose party it is!" There. Not my fault. My hands were tied.

"All right. But I've gotta tell you, Hol, don't be surprised if I slink off to get changed in the little boys' room, because if I see anyone famous in there, with or without you, I am crashing the joint."

"Knock yourself out, Cinders. But the pumpkin and I will be leaving by eight-thirty-five, with or without *you*. I guarantee it."

The rest of the day was as busy as I'd anticipated, and although Jess was unusually quiet I couldn't be sure if it was because he was sulking with me or mentally planning his outfit.
Both probably. When things died down in the afternoon, I
left him sketching out a rough design for the Argyll cake. I
had to hand it to Jesse—when it came to creativity, there was
nothing his hands couldn't do.

I'd managed to steal a few sneaky peeks over his shoulder,
knowing that whatever he came up with was going to rock.
Jesse was probably right. It would be his scene—everywhere
was his scene. Effortlessly good-looking and funny as hell,
there was little for anyone to dislike about him. Both he and
the cake would be able to hold their own at the party. Sure,
he was going to be contending with some beautiful people,
but Jess could *make* beautiful right out of nothing, and that
was a talent that couldn't be bought.

Before the end of play, Jess had finished sketching up the
cake and had emailed the quote over to them. I'd made sure
he'd signed it off so that they had a new name to chase. Martha
had called, warning me Mum had been on the phone, we'd
picked up a couple of last-minute telephone orders giving us
a nice even pace until the weekend and, with no weddings
booked in for Saturday or Sunday, one of us was going to get
a whole weekend off.

"Hey, Hol, there's nothing in for the next two Saturdays.
You knew that, right?" I knew he wouldn't be sore at me for
long.

"Uh-huh. Are you thinking what I'm thinking?"

"I was thinking you take this Saturday off, I'll take next?
If that's cool?"

"I'm easy, Jess. Whatever fits in with your plans. Going
anywhere nice?"

"Dunno yet. My mate's taking his girl on a road trip. If

she can talk her friend into it, I wouldn't mind a spot in the back with her." He flashed me a full set of pearly whites and wiggled his eyebrows until I burst out laughing.

"A road trip? Is there anywhere you won't go for a bit of skirt, Mr Ray?" Jesse was eternally in love, but with a different girl every week. I could see what every last one of them saw in him. I loved him, too. He'd played big brother when I needed it more than I'd known, and was like a kid brother to me for the rest of the time. I had a lot to thank him for. For things I didn't know how to say.

"Probably." He shrugged, all big brown-eyed innocence. "But I haven't found it on the map yet."

By the time I'd done my eight-hour stint, I was ready to call it a day, and left Jess to lock up at closing time. It had been a steady day, and with all the people coming and going, I'd hardly thought about teepees until the drive home.

It was still warm when I rattled down the track towards the cottage and, as I parked up, Dave walked out into the yard to greet me.

"Hey, fella," I called, creaking the van door closed with my bum. I reached into my shopping bag as I walked towards Dave, fishing for a little of the meat I'd bought from the deli on the way.

I slid the key into the lock and pushed on the peeling crimson paintwork. Dave followed me in, nearly knocking my legs out from under me, excited for the other contents of the grocery bag in my arms. Inside the hall, the answer machine was flashing red. I hit the button and went through into the kitchen.

"You have three new messages." I started picking through the groceries while wrestling my bag and cardigan from my shoulders.

"First new message, received today at eight-sixteen a.m.—'Holly

love, phone Mum, would you? She's getting a bit tetchy that you haven't called for a little while. I've told her you're busy but, well… just give her a call, love. It would be nice to hear what you've been up to. 'Bye, love.'"

"'Holly love, it's Dad again. Just don't tell your mother I called. You know it's just…she'd like to think you've just called her up. All right, love, 'bye for now.' Received at eight-nineteen a.m."

Seeing all the little pots on the counter made my stomach growl.

"'Holly, I know you are busy, but really? Is one call a week unreasonable? Martha's telling me everything's fine, and the scan was okay, but I'm not sure, Holly. I think that maybe she just doesn't want us to worry. I'm stuck over here and I don't know what's happening! Anyway, I hope you're taking care of yourself. Martha says you've lost a little weight? Call me. 'Bye.' Received at twelve-fifty-two p.m."

"Well, that's kinda what happens when you move to another country, Ma," I said, picking at a pot of olives. I had not lost weight. Martha had just temporarily outgrown me.

I stuffed a few more salty morsels into my mouth and threw my things over the newel post at the bottom of the stairs. I needed to work out a better warning system with Dad.

I deleted the messages and thought about calling them as I scanned the hall for the slipper I couldn't see. Maybe after dinner. Off the hallway I could see into the drab front room, and my other felt slipper waiting for recovery.

It was always cold in this room. We hadn't lit the fire in here since the first few weeks of Chinese takeaways and grand plans, and I'd since turned off the radiators to conserve energy. Until we'd knocked through the kitchen, this had been the largest open space in the whole house, and we'd used it as a dumping ground for all the furniture we were gradually rehousing around the rest of the place. It was a bit like an elephants' graveyard in here now, picture frames long unhung and lamps long unlit. There was still plenty of furniture in here, too, including the beat-up old chesterfield Mrs Hedley had insisted we have.

While I was being indecisive about what was going to be my favourite room in the house, Charlie had commandeered the smaller snug just off through the rear doors, officially declaring it as his man-cave. He had everything he needed in there, he'd said: sofa bed for when I was mean to him, and flat screen for when the boys came over on footy nights. It was just a cave now.

I scooped up my slipper and went back to sit with it on the stairs. The wood was hard under my backside as I changed out of my shoes.

The inside of one slipper was contorted enough that it scratched my foot as I tried to put it on. "Dave! You've been chewing again! You bad dog." Again, I really needed to work on my boss voice. I pushed my foot into the slipper—

A cold wet residue spread itself across my toes. *Gross.* "They're the third pair since April, Dave! What are you—a *fetishist*?" He whimpered at that.

I reached into my bag hanging next to me for a tissue to wipe Dave's essence away. The last thing I'd put in there was Charlie's mail. I left the tissue and pulled the pamphlet free of my bag for another look at that which had captured Charlie's imagination. The perfect couple, toasting their quirky getaway under a twilit sky. How could we have known how fragile it all was? The infinity of the world around us, the promise of our youth, the protection of our love. All gone in seconds, leaving nothing to believe in.

chapter 7

"Mrs. Jefferson!" came the boom of a voice I hadn't heard for a while. "How are you doin', darlin'?" The forest air was crisp and fresh, and exactly the pick-me-up I'd needed. I hadn't spent an afternoon in the forest for so long, and it had been a stretch of many more months since I'd last bumped into any of Charlie's crew. Dave ran ahead to the base of the tree from where Big Frank Stanley's familiar tone was emanating, and wagged himself silly until Big Frank shuffled down.

"Agh, get away, mad dog!" Frank jovially cried as I staggered through the mulch towards them. Frank was the biggest man I'd ever met, but still Dave looked like a monster as he charged playfully towards him.

"Dave! Leave him alone…. He's only little." I grinned as Frank pushed Dave aside to come greet me.

Frank grabbed hold of me in a bear hug. "Hello, darlin'," he rumbled, his beard bristling uncomfortably against my face. He smelled like Charlie after a long day. Of chainsaw fuel, and pine needles.

"Hey, Frank. How have you been?" I asked, fighting the urge to smooth the itch he'd left on my cheek. He had the look of a Viking about him, but if I thought Charlie's broad shoulders were well suited to working the forest, Frank made Charlie look as though he shouldn't be far from his mother. I hadn't missed being eaten out of house and home by him on footy nights, but seeing him now I realised that I had indeed missed him.

"Same old same old." He smiled through a covering of reddish whiskers thick enough to hide his lips. "Where have you been hiding?"

"Nowhere." I shrugged. "Just been busy with work and things."

"I know that feeling. I'm just trying to get a few extra quid in over a weekend."

"I hadn't expected to see anyone up here on a Saturday," I said as we strolled through the trees.

"It's all go up here at the moment." A seriousness settled in his features. "There's a few of the lads out today. Deckard and Jimmy are here somewhere, marking off the boundaries for the suits. You know about the slade, over on the west side?"

"I heard they were talking about it. But then it all went quiet. We don't hear much over our way without anyone to keep us in the loop." I shrugged.

"Three years fighting and now they're still selling them out from under us."

The campaigners had put up a good fight, but we knew there would be a domino effect once the sell-offs had started. Before long, none of these forests would be open to the public anymore. Worse still, they would be *developed*.

"I'm sorry, Frank." I really was. Sick with sorry, in fact. For all of Charlie's efforts here to come to nothing, it was beyond crushing. Here was the closest thing Charlie had to a legacy.

He'd invested so much time trying to think of new and tangible ways of keeping the forests an integral part of the local community. Then, one night, over beer and nostalgia, Charlie had his eureka moment. He'd been telling Martha and Rob about his awful school days, where he'd been expelled from one high school and forgotten by his next. He'd been aggressive, and disruptive—everything you didn't want from a teenage boy. Everything Charlie wasn't.

But it had all been a diversion. A mechanism for survival. Because no one had ever diagnosed Charlie's dyslexia.

Martha cried when Charlie told her the things he'd do to avoid being called upon for answers in class. He made light of it, but I knew how it had affected him, how he worried that our children would suffer the same way. School for him had been a demoralizing experience, and a lonely one, too, but even we were stunned when Rob told us the proportion of offenders he'd represented with learning difficulties such as Charlie's. Individuals who had all started off with expulsions for behaviour just like his, children crippled by shame. It had taken Charlie a long time to finally accept that he wasn't simply *stupid*.

Rob had raised the topic of forest schools that night. We'd never heard of them, not even through Charlie's work. The more Rob had explained what it was he understood forest schools to be, the more Charlie had hung on his every word. He'd thought that a forest school was the answer, to the sustainability of the forest and to the local children who could benefit from all that they offered.

"They're not talking about it now," said Big Frank, grabbing for a stick Dave was thrusting at his hand. "The slade's gone. Sold. It's all fenced off now by the new owners. They'll be moving into the woodland next."

I looked around me into the eeriness of the forest. It was

so beautiful here, I couldn't bear it if we lost the woods, too. Frank kicked at a few fallen pine cones as we walked, sending them spinning from the rich damp earth.

"I'd better let you get on, Frank," I said, reaching up to give him a hug goodbye. "Say hi to Annie for me?"

"I will. Watch for that mad dog of yours."

Another bristled cheek and Big Frank turned back towards where Dave had first found him.

Dave went back on his leash as we neared the more populated walks. The path led us through the woods, past the forest park where families were picnicking and chasing each other around on bikes, before taking us out onto the slade at the foot of the forest. All along the perimeter, iron stakes held aloft red and white tape, flickering uselessly in the breeze. Although it had quite obviously been demarked as somewhere we couldn't go anymore, it was hard to accept that so much space was suddenly off limits.

The pocket of my jacket flashed to life with the phone ringing inside it. It was Jesse's face on the screen.

"Hey. What's up?"

"All right, Hol, sorry to spoil your day off."

"No, you're fine. Is everything okay?" I asked.

"Yeah, yeah, everything's fine. It's just, I've got a lady on the shop phone asking if we can make two hundred cupcakes for Monday."

"Monday? This Monday coming?" I asked. It was unusual for anyone to have a function on a Monday, and be this late for ordering.

"Yeah, I didn't want to say yes without checking it with you first."

"Thanks, Jess. Did she say what they're for?" Dave was trying to pull me into the slade. He'd never been bothered before—now he wasn't allowed, he wanted in. I heard Jess running my query through the other phone.

"No, no function."

"Delivery or collection?" I asked.

"Collection." I couldn't help but be suspicious. You tended to get a feel for quantities and days, that kind of thing. This sounded like a wind-up.

"Okay," I said, "but they need to pay it all up front, today. Otherwise we can't start it when we get in on Monday. And no cheques, Jess."

"You got it. Catch you later," he said.

"'Bye."

Jess clicked the phone off. It was unlikely I'd be making those cupcakes on Monday; I could near enough feel it.

Dave and I were back in the old Land Rover Mrs Hedley let me use to cart him around in, and well on our way home when my mobile started ringing again. Jesse, Martha and my folks all had the same ringtone, so whoever this was I didn't know them, I didn't think. I ignored it and carried on for home. The sky had already started falling into that rich cerulean blue by the time I'd dropped the key round to Mrs Hedley. I needed an excuse to get out of movie night at Martha's.

As soon as I'd let us into the cottage, Dave went straight for his spot on the floor at the back of the kitchen. I crashed, too, on the window seat halfway between Dave's bed and the bottle of wine I'd left on the breakfast bar, and lay back there looking up at the rows of books on the shelves above me. I held my phone above my face and flipped through the menu to text Martha. I know, I'm a coward, but it's markedly easier to say anything when you don't have to use your voice to do it.

The call I'd missed was from a number I didn't recognise. They hadn't left a voicemail.

Martha returned my text within seconds, checking that I

was feeling okay and not having the meltdown my mother was always warning everyone to be ready for. Martha was surprisingly fine, though. I should imagine it was nice for them to have a Saturday night to themselves for a change without me as the third wheel. I didn't fancy Rob's chances for getting out of the grapefruit breakfast tomorrow, though.

My arm started to ache from mid-air texting, so I rolled onto my side. Martha had made a long mid-grey cushion to run along the cream timber seat, and had insisted on at least six scatter cushions in soft lime and grey to finish off "the look." Never mind how it looked, it was pretty damn comfortable here. Comfy enough to just slope off into a sleep. I pulled a cushion under my head. Across the kitchen, through the chunky legs of the table, I could see Dave's hulking frame already snoozing in his bed. He had an easy life. Reluctantly, I pushed myself up.

A glass of red and a soak in the tub were the only things that were going to get me on my feet.

Dave was already too far gone to come sit in the bathroom with me. I poured a glass of wine, grabbed one of the deli pots out of the fridge and headed up on my own. I polished off the feta chunks while I changed out of my jeans and T-shirt, and wished I'd bought more as I sank my tired body into the hot silk of the water. There were few things more pleasurable than sliding into a deep bubble bath. Well, there were a *few* things, though I could vaguely remember what those things felt like. Vaguely. I resolved to start making more time for baths and showering less.

The change in temperature rippled me with gratifying goosebumps. I lay back and closed my eyes, enjoying the drip, drip, drip of the tap into the otherwise still water at my feet. The stiffness in my shoulder from Dave's yanking gradually began to release. Through barely open eyes, I lifted a foot to the trickle of cold water, plugging the tap with my toe, and was more than shocked at how long I must have left it since last defuzzing my legs.

Bloody hell, Holly. You won't need to wear trousers through the winter if that grows much more!

I spotted my razor on the tray in the shower. "Oh, sod it, I'll do it tomorrow," I said, before settling cold shoulders back into the warmth beneath the waterline.

I relaxed again, the noises of the water swilling around me died away to nothing. Downstairs, I could hear Dave sucking in a deep, sleepy breath through his nose, then the dull buzzing of my mobile phone vibrating on the bed.

I thought Martha had given up too easily.

Just ignore it.

But then she'll worry.

Go answer the phone.

"Damn it, Martha!"

The towel I grabbed had spent just long enough to warm through on the radiator. I pulled myself free of the water's reluctant release and wrapped myself in the towel, then treaded wet feet over the rug on the landing and into my room at the back of the house. This was the only room in the house with carpet, thanks to my sister, and I was glad for it as I padded across the floor to the heavy four-poster. The phone stopped buzzing before I reached it, of course. I dumped myself on the soft give of the simple ivory quilt Martha had said was to die for, and looked at the screen. The same unfamiliar mobile number sat at the top of the list of missed calls. Martha's and Jesse's names took all remaining spots.

I started towelling the ends of my dripping hair and pondered who had pulled me from the tub before I'd had a chance to wash it through. Maybe it was Annie, Big Frank's wife.

She'd tried her best to get me to go and spend some time with them; it was probably her off the back of our catch-up today.

Still no voicemail, though. I wasn't calling her back now. I'd do it tomorrow sometime, right after I finally called Mum. *Crap.* I was going to get an earful.

I was thinking of my mother's impending annoyance, mobile phone still nestled in the palm of my hand, when it rang back to life. Annie's attempts at being friendly had always been persistent, and I hated myself for holding it against her. I just didn't want the therapy she thought she could offer me. My thumb hovered over the reject button but it seemed a little harsh—ungrateful, too, probably. And I had enjoyed seeing Frank today. Maybe I was starting to mellow. *Just answer it.*

"Hello?" I said, waiting for Annie's buoyant voice.

"Hello?" came a man's answer.

"Frank?"

"No. Not Frank. Is this the correct number for Miss Jefferson?"

I didn't know why I'd thought Frank. Only it definitely wasn't Jess or Rob, which left me searching through a very limited list of male names.

"Who is this?" I asked, checking the time on the dresser clock. It was a bit late for mobile phone companies, or telemarketers. There was something familiar, though—

"It's Ciaran. Argyll."

The faintest involuntary gasp of breath kicked off a sudden thumping in the side of my neck and the wash of a tingling sensation over my cheeks. My body was already starting to react to some sort of stressful situation my brain didn't understand yet.

"Or…occasionally I go by Bond. James Bond."

I knew it. As soon as the name started to trip off his wistfully Scottish tongue, I knew what was coming. For some reason, I felt like I'd been caught out by him again.

Think of something to say….

"And on occasion, Handsome S—"

"Ah, Mr Argyll…what can I do for you?" I asked, searching for what the hell the answer could be. *Thump, thump,* continued the percussion in my neck. I tried to breathe quietly and evenly, to not allow the unsteadiness to give me away.

"I'm sorry to call you out of hours, Miss Jefferson—" I could hear the smile still there in his voice "—but I'm afraid I have a few queries about my order."

In the dresser mirror I could see the look of absolute confusion all over my daft pink face, but at least at the mention of work some part of my brain found a foothold and started to climb its way up to the light.

"How did you get this number?" I asked, allowing myself the first stirs of what could be annoyance, hoping that they might chase off whatever else was stirring back there.

"Nothing's sacred these days, Miss Jefferson. I find a little research saves time. I hope you don't mind?" It was one of those statements that had few answers which wouldn't leave you open to one implication or another. I wasn't sure exactly what *a little research* involved, or whether I liked being the subject of it, but whatever he wanted, it must be important to call out of shop hours, and to *research* me enough to do so.

"Is there a problem, Mr Argyll?" I asked, the annoyance warming up nicely. "Because if there is, Jesse will be able to deal with that for you first thing on Monday."

"Jesse?" he asked. "And will Jesse be taking care of my order throughout?"

"That's right. So if you have anything to discuss regarding your cake, he'll be able to help you out with that. On Monday. During shop hours."

The other end of the line went quiet for a few seconds.

"I was just wondering, and I'm sorry to keep you, but you *are* the boss and so I think I should really run this past you." His voice was relaxed, and carried with enough softness that his referring to my snippiness in the shop didn't bug me. "There are going to be a lot of people at the event we've hired you for. We don't really want them all wandering over and helping themselves to your masterpiece. It could get messy." *Jess's masterpiece.* "I was just wondering to what extent your business's services could be utilised?"

"I'm sorry, Mr Argyll. I'm not sure I understand the question."

"I was just thinking that it might be an idea to employ you to oversee the cutting and serving of the cake. After seeing the detail of your work, I don't think the staff are going to know what to do with it."

"I'm sorry. Are you asking if we can *babysit* the cake for you?"

He laughed then, an effortless press of breath against the phone. "I suppose I am. Of course, you'd also get to spend the evening at the Gold Rooms. I think you'd enjoy it."

Across in the mirror, the redness had definitely started to leave my cheeks, but I looked even more confused now. *Why would I want to stay there? Why would he think I would?*

"Ah, we don't offer that kind of service, Mr Argyll."

"Call me Ciaran."

The faintest prickle rode over my neck. I reached up to rub it away.

It was hard to decide if that gentle edge to his voice had come from a childhood left behind, or his father's intonation influencing his own through the years.

"We don't cake-sit, Ciaran. The venue's banqueting team will be able to accommodate you."

"You're right. They should do for what they charge. Have you ever been there?" *Were we chit-chatting?*

"No," I answered, more than bemused. "But Jesse's told me *all* about it," I said in a voice that must have shown my disinterest.

I felt a large droplet of cold fall from my hair onto my thigh.

"Then he's told you how exclusive the venue is?" What was he getting at?

"He mentioned it."

"That it's notoriously difficult to get into?" This was getting weirder. The place was seriously swanky, I got it.

I was about to disappoint him. "As Jess explained it to me, it's not *difficult* to get in there. You just have to pay your way in."

"At an eye-watering price," he added.

"I heard that, too."

"And you wouldn't take the chance to enjoy an evening there? *Without* having to pay your way in?"

"The cost of entry isn't what puts me off, Mr Argyll. Well, it would, but places like that just…" I remembered to choose my words carefully. I might be sat on my bed, for some bizarre reason talking about frivolous haunts, but I was still talking to a customer.

"Not your thing?" he offered. *Exactly.*

"Nope. Not really," I said, wondering how to round this chat off before I did offend him.

"And is it Jesse's thing?"

I gave a small laugh myself then; his question had surprised me. "Anything with gold, music or overindulgence is Jesse's thing."

"Then the Gold Rooms must score highly on places he'd like to visit?"

Jesse had already made it perfectly clear how much he'd like to visit. It would be mean to head off a chance for him.

"You're welcome to ask him if he wants to cake-sit. But your best chance of catching him will be on Monday...when we're open."

The line went quiet again for a few moments. Maybe I'd gone in too hard. "Sorry. I've kept you. I'll deal with Jesse, then, from now on?"

"Jesse's your man."

"Thank you for your help, Miss Jefferson. I'm sorry to have disturbed you. Enjoy the rest of your evening." He clicked the phone off before I had chance to say 'bye.

chapter 8

Jesse was grinning like the cat who had the cream. I ignored him; this hadn't been my idea. And he looked like Liberace in that tux.

Above us, great swathes of twinkling fabric pitched away like the insides of a circus tent, and gathered at the point an enormous chandelier, fashioned in sweeping strands of golden chain mail, hung regally over us all. It was dizzying looking up at all that glitz, but down here there was even more going on.

Jesse had my hand, and was pulling me deeper into the bodies, dancing furiously around us. I didn't want to dance but Jess wasn't listening. I wobbled on my shoes as he pulled me further into the heaving mass. At least if I fell here, I'd be swallowed up by a pit of legs and shaking booty.

These were beautiful people, all right. The men all looking every bit as tweezed and polished as the women, the women all dressed like each other in gold evening gowns, sparkling cocktail dresses and—*was she dressed as an ancient Greek?*—the odd historical fashion, apparently.

Some five or more bodies into the crowd behind Jesse, a

large chap was throwing crazy shapes to the music pulsing around us. The people immediately next to him had all moved back to give the big guy some space. Smart move—*somebody* was really enjoying themselves. Suddenly I didn't feel so self-conscious about falling off the heels I was stupidly wearing, or drawing attention to my limited knowledge of dance.

I wasn't really dancing anyway, more swaying with the motion of the sea of people around me. Jess hadn't noticed my lacklustre efforts, demanding that I get more into the party spirit, so I was good for now. Besides, I was busy people-watching. It was hard not to stare at the big guy through the other dancers. He was way too interesting not to. I'd only caught him from behind, arms flailing wildly to the music and head of perfectly coiffed deep red hair swaying and bobbing to the beat reverberating through my feet.

As is so often the case when you're rubbernecking, though, Twinkletoes started to turn that hairdo this way. *Big Frank? What the hell is Frank doing in the Gold Rooms? And what has he done to his hair!* Frank was lost in the music, and turned back before I could catch his attention.

"Jess?" I shouted. I caught his eye for a second. "Is that Frank over there? You remember he worked with Charlie?"

Jess frowned like he couldn't understand me. I looked for a way through the crowd to get closer to the person I was sure was Frank. The crowd wasn't budging, though—we were packed in. I turned to look out across the rest of the partygoers in various shades of golds and creams.

Up on the podium, the only normal-coloured suit in the room had gone against the grain and was looking out in grey over a sharp white shirt, surveying the crowds beneath him. I watched curiously as he finally turned eyes to where Jesse and I stood.

Ciaran Argyll looked down at us and nodded. Next to me,

Liberace was too busy throwing crazy shapes of his own to catch Mr Argyll's greeting. I looked back up to the podium, and saw that the ice maiden had made her way to his side. Her impossibly blonde hair was loose now, a little shorter than mine, sitting just above her shoulders, just short enough not to detract from the line of her neck. She was dressed in a strapless white bustier, pinching in at her tiny waist before a full tulle skirt burst away from her in every direction. She looked like Miss Universe, and all of us in the crowd knew it. It didn't matter how any of us dressed; in this place we were the commoners, looking in awe to the king and queen in their tower.

It wasn't like me to care, really, but I found myself checking down to see my own clothes against theirs.

I'd gone strapless, too, an unusual choice for me. I liked dresses, but I was more for a light floaty tunic in the summer, at a push a tea dress maybe for an evening drink in the village pub. Nothing that required anything with more faff than flip-flops. I really had broken with tradition tonight.

I allowed my hand to investigate the fabric wrapped around me. It was cream, better than gold at least, but rough, and soft…all at once. I rubbed it between my fingers.

"Glad you could make it," called a satin-smooth voice over the music. Ciaran Argyll stood behind me, every bit as casual as he'd been at my shop counter. I knew this was all a little odd, but I was going with it. Going with the feeling in my chest was the oddest thing of all.

I looked up to face him with more assuredness than I'd managed in the shop. I was wrong. He was rocking a little gold, but it was the gold the sun had given to the edges of his hair. In a roomful of finely groomed excess, his simple charcoal suit and rugged hint of a beard made him even more attractive than I'd remembered. Assuredness gave way to a smile, and I liked how it felt. *Long live the king.*

"Holly, what are you wearing, darlin'?" A very sweaty, but dapper-looking Frank had appeared at my side as I'd been thinking of something to say to Mr Argyll.

"You look beautiful, Hol, ignore him. Frank—shut up, man." Jesse had stopped dancing now, too. Ciaran Argyll hadn't moved. He was just standing there watching me, his approving eyes almost as brown as Jesse's. I looked down at my dress and felt the smile fall from my lips. With a sickening lurch, I realised that I was still wearing my bath towel.

Right on cue, of course, the ice maiden took her place at Ciaran's right arm, just as I started to hyperventilate. "Would you like me to take you to get those waxed?" She smiled sweetly.

A vicious intake of breath and I jolted back to life on my bed. Dave was looking at me from the edge of the sheets, panting warm doggy breath my way. On the bedside table next to him, an empty pot of feta had a lot of explaining to do. *No more cheese before bedtime.*

Kicking off the covers, I dragged my pyjama leg up. Right. They were being sorted today. I really had to stop snacking before bed. It had been the strangest dream I'd had for a while, but at least it wasn't a bad one. There'd been a real mix of those lately and at least I wasn't in the reservoir again.

I sank back into my pillow. Frank's hair had been *disturbing*.

The clock on the dresser declared it was already past eight. I must have been zonked. I had to have slept for more than ten hours. No wonder Dave was waiting for breakfast. His appetite hadn't been off the rails for long once the vet had pulled the shard of bark from his gums.

I flopped out of bed and trudged over to the window, patting Dave's sturdy head on the way. My brain was trying to hang on to the sense of panic it had felt at the prospect of clubbing in towel and heels.

I was not going to spend today dissecting that dream. I pushed the voile drapes aside and looked out through the window at the day waiting for me. It was a little greyer than yesterday, but dry at least. Dave wouldn't be treading mud in all day.

Mrs. Hedley was collecting eggs from the henhouse in her garden.

"Do you fancy a boiled egg, Dave?" He didn't answer.

I let go of the drapes and they settled themselves back into position. They were useless. Martha said they looked right for the window, but they didn't keep any of the light out and, since I last checked, that was the whole point.

"Come on, big guy, I'll fetch you breakfast." *And while you're eating it, I'm shaving my legs.*

chapter 9

True enough, over the following weeks October proved to bring about a dip in temperature, and along with it, a noticeable dip in passing trade.

Usually Jesse and I would have used the time harvested from our scaled-back cupcake schedule to start working on the next season's range of wedding cakes, and the dummies we'd need ready to exhibit in the new year's big-bucks wedding fairs. Jesse had an eye for fashion trends and so long as he got to spend a few hours researching what noises were being made by all the big fashion houses, he'd always come up with a way to work their magic into ours. We had to get the exhibition cakes prepped in October as the work involved in the run-up to Christmas always squeezed us either side of the season.

The last few weeks, however, had been a little off-key. The cupcake order Jess had run by me had turned out to be genuine, and seemed to bugle in a spate of sporadic last-minute orders that had kept us nicely busy over the last fortnight. It wasn't that people always booked us weeks in advance, but most of our business was called in by women, often mothers, charged with arranging a party somewhere, and they were largely a militant breed. Last-minute orders always came in, but very rarely for gold-level cakes, and recently, it had been all about the gold.

Jess was sat on the sofa in the bunker, flicking through one of the magazines he'd brought through from the consultation area, while I sat at the desk and checked through the accounts. October was also a good time for getting paperwork up-to-date for the January deadline. I always left our tax return until the last minute.

"No way. Aleta Delgado was snapped in town! Aleta, I love you. I've got to start reading these things—give me the edge over the honeys."

I cocked my head round from the spreadsheet to look at Jess. I'd been waiting for an excuse. "Aleta Del who?"

"Who's Aleta? Hol, sometimes I think you don't pay me any attention."

"Go on, then, educate me."

Jess cast me a look that wasn't at all convinced by my expression of interest. "Paperwork a bit boring, is it?"

"Actually," I said, spinning back to the laptop, "it's making for *pretty* nice reading. First October ever."

"Yeah, we're having a good run," Jess replied idly as the sound of pages turning resumed.

I studied the figures I'd inputted outlining the value of cakes against the dates they'd been made for. We were into our third week of the month, and had taken on an unusual amount of high-value orders. Roughly four a week, actually, all over the five-hundred mark, all ordered last-minute.

"Jess? These bespokes we've been making lately…"

"Mmm."

"What have the customers been like?"

"What do you mean?" he asked, still flipping through his magazine.

"I've taken a few of the orders over the phone, but out of—" I ran my fingers down the list of entries on my spreadsheet "—eleven cakes, I've only seen two Friday collections. The rest have all either been delivered by you, or picked up late afternoon on Mondays and Wednesdays."

"Yeah, and…?"

"So, what are they like?"

"What do you mean, 'what are they like?' They're like people, Hol, hungry people." Jess went back to his mag. "Very hungry, some of 'em. None of those cakes have been small."

I skimmed over the order values in front of me. Five hundred, five-fifty, six hundred, six hundred, five-fifty. "Jess, have *we* priced any of these cakes?" The numbers looked too rounded all neatly stacked up in their column. Too many zeros. Jess gave me a little more attention. "I've taken three of these orders over the phone, and now I think about it, they were all really easy-going about the price. They all gave me a budget to work to," I said.

"And basically told you to get on with it?" Jess added.

"Yes. Weird, right?"

"I guess," Jess said, thinking it over. "But not really. They were all last-minute, Hol. People in a rush don't want to wait for quotes, not if they can just give you the go-ahead."

"But all of them, Jess? All eleven cakes just giving the go-ahead? On cakes with values of five hundred pounds and up? We've done enough business to know that people don't just do that, Jess. It's weird enough that they were all last-minutes."

"So what are you saying?" he asked, eyebrows reaching for the purple brim of his cap.

I didn't really know what I was saying as it went. I shrugged my shoulders. "I'm saying it's weird."

"It's business," Jess answered, throwing the spent magazine down onto the coffee table in front of the sofa. "I've got to go crack on with number eleven now if I'm going to deliver it Friday," he said, walking to the sinks.

"Where's it going to, Jess?" I called around the wall, still curious about our recent activity.

Jess walked over to the workstation where his order sheets for the week were all lined up on the wall in front of him.

"It's in town. St Harry's Square. Er...number nineteen." By town, Jesse meant *his* town—the city. Not the town we were actually in.

"What is that, a bar?" I asked, nowhere near as familiar with the city as he was.

"Nah, a flat. St Harry's is a nice little neighbourhood. It's where the yuppies live and get together for canapés and co-caine."

"A house? Why is it going to a house?" I said, moving over to look at the sketch on the order sheet in front of him. "All that's going to a house? Why haven't they had it delivered to the venue?"

"Everything I've delivered in the last two weeks has gone to someone's gaff. Not the same one, obviously, but all residential addresses. All nice, too." Jess watched me start to chew at my lip. "What?"

"I don't know," I said. "Something just feels off. Where are the rest of the order sheets?"

"In the folder. Why do you care, though, Hol? Money is money."

And there it was.

I sat back into my chair and couldn't help but lock down on the name Ciaran Argyll. Jess didn't realise, but he'd thrown a thread of suggestion out there, and it had snagged on something in my head. He shook his head at me and left me to it.

Over in the bunker, I pulled the orange completed-jobs file from its shelf, and dug out the order sheets for everything bespoke over the last three weeks. Flicking through them, they all looked reasonably inconspicuous. All of the order names were different women, as were the contact numbers, and addresses where delivery had been required. The designs had ranged from a deep-sea theme to butterflies and pearls to chocolate cherubs. In fact, the only thing any of them had in common was the limited specifications scribbled on the sheets.

When people were spending this much money, they were usually very particular about what they would like us to achieve for them. But with each of these cakes, the notes were equally scant. Contact details, a nice round budget, a theme and choice of flavour. I whizzed through them again.

The first Monday's cupcakes had been elderflower, two days later and three tiers in honey and walnut, the day after that and toffee apple, the next cake—coffee and walnut, then banoffee, then chocolate and maple. The orders were reading like our flavours list, as if a group of customers had got their heads together and decided who was buying what, so they could all have a try.

Like the pick 'n' mix girls.

The phone on the shop counter started to ring, and Jess went through to answer it. He was still helping whoever he was talking to when the bell over the door jangled at someone's arrival.

After tucking the orders back in their file, I went through the front to serve.

Martha cut a flustered figure as she lay in a collapsed state across the leather sofa reserved for blushing brides-to-be. She was blushing, all right. Scarlet cheeks are quite the shocker next to a lemon-yellow dress and sticky blonde hair, plastered haphazardly to one of said cheeks.

The whites of Martha's eyes told me she'd been overdoing it, and she knew it, too.

I was just taking in the rare view of my utterly dishevelled sister when Jess put the phone down behind me. "All right, Marth?" He half chuckled.

"Need water" was Martha's strained reply. The pile of shopping bags next to her on the couch made it all become clear. Half of them had fallen onto the floor. Next to them, two very swollen ankles disappeared into nude satin courts, with heels at least as high as Jesse's afro the last time I'd seen it.

"Martha, when your ankles get to be as wide as your husband's neck, it's time to leave the heels at home, honey," I said, moving around the pile of discarded goods to sit with her. Jess had already gone for water, so I peeled the hair off her face and tied it back with the spare hairband I'd had on my wrist. "Are you all right, sweetie?" I asked, watching her for the truth.

"I can't do it," she panted. "I thought I could, but I can't." Jesse returned with a glass of water and Martha gulped it down.

"Can't do what, Marth?" I asked. "Power-shop around town in these?" I nodded to an offending shoe.

"Nice shoes, Marth," Jesse added before taking her glass back off to the bakery.

"I can't be a glamorous mummy," Martha said, her eyes dewing over as I watched.

"Martha, you mentalist. There's nothing glamorous about sweating your way around town on tippy toes. Don't be so ridiculous. You look a million bucks."

"Do I?" she asked, all little-girl-lost.

"Always, Marth. But do yourself a favour and chill out. This can't be good for little one, can it?"

"No. You're right. I need new shoes. I never thought I'd say this, Holly, but I need shoes…like *yours*."

I made a point not to take offence where it wasn't intended, although I was tempted not to tell my sister that I had a spare pair of flats for her big fat feet back in the bunker.

"Where did you park, Martha? Or is Rob in town somewhere?"

"No, he's home. Learning how the sterilizer works. I've parked in the multi-storey but it was just too far with the bags." Her breathing was evening out and normal colour had returned to her face.

"Okay. Well, just relax for a while. I'm nearly done here, so I'll get you a cuppa, and then I'll drive you round to your car. Okay?"

Martha nodded and looked just like I remembered her when we were little and she'd hurt herself, so Dad had her sit on his knee until she stopped crying. I kissed her on the head and started for the bakery.

"Hol?"

"Yep?"

"Would you mind if I took my shoes off in your shop?"

I grinned back at her for being so prim. What a burden. "Sure. I've got some flats you can use."

"Hol?"

"Yep?"

"Can you pull them off for me, please? I can't reach."

Martha eventually dragged herself through to the back and found no end of enjoyment nibbling on the plate of cupcakes Jesse had brought out back for them both. I finished on the laptop while Jesse added the final flourish to tomorrow's cake and Martha chatted seasonal colour trends with him.

Jesse showed Martha the latest object of his affection in one of our mags, and Martha showed Jesse her favourite wedges in a magazine she'd brought in with her.

"I can do better than those," Jess said, dragging her over to the bunker, where he reached up for the paper bag I'd forgotten we'd been safely keeping on the shelf there.

Martha's eyes widened when she saw the shoebox.

"Oh, hello, my little Dior-lings," she cooed over the pretty black heels. "Go on, Jess, pop one on my foot for me," she said, flopping back onto the plum sofa.

"No," I said firmly. "They're at least an inch higher than the ones you've just rode in on. I'm sorry, but you're a week off your due date, Martha. I'm putting my unfashionable yet unswollen foot down."

Martha pulled a face, settling for just looking some more. "They're brand-new! Oh, what a waste, Hol. I can't believe you haven't been pottering round in them."

"Ha, I value my life," I said.

"But they're so pretty! How come they're here?"

"Some bird gave them to Hol. What a waste, huh?" Jesse was winding us both up.

"A tragic waste." Martha sighed. "Although, we could share?"

"Martha, they don't belong to me, or you could gladly have them. We're just hanging on to them until someone comes back to collect them."

"She won't be coming back, Hol. You know she won't."

I had to admit, it did look unlikely.

And they were both right—it was a waste.

chapter 10

Autumn had really started to push in on Hunterstone come Friday, by which time I'd already told Jesse that I was taking the eleventh mystery cake to its final destination, a skateboard-inspired super-cake for some lucky teenage boy. Whoever he was, his folks had gone to town on him. I'd never seen such a detailed cake. As ever, Jesse had outdone himself with intricate models, a hand-painted graffiti-daubed wall, half-pipes and other crazy stuff kids threw themselves around on these days. I was more than a little concerned I might break it, and half of me wished I hadn't said I'd deliver it, but I was still niggled about the coincidence of so many random orders.

Jesse was right, though—we were having a good run, and when he pushed me on it I really couldn't think why I was prodding at it.

For so long, the shop had been demoted to no more than a distraction, but the last few weeks had reminded me what going to work used to feel like. With such loose design briefs, we'd been allowed to thrash out ideas and play with techniques we hadn't seen much chance to use. And there had been enough money running through the till that I'd even dug out the catering-equipment brochure. We did desperately need a new oven. I'd also considered getting the van suspension looked at, amongst other things.

"So Rob's going to be emptying the storeroom and repainting it?" Jesse asked, as I was about to drive off with the cake.

"No, Rob's going to be hiding from his wife. We just need to supply a bogus list of jobs to throw her off his scent. She'll be spending the last week run up to D-day eating Häagen-Dazs in front of the TV, but if she calls we need our story straight." I smiled, turning the key over in the ignition. The van choked to life.

"Sure you don't want me to take it?" Jess asked.

"It'll warm up. I'm going straight home from there so I'll catch you later."

"Yeah, okay. Drive steady."

"See ya."

After two unfortunate misunderstandings of the city's one-way system, St Harry's Square finally peeked into view slightly later than I'd intended.

The square itself sat back off the road, segregated from those who weren't *residents only* by a long run of old brick wall, crowned with tall iron prongs of ornamental railings. On the other side of the enclosure, uniformly planted maple trees stood ablaze in angry bursts of oranges and scarlet—nature the arsonist. The contrast was staggering against the lush green of cool grass at the square's centre, and it was as though the refurbished town houses behind in pale stucco and shiny buzzer panels had gathered around the spectacle to watch them burn.

The van had warmed up, thankfully, and pulled smoothly into the gated square. Everything was so orderly here, it was easy finding the right address for the lucky skater. It was slightly harder finding a spot close enough to park the van. Eventually, after looping the square again, I settled on the only space that would allow me the room I needed to get the back doors open.

I walked across the square and punched the buzzer for 19 Richardson. A clunk before the door opened and a young hipster in a blue checkered shirt and Ronnie Corbett glasses looked out at me from underneath a mass of blond hair.

"You're late," the kid said, face full of disdain. I was late; he was right. I didn't really have anywhere to go with the snotty little git.

"Sorry. Road trouble. I'll go and get your cake." I smiled.

"You do that," I heard him say as I walked back to the pavement outside his house. *The customer is always right*, I thought, closely followed by: *And next time Jesse's delivering, leave him to it*. I bet the little twerp wouldn't have been so smart with Jess towering over him.

After trekking around the corner with Jesse's edible art, I made the delivery as short and sweet as possible and then got myself back into the van. The seat belt finally clicked home after the usual fumble, and I turned the key over. A spluttering of ignition, then nothing. I tried again. Nothing.

"Oh, come on! You've warmed up already!" I yelled, grateful that I hadn't parked where the kid could see me from his ivory tower. Another fruitless attempt and I knew I had to get this van sorted out. My head flopped back into the seat and I took a deep breath. This wasn't the first time. The van just needed a few minutes to consider its future on the scrap heap, then I'd start it up and we'd be on our way.

I needed a new van. Thanks to all the recent orders, there was extra in the bank, and after delivering to the little creep at number nineteen and finding absolutely nothing to add weight to my paranoid suppositions, I gave in. It really didn't matter where the work came from so long as Jess got paid and Cake kept ticking over. Maybe it was time to start thinking about moving forward a bit more. I could put a down payment on a proper van that would get me home after a delivery. Charlie would still be right—this van would have more character than anything I could buy from a dealer—but it would be great to make deliveries a little easier.

What I needed was a van that I could rely on, something that would keep me warm and comfortable. Something like the sleek black Range Rover crawling through the gates onto the square now, with huge silver wheels and blacked-out windows so no one could see me sat in the front like a doughnut when the engine refused to start.

Yeah, right.

I wasn't really much for cars, but it was nice, and— *Oh, look at the size of that boot. Multiple cake drops—every girl's dream!* I watched as it came around the square on the right of me then cruised around two more sides before drawing to a halt in the middle of the road behind me. I watched as the shiny truck waited outside number nineteen.

From the top window, the kid with the attitude glared at the Range Rover outside. The driver's door popped open and out stepped the unmistakable figure of Fergal Argyll. I almost leaned against the horn as I scrambled to turn around in my seat for a better look back there. *Fergal Argyll?* What was he doing here? He looked more normal without his kilt, but not normal enough to be here. He was wearing some sort of leisure gear, golf I think, and had rounded the truck to open the passenger door. With the door still open I couldn't see whose hands had found themselves wrapped around Fergal's back—obviously a woman's but I very much doubted that they were his wife's.

Fergal closed the door as the ice maiden walked from the car to the door of the town house looking every bit the golf enthusiast as her boss. They'd been friendly, but—I thought she was with Ciaran. The look on the kid's face had said it all. They were at it and he didn't like it. By his colouring, I was guessing at kid brother. Well, no wonder he had an attitude.

19 Richardson. Penny Richardson? PA to the chairman and chief exec of the Argyll empire? I was guessing so. *Personal assistant*—so that's what they called it now. Well, good luck to her. If she stuck it out hanging off the arms of rich men, maybe eventually she'd find something for her, and her brother, to smile about.

How one of our cakes came to end up at her place was a mystery, though. If she'd wanted a cake for the kid, why didn't she email it through like she had done Ciaran's order? Most people would have tried for a discount. Maybe she did and Jesse forgot to mention it.

The Range Rover purred towards where I was still sat in the van. An unexpected thrill of panic sent me slumping down into my seat. As if that would help. This vehicle was not made for stealth. That it was the only car on the street older than a year paled against the other comparisons it would draw. Colour, form, *Cake!* in foot-high lettering. I cringed as Fergal rolled past me and out of St Harry's Square.

Lately, it seemed, whenever anything out of the norm occurred, an Argyll wasn't far away.

I readied the key to try the engine again. I had my AA card in the glovebox if I needed it. As if the van had had a complete change of heart, the engine growled into a nice steady rumble.

As I left the dim streetlights of the city and drove north past Hunterstone, I thought about the collection of characters that had seemingly appeared from nowhere in my life. It had been a month since I'd taken the order for Argyll's Dior heel cake, and since then had felt as though they'd never been off the radar.

I was already driving away from Hunterstone when my arms decided to steer back towards the shop. I was being stupid, and anal, and there was no sense or reason to it, but the Argyll link—no matter how tenuous—would keep me up tonight, I knew it. And that, more than anything, bothered me.

I let myself into the shop, flipping the lights on as I went. The bakery clunked into view, one area at a time as the overheads flared up. I only needed the order sheets. I could have asked Jesse for the info I wanted over the phone, but then he'd know that which up until now he'd only suspected. That I was nuts.

Within minutes, I was back on the road for home and, if I'm honest, feeling a little bit of a berk. But then, only I knew it, so that was fine.

Dave's annoyance at my late return was about as masked as the skater kid's. Dave had taken it one step further, though, and had vented his emotions on my slippers. They were officially dead.

"Okay, I get it. I'm late!"

Dave wasn't hanging around for excuses. Instead he went over to wait at his food bowl. Once he'd been sorted, I jumped on Charlie's laptop in the man-cave. Within minutes, I was looking through Penny Richardson's profile on Argyll Inc.'s website. She didn't look as pretty in her headshot. Her smile didn't suit her as much as I thought it would. Maybe she didn't use it outside of marketing shots. I hadn't seen it in the flesh yet. I pulled ten other sheets from my jean pocket and started to flick through the names on the orders.

Ms Beirne, Mrs Copeland, Mrs Peterson, Mrs Stephenson, Mrs Krohl, Mrs Randall… I came out of the ice maiden's profile and scanned the screen in front of me. Argyll Inc.'s team ran to some thirty or more hard-hitters, all with artsy head-shots in rows of five along the screen. Jesse had said that all of the houses he'd delivered to had been nice, so the top of the screen seemed a good place to start.

First up was Fergal himself. He looked good in his picture, handsome. The grey tones of the black-and-white photography became him, and I could see what the ice maiden might see in him, other than his fortune obviously. Alongside Fergal, a few names that meant nothing to me. Then, a few names that did.

Donald Stephenson, Head of Residential Estates; Carl Copeland, Development Director; Jamie Peterson, Construction Director. Further down the screen, Heidi Beirne, Head of Customer Care; Andrzej Krohl, Director of Asset Management; Bert Randall, Acquisitions.

We'd been making cakes for the whole bloody company! A wave of annoyance flooded through my brain. *But why?* Why the secrecy? Which Argyll was it, for a start, and what the hell were they up to? I tallied up what they had spent with us over the last three weeks. Excluding the Hollywood cake, the figure stood at five thousand, six hundred pounds. What the hell were they playing at? Were they trying to size us up or something?

My eyes followed the screen all the way down from the heavyweights, until one photo stood out, every bit as photogenic as his father. Ciaran Argyll, Chief Brand Officer. Black and white became him, too, making already dark eyes abyssal. I stared, the annoyance slipping like snow in an avalanche as I tried to decipher why I cared so much.

chapter 11

A little light fishing was one thing, but I had gone too far last night, Ciaran's name scattering off my fingertips as effortlessly as my own would have.

I'd thought that shedding light on the whole cake-gate situation would increase my chances of a decent night's sleep. I was wrong. For much of last night I wrestled with insomnia and the many images of Ciaran Argyll's party lifestyle whizzing around my head. Along with feta, cyber-snooping was not something I would be indulging in before bedtime again.

At first sight, there hadn't seemed to be much about Ciaran on the Net, other than references to *Fergal Argyll's only child*, and *heir to Fergal Argyll's fortune*. The images of Ciaran Argyll, though, were altogether more inclusive. Partying with a brunette, partying with a blonde, partying with two blondes, this year, last year, three years ago, snap upon snap of a man enjoying his father's money and the lifestyle it afforded him. Fergal was often in the background, but all the cameras had preferred the antics of the younger Argyll, who seemed more than happy for the attention.

Today was going to be one of *those*, I could already tell. I felt so pent-up this morning, so...so frustrated. Just, niggling and niggling.

Dave had picked up on my mood and stayed out of my way, as had the van, which started first time. I had two hours before opening up at ten, just long enough to get to Hawkeswood, say my piece and get to Hunterstone. All I had to figure out now was whatever *my piece* was.

The journey there didn't clear that one up any. Mist hung a few feet from the grounds of Hawkeswood Manor, making it seem more Gothic than the last time I'd been there. It also looked more formal without the bustle of merriment. Seeing Fergal's Range Rover next to the sportier car Ciaran had parked outside the shop almost made me lose my nerve, but I was here now and if I left...well, I'd be a chicken.

Stalking across the courtyard seemed to set me up nicely, my disgruntlement good and ready once I'd banged on the knocker. But I hadn't prepared myself for the brunette lady's cheery disposition, and the dent it would instantly make on my mood.

"Hello, dear," she said brightly. "Come on in. It's brisk out there this morning." I felt my grimace slip immediately at her cheerful welcome, knowing I was failing already. I needed the grimace back in place before I set eyes on either Argyll.

"Hi, again." I smiled, entering the main lobby again. She was still smiling, too, waiting for me to state my purpose. How was I going to put it exactly...?

"It's a bit quieter this morning."

"Oh, yes, nobody's awake yet," she replied.

"Oh," I said, not factoring that into my loosely planned campaign. "I was hoping to catch a word with Mr Argyll." Good start. Nice and vague enough.

"Well, which one would you like to see, dear?" she asked,

still as friendly as ever. "Fergal is closer, although—" her voice tailed off to a whisper "—he's probably a little harder to wake. Or," she said, volume returning to normal levels, "I could wake Ciaran for you?"

"Wake Ciaran for who?" came a voice from the landing above us. I turned to look through the stairwell as two bare feet, followed by legs in baggy grey marl sweatpants, were treading their way down to us. If the voice alone hadn't told me which Argyll was coming, the athletic line of his thighs and other things through those joggers did. I tried to get my grimace back, but when I looked at the woman next to me I was met with an expression of total bafflement. I couldn't do this! I couldn't be friendly, and annoyed at the same time!

This was already going badly. I already felt embarrassed!

As the stairs led him lower, sweatpants gave way to a naked and exhaustively ripped torso. I heard myself swallow.

Ciaran Argyll's body hadn't shown up shirtless on the endless pictures of him I'd seen last night. If it had, I might have been able to prepare myself—as it was I'd just walked myself straight into the jungle without so much as a fly-swat.

The warm rush was already creeping up over my chest. *Be cool, Hol. They're just pecs...just well-defined pecs.*

"Hello, again," he said, sending me a polite smile. "Morning, Mary."

"Morning, Ciaran. I didn't think you'd be awake yet after all that racket last night." There was an edge of a mother's rebuke in there. "Are you ready for breakfast?"

Ciaran crossed the hallway and planted a kiss on Mary's head. "Yes, please, in the orangery?" Mary smiled a mother's smile and then looked back to me. Ciaran was looking at me, too—everyone wanted a reason for my being there and I couldn't remember myself what it was.

"Are you here for me?" he asked, running his hand back

over his head to settle bed-ruffled hair. As he lifted his arm, my eyes fell to that line alongside his hip, happily disappearing into the waistband of his joggers. "It's just that I thought I was dealing with your friend Jesse. Exclusively. On Monday mornings."

He delivered the sarcasm with a smile that could have softened granite, and without anything to feel defensive about, the flush carried on its skyward crawl.

"I'll just go and arrange breakfast. Will you be staying, Miss...?"

At last, something manageable... "Holly," I said, without allowing the catch in my throat to betray me. Mary carried on beaming at me, and again I was lost for words.

"Will you be staying for breakfast, Holly?" she repeated.

"Oh!" I stammered. "Oh, no...thank you. No."

"Then I'll leave you two to it."

Ciaran's eyes followed Mary as she passed him, and I could tell she was watching him, too. Then, he turned them back on me.

"Do you mind if we don't stand around here?" he asked, pulling on the matching grey hoody to his sweatpants. "The floor's a little cold."

Already I felt stupid for even being there, and following Ciaran as he walked off through the passage behind the stairs did little to make me feel any less so. At least from there I couldn't see any flesh.

"So, to what do I owe the pleasure, Holly? Or is this business?" he asked.

"I, er, wanted to run something past you. Well, I think you should just know that, er..." Ciaran had led me through an enormous reception room, where Fergal was slumped in boxer shorts and last night's shirt over one of the settees. He looked something between a sleeping baby and a hog, the depth of his snoring leaning more towards the latter.

"Don't mind Fergie," Ciaran said, this time not bothering to turn his head. "He's just getting his beauty sleep."

We left the thrum of Fergal's snoring behind and crossed two or three smaller rooms, these ones facing the grounds to the back of the manor, I thought.

I waited for Ciaran to ask me to finish what I was saying, but he didn't.

I didn't know where I was in the house now, and could only follow like a little lost sheep. Ciaran took us left into a much lighter, brighter space. The room wasn't overly large, not so much bigger than my open kitchen at the cottage, but I felt as though I'd just walked straight out into the gardens.

On all but one side of me endless lawns rolled away into a landscape punctuated by pockets of trees and occasional garden sculptures. Behind the pavilion, the river wound off into the distance beneath uninterrupted sky for as far as I could see.

Ciaran allowed me to take it all in, sitting on one of two sofas. He scooped up one of the two coffees he'd just poured for us.

"Do you take sugar, cream?" he asked, waiting for me to finish with the great outdoors.

"Just milk, please. Or cream. Whichever." *What are you doing? You're not staying.* I caught him up at the sofas and moved to stand beside the one he wasn't sitting on. If I thought the hoody was going to spare any more blushes, I was dead wrong.

Ciaran casually sat forward on the edge of the sofa, stirring the cream into my cup. His grey hooded jacket gaped open over a tan body, the chunky white pull cord on either side of his collarbone dangling down over the flat expanse of his chest. Beneath that, stomach muscles bunched as he leaned forward, a neat little belly button crowning the beginnings of a hairline running down to other things best not to think about.

I was ogling. I'd been in here minutes and so far all I'd done was stare at stuff.

"Would you like a seat?" he asked, gesturing at the sofa I was standing idly alongside.

"No. Thank you. I'm not staying." There was a snip in my voice, which was good, but even I couldn't help think its timing was off.

"Well, you're staying for your coffee, aren't you?"

I reached for the coffee cup on the table and began to glug it down. *Crikey, that's hot! I think I've just given myself third-degree burns!*

I did that thing then that all idiots do when they've hurt themselves—I pretended I hadn't.

"I've only come because I thought you should know some-one from your company, I *think*, has been placing a lot of or-ders with us lately, and maybe that was something your father needed to be aware of?" Ugh, that could have been worse but it still sounded bloody ridiculous.

"I see. And why do you think that?" he asked, sipping sensibly from his cup. His chest was playing peekaboo with me. I ignored it. I was rolling now. Mary came back into the room, still smiling, with a tray of toast and fruit and weaved her way between the sofas to place it on the table between us. If I stopped now, I might not get started again.

"Because in less than three weeks we've pushed ourselves to finish eleven last-minute orders, all of which have been delivered to the wives of people featured on your company website."

It had sounded a lot less sensible out loud.

Mary stiffened and looked worriedly at me, before turning

to Ciaran. Ciaran smiled at her and shook his head a little—to reassure her? That one gesture made me a little braver.

"And it's not that I don't appreciate the business. It's just the lack of transparency I don't understand."

"I'm sorry, Ciaran. I just thought that when you said that it would be nice for the wives… They'd appreciate the thought, I thought." Mary looked positively mortified now, and whatever it was that I'd said to make her look that way, I regretted.

"It's okay, Mary. I think that was a great idea, and I'm sure they all loved Holly's artistry."

Mary looked apologetically at me, and it made me squirm a little.

"I'll bring the dishes through when I'm done, Mary," Ciaran said.

Mary took her leave and left me alone with him again.

For the first time so far, I looked straight at those serious umber eyes without flinching. "Did I just upset her?" I asked.

Ciaran didn't flinch, either, meeting my stare just as assuredly. "My father wanted to give his staff a token of appreciation for their dedication over recent months. I suggested we do something different, unusual. Your business fitted the bill."

Made sense. I guess.

"So why not just get the ice—Ms. Richardson to email us? We would've offered you a discount for multiple orders."

"After Fergie's behaviour, I wasn't sure you'd be in a rush to work for him. So I asked Mary to arrange the cakes, and allocate them accordingly." Ciaran's explanation had knocked the wind out of my sails. "I'm sorry if we've put any unwelcome pressure on your team to get the orders fulfilled," he said.

"It's not that we didn't appreciate the extra work. It's just…" *What was it just again?* What was my problem? I felt like I had something to apologizc for.

Fergal Argyll grunted his way into the summer room, still

just in pants and shirt, smoothing back his hair as his son had done. If he were anything like his son from the neck down, it was well hidden by years of overindulgence. He looked at me and an unnerving smile broke across his sleep-filled face.

"Ye havenae come tae feed me more body parts have ye, darlin'? Ma guts couldnae handle it this morning!"

"No, not today, Mr Argyll," I said, eyeing for another spot in the room I could safely look towards.

"It was very good, you know, and I dinnae normally eat the stuff. I'm more of a meat-and-tatties man," he said, surveying Ciaran's breakfast platter.

"Right, I'll be going, then," I said to Ciaran, before turning to his father. "Thank you for the cake work, Mr Argyll. I appreciate the business."

"Business? I don't think she'll be back fer another!" he laughed. "That was probably a one-off te accompany the divorce papers."

I didn't understand what he meant.

"And don't rush off on my account, darlin'," he continued, not at all bothered about his state of undress. "I'm goin' to see what the kitchens have got that doesna involve rabbit food."

"Fruit won't kill you, Dad. Go easy on the sausage, eh?" Ciaran responded.

"Why dinnae ye take Holly here back into the kitchens? Ye can show her what your mother said was the best oven she'd ever used. It is Holly, isnee it?"

"Yes," I said, confused, "but really, I don't need a tour of your kitchen, thank you, Mr Argyll. I spend enough time in my own."

"Oh? It's just that Mary said Ciaran was helping you replace your oven? Is that no right?"

"Replace my oven?" I said. "Why would you think that?" I smiled.

Fergal looked at his son. No one said anything.

"Why would your dad think you were helping me replace my oven?" I asked Ciaran.

"Right then, about those sausages," Fergal said, and without offering any more goodbyes, he left through the door Mary had taken.

"What does he mean?" I asked again.

"Look, I overheard that you were in need of a new oven. I just thought that you might like the chance to earn enough to meet your needs."

"But...*what*? So *that's* why we got the orders? *That's* the reason?"

"It killed more than one bird. You can't operate efficiently without working equipment."

"Why would you do that? It's not your place!" My voice was getting higher.

"I really don't see what the problem is. You've increased your turnover, I've made amends for my father's indiscretion and your product has been exposed along the way."

"So, you've ordered cake after cake, because you thought I needed the money? You've spent a *fortune* on cakes nobody wanted," I asked, disbelievingly.

"Sure they did. They just didn't know they wanted them until they took a bite. I don't understand the problem. You should be gra—" He stopped himself short.

"*Grateful?*" I finished for him. "For making a mockery out of my business? I never asked for your help, Ciaran. I wouldn't have even if I'd needed it."

"Then you're saying you weren't glad for the additional money coming in? Come on, I heard you say you needed a new oven."

"Yes! And would have bought one *myself* with my *own* money. And yes, as you've asked, I was glad of the extra work, but not because there was more money in the till. It's not *just* about money, you know."

Ciaran rose to his feet and cocked a wry smile.

"It's always about money."

"No," I answered him defiantly. "It's not. But it must be nice to have enough of the stuff that you can convince yourself of that."

He wasn't so good-looking when he talked like an idiot. I turned to leave him there, hoping I'd be able to find my way out of the myriad rooms I had to pick my way through.

"Holly, look. I thought you had a problem. I was simply making it go away for you."

I watched him walk barefoot across the rug to me.

"Well, it must be very nice to be able to just pay your way out of a problem," I said, trying not to look anywhere near his torso.

He laughed then, and it irritated me. "In my experience, money can buy most things."

I was brave enough to look at him then, into eyes that were hard now. "Well, I guess that depends on who's selling."

I'd take my chances with the rooms. Storming my way out seemed to help my sense of direction.

Somewhere behind me, the floor creaked.

"So you're a traditionalist, then?"

I halted beside a long occasional table where silver-framed photographs catalogued the life of a family here. "What?"

"I bet you're just waiting for Prince Charming to come rescue you from your broken oven every night, huh? Before taking you away to your happy ending?"

"Happy ending? I'm not waiting for my happy ending, Ciaran."

"Sure you are. You're a woman. I bet you've got it *all* mapped out."

He was annoyed? *He* was? He didn't know me; he didn't know anything. I did believe in Prince Charmings once. I'd even met one. But no, I didn't believe in happy endings. Either they didn't exist, or you couldn't have them as well.

chapter 12

"No, Pattie, I won't leave my phone anywhere irresponsible. No, no, I won't do that, either.... A *what* pump?"

Jess and I giggled in the back as we listened to Rob being read the riot act by my mother for the second morning in a row. Normally, I'd have felt sorry for him, but after knocking over the bin of flour yesterday, as well as twice drinking the hazelnut praline latte Jess had bought specifically to lift my mood, it was difficult not to enjoy Rob's ordeal now. He was as good as my brother, so I was allowed to delight in his misfortune. He was as good as Mum's son—she was getting her allowance, too.

We were on the countdown to the baby's due date, and despite him being in the way, I still thought Rob could use a few last days of normality before he succumbed to Martha's colour-coordinated baby outfits, my mother's inescapable visit from Minorca and debilitating sleepless nights.

Please, it had to be someone else's turn for the sleepless nights.

Maybe I was coming down with something. Maybe by some weird sisterly marvel, I was experiencing Martha's hormonal imbalance. Whatever it was, it needed a steady stream of hazelnut lattes.

My spat with Ciaran Argyll, the pretentious git, hadn't eased my mood any. It had been refreshing, though, arguing with someone. No one argues with you when you're a widow. I took a deep breath and let it out slow. Come Saturday night his Hollywood cake would be delivered. His name would be crossed out of the diary, his order sheet deposited in the Jobs Done file. Ciaran Argyll would finally be out of my hair.

Rob appeared in the doorway to the bakery looking emotionally drained. "Your mother wants a word."

I mentally corrected myself. *Some people argue with widows.*

"Hi, Mum."

"Holly, I see Robert's back there again this morning?" my mother trilled.

"Yeah, he's really helping me out around the place." On the counter in front of me there was a conspicuous mound of crumbs where Rob had covertly devoured a cupcake.

"But that's what you pay Jesse for. Don't you think Robert should be at home, with his wife?" Even from Minorca she had to interfere.

"Oh, I don't know, Ma. I'm sure Martha's glad of the peace and quiet." *She's probably vacuuming less, too.*

"She's due to give birth in three days, Holly. I don't expect you to understand but your sister's body is under a lot of pressure right now."

No. What would I know about my body being under pressure? I hadn't slept properly for weeks in the run-up to Charlie's birthday, but no, she was right. I'd never been pregnant.

"Martha is fine, Mum. If she needs anything, she'll ask. We're less than ten minutes from their house," I said.

"Well, just encourage him to get a move on, Holly. A man's place is with his wife. She needs him."

I stood waiting for her to finish her point, to finish educating me on all the ways a woman needed her husband. I felt the colour draining from my face, edging nearer and nearer that grey tone Rob's skin had been before he'd handed me the receiver. It was so good to feel all that Minorcan sunshine, right down the phone line.

Mum was saying something about not giving the baby too much attention, when salvation walked in through the door.

"I've gotta go, Ma—customers. 'Bye." I clicked her off before she had time to argue.

The wide set of the shop door gave just enough room to allow the couple to walk through it near enough side by side. "Hi!" we all said in synchrony. Yay, friendly customers. They had the power of at least five lattes, and engaged couples who came in without a pernickety mother were usually the sunniest of the lot.

Both dressed like a pair of Ralph Lauren models, he with darker features than Jesse and her a very cute befreckled redhead. I was instantly taken with how perfect they looked together.

The cute redhead went first.

"Hi, we're looking to speak with the person dealing with Mr Argyll's commission?"

If there was a moment this week where the sound of a needle scratching gratingly across a record was to feature, this was it.

Her smile was going nowhere so I held mine, too.

"Jesse!" I yelled sharply. She jumped a little. I reiterated the smile as compensation.

Jesse poked his head out into the shop. "Yeah?"

"Somebody here to speak to you about the Hollywood cake."

"Actually, it's not so much about the cake itself... Well, it *is*. Hi, my name's Nat and this is Ryan," she said, offering hands to be shaken. Ryan followed suit. "We work for a company called Cinder Events and will be overseeing things at the Gold Rooms this weekend. Mr Argyll is one of our most valued clients, and when he mentioned that Cake was providing, well, the cake, we thought we'd better come see what you guys were all about."

A tension pulled in my stomach. I was definitely coming down with something.

"He wasn't exaggerating, either. These are impressive. How come we haven't heard about you?" Ryan asked, wandering along the displays.

Jesse looked at me to take the helm.

"We don't really advertise, outside of wedding fairs," I said.

"Wedding fairs? You guys need to get yourselves on the events circuit. Our clients would go berserk for something like this."

Ryan was a nose away from the tallest cake on display, a six-foot-high chocolate masterpiece Jesse and I had created for this year's fairs. Detailed water nymphs interspersed with insects and toadstools, all sculpted by hand in rich dark chocolate.

"And that's the reason for our visit," added Nat enthusiastically. "Saturday's event is going to be very special, attended by a broad mix of society types. We can't wait to see your finished creation for Mr Argyll! But another of our clients will also be there, and we just so happen to know that there's an engagement in the pipeline."

"Sorry—how does this relate to us?" I asked.

"Well, when Ms Delgado and Mr Benini formally announce their engagement, we'll be managing the ensuing parties. They've already booked events in their native Spain and Italy, but as Modesto is signed to play for an English team and Aleta's new film will premiere in London in the spring, they're both keen to celebrate their union in the UK also. We're looking for a cake supplier, someone who can provide a centrepiece that stands alone from the average, and I have to say I think we've found one," Nat said, joining Ryan at the displays.

Jesse turned to me and raised enthused eyebrows.

"Wow," I acknowledged, "that's fantastic. Thank you so much!"

Wow, wow, wow! It really *was* fantastic. This could be the job! That one commission that could see us catapulted into a new realm of work! Another thought piggybacked the first.

Crap.

Somewhere along the line, I had Ciaran Argyll to thank for it.

"Well, it's not in the bag yet," Ryan added. "Aleta's quite fussy about who she uses. She'll have to meet you first. As Nat said, she'll be attending this Saturday's event, and so as you guys are both going to be there it would be a great opportunity for us all to touch base. If you're interested?"

Ryan laid two very simple-looking black cards on the counter and slid them over towards me. I lifted one up, inspecting the gold italics on the reverse. *Guest* it read, nothing more.

"If we're interested?" Jesse asked, eyes growing wider. Ms Delgado, and invites to the Gold Rooms. Jess was having a good day. "We are interested, aren't we, Hol? Please say that we're interested."

"I have to point out that there is a strict dress code, either formal evening wear or Hollywood hero or villain... If you do stay at the event after you've set up for Mr Argyll, you would have to adhere to that."

"Hol? We are interested, right?" Jesse prompted.

A shuddering breath, the kind that slips out after crying, pulled all eyes on me. Maybe, if I were lucky, Ciaran would be necking with some leggy lovely all night, too busy to be thanked. If I were lucky.

I looked at the simple invitation, still sat in my hand.

"Yes, Jesse. We're interested."

chapter 13

Jesse really wanted the Delgado commission. It was bitter-sweet for him, the chance to meet the girl of his dreams, in the company of her international-football-star fiancé. Jesse had been working on the cake all week, and I knew it would blow everyone away. But I also had a sneaky suspicion that if Jess thought he saw a chance of swaying Miss Delgado's heart, he'd probably take a shot at it.

The cake was incredible.

Jess could have so easily gone down the obvious route of colourful superheroes and arch-enemies. Instead he'd incorporated iconic imagery from Travis Bickle and his taxi, to Audrey Hepburn draped over a chaise longue. At the head of the cake, a large Hollywood Boulevard star with *30* sparkling in gold.

Cinder Events had arranged a parking spot at the back of the building, and clearance to get up through security.

Due to the guest list, restrictions would be in place on who would be accessing the lifts and the skyline Gold Rooms on the twenty-fifth floor.

Jess and I both knew what services we were going to offer Miss Delgado—basically whatever services she required, with Jess prepared to go way above and beyond what I paid him for.

The cake was perfect, the guest passes safely in the van glovebox. We'd be back to collect the cake on the way to the city.

I had only one problem. I had nothing to wear.

Jess had gone back home to have his mum fix his hair and was going to get her to give him a lift all the way over to mine so that he could vet the outfit I picked out. As instructed, I was showered, plucked and ready to state my argument for trousers when Jess arrived with a bang.

"Jesse, you look amazing. Just wait there a sec." I closed the door in his face and skipped off to contain Dave.

I let Jesse in, absorbing every inch of him. He looked like some kind of movie star.

"Your hair!" I sang. "Jesse, you look *incredible!*"

Gone were the cornrows he'd had all through the summer, replaced now with a very grown-up mass of individually defined twists.

"And your suit—I don't think I've ever seen you wear black!" Other than the one day.

"Actually, it's licorice—the licorice looked better with the tie and hankie."

Beneath Jess's jacket, a *licorice* waistcoat over *licorice* shirt held back the tail end of his fat coppery tie; a matching handkerchief in his breast pocket completed the look.

"The licorice works." I grinned. "It's a good look for you."

"This is my neo-soul look, girl. I am on the prowl tonight. So you think I've nailed it?"

I couldn't stop looking him over.

"I think you've just lost us the Delgado engagement cake."

That girl had to be seriously in love not to throw Jesse a second glance tonight.

"So, did you come up with anything?"

The truth was, I hadn't really looked that earnestly. I'd thought that the trousers were smart enough, and black flats, but now I wasn't so sure.

"Come on up. You can tell me what you think," I said.

Jess hung his jacket with meticulous care and sat on the chair at my dressing table. I'd changed in the next bedroom so that Jess had somewhere comfortable to wait before giving me his expert opinion. I teamed the trousers with a white chiffon blouse, and threw a black tailored jacket on over the top. I thought I looked okay, but Jesse's face said it all.

"No good?"

"No, it's fine. You look nice…but we need to see your legs, Hol. People are going to be asking you to take their drinks orders all night."

"But I haven't got anything like that, Jess. I don't…party."

"Did you look?"

"Yes," I lied. "Okay, no, I didn't. But I know there's nothing in my wardrobe."

"Yeah, well, we've got to leave in an hour. So I'm just going to take a look now if that's all right with you?"

I felt like a student who had failed their assignment as Jess began thumbing through my wardrobe.

"No, no, no," he said. Well, I had told him.

"Wow! Do people still *own* these?" He poked his head back to see if I was biting. "When was the last time you cleared out your closet, Hol? No, no, definitely no… A-ha! I knew you'd have *something*. What's up with this?" I looked in the dressing table mirror and saw Jesse inspecting the little black dress in his hands. "It's a bit dusty, Hol!"

"I haven't worn it for two years, Jess."

"Well, it's a little bit long, and the neck's a bit high."

"I like bateau necklines," I interjected. See, I knew some stuff.

"But it's sleeveless. You have nice arms, Hol, one of the perks of rolling fondant all day. Where does it come to on your legs?" he asked, leaning back out of the wardrobe.

"Just above my knee."

"That's a shame. You have good legs, too, Hol, I've noticed." He winked. "So what was the occasion?" he said, dusting the dress. "And why wasn't I invited?"

I looked at him in the mirror and smiled as he made the leap.

"You were." I smiled. Jess took a deep breath.

"That's flown round, Hol." He winced, carefully draping the dress over his arm. It wasn't quite two years. We had a couple of weeks yet. "Hol, I'm sorry. You should've said as soon as I pulled it out."

I felt bad for Jess, but actually I quite liked the dress. After my expectations of what this party would be like, at the very least it wasn't too attention-grabby. And I wasn't keeping it under glass; I just hadn't found another reason to wear it.

"I like the dress, Jess, but I've only got flats to wear. Don't you think that trousers will be better?"

Jess twisted the hanger in his hand to spin the dress around. "Are shoes your main issue with this dress, Hol? Be honest."

"Jess, honestly, it's a nice dress," I said. I didn't want him to feel bad.

"You're sure?"

"Yes, but—"

"Wicked. Well, I've got a surprise for you, then. You get out of your hotelier gear and slip into that. I'll be right back."

Jess left me to dress. I was going to need tights. My legs were like silk, but they hadn't seen the sun in a while. I dug around in my drawer for a pair, listening to Jesse stamping on the stairs.

"When are you getting this place finished, Hol?" he called from the next room. "You know I can cover the shop if you wanted a bit of time here."

"Soon. When I get round to it," I yelled back. "It's on the list."

Aside from the zip I couldn't fasten up the back by myself, I was ready for Jess's critique.

"Come on, then. Feast your eyes."

Jess came back into the bedroom behind me and went straight for the zipper. Helping a woman *into* a dress must've been a real novelty.

We both checked over my reflection in the mirror. Jess got distracted and started messing with his own hair. I couldn't blame him; I'd rather look at him, too. I didn't look bad, though. Not bad at all. It did still fit, better than before even. I'd been skinnier then.

"So? What's the expert's opinion?" I asked.

"You look hot, Hol. Pull your hair out, though."

I did what I was told and shook my hair loose. It hadn't been completely dry when I'd tried tying it back with the trousers, the damp setting it to loose waves just below my shoulders.

"Yeah, very nice," Jess said, checking me out.

"Are you *checking me out*, Jesse Ray!" I teased.

"Well, we could always have a go if you like?"

I laughed. "This bedroom is a sex-free zone." When I was awake, anyway.

Jesse delved into the bag he'd brought in.

"Right, you look hot, Hol, but I have something that's going to take you from hot to *sizzling*."

Jesse pulled a box from the bag and opened it.

"Oh, no, no way, Jess."

"Hol, you've been shying away for too long. It's time." He laughed.

"Time for what! To fall flat on my face with a very expensive cake in tow?"

"The cake will be fine. The restaurant is providing a trolley. You can use it to lean on…like a walker."

Jesse held one patent shoe out to me. "Now who feels like Cinders?" he asked, grinning profusely.

"Jesse, I can't walk in those shoes. I don't know how!"

"Holly, my sister has a bigger ass than Martha, and she could chase the ice cream van in these. Now get them on, you'll look the bomb, and we can go to the ball…unless you want to take me up on that offer?"

A few unsure minutes later and I was making my first unaided journey downstairs, hanging on for dear life to the banister. I tried to ignore my entire collection of six or seven pairs of lovely flat shoes, sitting one pair to a step, as I teetered past them. Halfway down and I'd made it past my trainers, two pairs of flip-flops and my ballerina pumps. At the bottom of the stairs, I steadied myself enough to walk out across the hall.

An hour later and I still hadn't lost the uncertainty. But, after wobbling only once and a promise from Jess to catch me, I found myself hobbling over the yard to the van.

Back at the shop, I let Jesse struggle with the cake as I waited, shivering, in the nearly warm cab of the van. A few grunts and groans, and an emergency cake first-aid kit and we were on our way to the bright lights of the city.

"Can you hold these for me, Jess?" I asked, reaching down by my ankles for the discarded heels.

"Are you driving barefoot?" he asked, taking them from me.

"Yeah…I forgot to pick my pumps up."

"Well, I'd have gone back in for you."

"I'd left the kitchen door open. Dave would've trashed your suit." I wished Jess lived closer. We could hang out more. It was nice having a man around the place.

I traced my hand over the dress and remembered that day, standing in a frozen churchyard.

Life had gone on for nearly two whole years, and I had absolutely nothing to show for it.

chapter 14

My neck ached gazing up at the bright throb of the Gold Rooms, pushing out against the darkness, twenty-five floors above me. A shiver ran over me while I stood guarding the back of the open van. Guarding against what? There was nobody else back here. The rear fire escape we'd been told to use was shut fast, so Jess had run ahead around to the front of the building to find out what was going on. *Come on, Jess, it's freezing!*

The sudden slam of metal shattered the quiet of the service yard and the door swung out from the building. With it, the light from inside threw the only sliver of colour into the yard, and the flashiest looking maître d' this side of Vegas wheeled a shiny chrome dinner trolley my way.

"You took your time," I said, rubbing the cold off my arms.

"I got lost. I ended up in the underground car park instead of the street out front. You'd have thought they'd have stretched to signage." People who needed signs wouldn't find themselves back here. Why were back-of-house areas always so bleak?

Jess expertly manhandled the cake onto the trolley and I followed him back into the building. I hadn't used the trolley as a walker yet. Maybe I'd survive the night.

A mountain of a man with a detached expression and an earpiece running over the fold in his neck followed us into the lift. I concentrated on the flashing buttons, higher and higher up the pad, ignoring the prickle of claustrophobia.

The doors slid open just as I started to wonder how quickly the man-mountain could spend all the oxygen we had.

Security stepped aside, and the full effect of the Gold Rooms vista hit home.

The trolley rattled forward and I automatically stepped out with it into a space stretching what must have been nearly the whole expanse of the roof. And what a roof. Even up on the twenty-fifth floor, my neck still ached looking to where the ceiling reached away above us. It had to be at least double the height any of the floors we'd pinged past, triple even. The square bar at the centre of the room drew my eyes next. It drew the partygoers, too, like butterflies to a flower—beautiful creatures delighting at the nectars on offer there. Above the bar, held suspended by some invisible feat, a large sculptural piece hung over the immaculately dressed staff below. It reminded me of the oversized straggly hazel wreath they hung over the public entrance to the forest each year, only...posher.

"Hol?"

"Huh?"

"Beat a path," Jess said, nodding across the crowd.

Nat's red hair was like a beacon against the muted tones of her dress. She was smiling and beckoning us her way, a distance I hadn't had to walk in one burst yet. The cool metal of the trolley handle felt reassuring in my hand as I politely asked body after body to let us through. Exclamations of *ooh* and *ahh* bobbed over each of my shoulders as Jesse's centrepiece basked in the glory it was so deserving of. He had nailed the design. Most of the people here were dressed as refined Hollywood icons, not garish comic book characters. At least one Ghostbuster had crossed our path, the Terminator was waiting patiently at the bar, but mostly we were in a room of Godfathers and Dirty Harrys.

Nat's hair helped me to keep her picked out from the crowd as I led Jesse awkwardly between gently aglow booths, and the vast expanse of glass separating the lounge from the terrace outside.

Nat stood in front of a feature wall, a mosaic of giant metallic plates showing every depiction of gold, looming behind her petite frame.

Light dappled over all that shiny loveliness and I turned to see just as Jess did the same.

"Holy shit!" he exclaimed, gawping through the glass curtain.

"It's something, isn't it?" Nat asked, admiring the pool, too. "We're going to set the cake up through here, where it won't be knocked over."

I looked at her, just long enough to be polite, before turning back to the terrace.

"If you want to take a dip later, there's complimentary swimwear in the spa over there." Nat pointed to the far end of the water, where the pool ran underneath a pillared canopy. There were people in evening wear and bikinis peppered all around the timber decking of the poolside, sitting casually in clean-lined furniture and conversation.

I didn't realise the city had places like this.

"Do you like to swim?" Nat asked, humouring us.

Some guy in a Speedo was just walking out through the

doors of the building Nat had said was the spa. Jess and I both watched him step down into the lit waters.

"Hell, yeah," he said. I just hoped he'd keep his clothes on until we'd met with Aleta.

"Lead the way, Nat," I called, trying to rein in my awe.

At the end of the metallic wall, black carpet ran away to a dozen or so vertical glasslike panels breaking up the space, designating the area beyond them. The panels towered over us like monoliths some twenty feet high, highly polished stone in golds and bronzes and fusions of the two. I had a tiger's eye bracelet they reminded me of.

Nat slipped between two of the panels and led us into the buffet area. At its centre a large pedestal waited for Jesse's triumph.

"Once you've got it in situ, the kitchen staff will complete the buffet display around the foot of the cake," Nat told us, checking her watch.

"There's more food?" I asked, trying to take in the abundance of edible delights on offer around two-thirds of the room's perimeter.

"The birthday boy's a very popular man." She smiled, still checking her watch. I knew that already. Argyll had paid a small fortune for his friend's cake. "So you guys are going to hang out, right? Once you're done here?" she asked.

Jesse grinned. "Yeah, man. We're going to hang out, and dance and have a blast, aren't we, Hol?"

"Well, Aleta doesn't usually turn up on time, but they won't do the happy-birthday thing until later, so the cake will still be in one piece when she gets here. I hope."

Jesse carefully lifted the cake from the trolley and positioned it at the centre of the pedestal. Even through his jacket, his back felt warm under my hand. The cake had been heavy, even for him. "Good job, Jess," I whispered.

★ ★ ★

We left Nat in the buffet to discover the bar now packed with beautiful people. "An orange juice and a… Jess?" Jess's eyes were gathering intel. I knew who he was looking for.

"The champers looks a popular choice. I'll have two," he said, still casing the joint.

The bartender was leaning forward through the thick sounds of music and conversation, explaining to me that all drinks tonight were on the house. That was a relief, with Jess ordering two at a time. I held the two elegant glasses out for him. He took both, then passed one back.

"They're not both for me," he said, taking a sip.

"Jess, I'm driving," I said, holding the glass forward again.

"You can have *one*, Hol. It'll loosen you up a little. You won't be driving for at least an hour anyway."

I guess he was right.

Over the rim of my glass, the only Monroe I'd seen yet was watching a band of gentlemen greeting and slapping each other the way men sometimes do. It would seem the ice maiden was never very far from an Argyll, although I hadn't heard Fergal in here yet. Perhaps she knew the birthday boy, too, but something about the way she was watching Ciaran, as he laughed with the others, told me why she was here.

"I didn't think he'd go for the fancy dress," Jess said over my shoulder.

"What do you mean?" I asked.

"You know who I'm talking about. Moneybags. He's in a suit."

I looked away disinterestedly to the pockets of people hiding in the shadows of booths behind the dance area.

"Do you wanna dance?" Jesse asked.

"No, thanks! You go ahead, though. I'm going to go check the cake."

"The cake's fine, Hol. Relax."

"Technically we're working, Jess. I prefer it up that end anyway. More places to sit in these shoes!"

I took Jesse's glass from him and watched him cut through the people hanging around the periphery of the dance floor, not yet drunk enough to join the braver few. The baseline changed and Jess found himself. The women there were pleased to have him, the men less so. He moved like water around them, graceful as a shark and just as deadly. No wonder he was so popular with the ladies. I'd have fancied him right then and there if it wouldn't have felt so icky. I wasn't the only one who couldn't take their eyes off him. He was already drawing a crowd.

Before he did anything rash, like pull me on there with him, I turned to make my way back towards the buffet lounge.

Someone was blocking my escape.

"Nice shoes," he said, his hands in his pockets.

The champagne was warming my cheeks, or it might have been the embarrassment of being caught wearing someone else's footwear.

"Nice cummerbund," I replied, trying to put something, anything, back at him.

"Thanks," he said, a boyish smile reaching to eyes that were anything but. "I was lost for inspiration until you put me on track." I didn't follow. He opened his jacket, showing off the cummerbund in all its glory, and an aqua-blue water pistol poking from the top. Still, I was none the wiser.

"What, only Jesse's into Bond? That's too bad." He smiled.

How long was I going to have to suffer that one? Jess had started it. I could kill him. I glanced round, hoping to see an outdanced boyfriend doing it for me.

"He's a multi-talented man," Ciaran said, watching him, too.

I took the champagne flute he offered me, grappling with the awkwardness I always felt around him.

"About last weekend…" I tried, searching for the most efficient way to thank him for his obvious attempts to help Cake along.

"Have you cut yourself?" he interrupted, his fingers slipping between my glass and my hand. The move was so subtle, so unexpected. Lightly, his thumb ran over my knuckles. His hands were too soft, so unlike Charlie's. I felt myself stiffen.

Gently, he raised my hand to investigate the poppy red of my fingertips, clasped around the drink bubbling in my hand.

"Oh, no. That's just, er, food colouring," I stammered, nimbly pulling my hand away.

His eyes narrowed. "Did you get food colouring here, too?" he asked, softly stroking his thumb over my neck. A shock of adrenaline rushed through my body, the heat under my skin blooming in response to his touch. He smiled shrewdly. "Now that I think of it, I've seen you blush that way before."

Ciaran watched me as he sipped from his glass. I mimicked him, only gulping the lot down. *Talk about work, talk about work.*

"Are you pleased with your friend's cake?" I babbled, the fizz in my nose.

"Well, actually, I was hoping you could talk me through it," he said.

"It's all Jess's work. You should go speak to him." There, that was better.

Ciaran looked over my shoulder to the dance floor behind me.

"I don't want to disturb him. Would you take me to look at it? I haven't seen it yet."

Ciaran's arm waited for mine.

Tentatively, I slipped my arm through his and saw something in his eyes grow warmer.

It was both easier and harder, I found, to move through the guests when on Ciaran's arm. I hated that expression, but it was exactly where I was.

"Happy birthday, Ciaran," cooed one woman over her partner's shoulder.

"Happy thirtieth, mate!" said an already merry chap in a blue tux and wig.

"Nice party, Argyll—" came the cool tone of a voice noticeably more relaxed than Mr Blue Tux "—but you need more women."

Ciaran stopped pressing forward while a thirty-something with dark waves to his ears reached to shake his hand. Automatically, my hand began to slip from its cradle, allowing him the room he needed.

Ciaran's hand chased mine down to my side. Gently, *secretly*, he held mine in his for a moment, and then just like that, it was gone again.

"Ludlow. How's things?" Ciaran asked.

"Better than they are in your camp," Ludlow sneered. "I hear Fergal's about to lose another bid to Sawyers?"

"We're not losing anything to anyone," Ciaran said, a coolness to his voice.

"So Fergal's behaving himself, then? It's a shame he hasn't kissed and made up with James Sawyer," Ludlow persisted.

"There'll be no kissing there," Ciaran replied, coolness giving way to nonchalance.

"Ah, don't worry about it, pal. You'll get over it. Eventually." And Ludlow burst into a deep throaty laugh. "By the looks of it, you're doing your best, as usual." He sniggered, turning grey eyes on me. Ludlow was a handsome man, but something in the way he laughed made him less so. "So who's your plus one?" he asked.

Plus one? I ignored the question, but Ciaran humoured him.

"Holly, Freddy Ludlow. Holly's done some work for me. Holly, I believe you've already met Freddy's mother."

"Really?" Ludlow grinned. "Poor you. So you work for Argyll here? I'll bet he's had you doing all sorts for him." He leered.

My hand was ambushed again and I watched as Ludlow raised it to receive his kiss. A waft of cigarettes and booze came back with it.

Behind me, Ciaran's hand laid itself gently at the small of my back.

"Worked," I corrected him. "As in the past tense, not the continuous."

Ludlow's eyes momentarily widened, then he turned them back on Ciaran. "A bit feistier than your normal accessories, Argyll. You'll have to watch that one."

Accessories? I wasn't an accessory, and in case either one of them thought so, I left Ciaran's side.

"The cake's in the far lounge, when you're ready," I said to him, walking a few steps ahead.

"Enjoy yourself, Ludlow," Ciaran said. "But not too much, eh?"

I felt him close behind me as I moved more determinedly through the throngs of people. I half caught his responses to numerous sentiments of the well-wishers around him, but I wasn't in a hurry to meet any more of them. For a short silly while, the spot next to him had been a warm sunny one. I shook the thought away.

We'd nearly made it across the great expanse when a bustle of security caught both of our attention.

A gaggle of women with legs up to their eyeballs stepped

like gazelles from the burnished lift doors. All of them had the skin of women used to the kisses of a tropical sun, and the obvious poise of those plenty used to being admired. Ciaran hesitated behind me, taking in all that beauty. It was a fine display of high fashion and killer heels. Hell, I was dazzled by them. But there were more celebs in attendance tonight than Aleta.

I'd recognised a few faces in the crowd, famous enough in their own right to not be affected by Ms Delgado's entrance. Unperturbed, demure people, people not at all like Jesse, now stealthily shouldering his way to the lifts.

It would be interesting to see how this played out. Ciaran was obviously going to rain-check the cake to welcome his guests. This was his party, after all. At least I'd be free to rugby-tackle Jesse when I needed to.

"Ciaran? Aleta's arrived."

Ciaran and I both snapped our heads around to the ice maiden. *Of course he has to go*, I said to myself.

"Aleta's fine. She'll have plenty of people to keep her occupied while Holly shows me my cake."

The ice maiden shot me a scornful look. "You don't even like cake, Ciaran. I really think you should—"

"Penny, go get yourself a drink. I'll be back in a while."

"Fine." Her voice was sharp for an employee, too familiar with him. But Penny left us to continue to the buffet room.

The tiger's eye panels had been rotated, forming an uninterrupted partition now. Ciaran hit a button and, with a muffled thrum, the sections began to revolve.

"Incredible," he said softly, approaching the cake.

I followed him into the room. "Jesse's a talented guy. I'm lucky to have him."

Ciaran's attention turned back to me, his eyes falling to my dress. Immediately I found a small sharp edge of a fingernail to bother at.

"He's a nice guy, too," he said.

Stop fidgeting.

I breathed steady and smiled. "He is. The best."

"You must think so to bring him along tonight. You had two passes, right? I'd thought you might bring a partner."

I found another unevenness to my nail. *Stop. Fidgeting. Talk shop.*

"We're meeting with Miss Delgado this evening. She may have some work for us. I wanted to thank you actually, for telling the Cinder team about us. I appreciate it."

Ciaran looked at me thoughtfully. "So…I'm not making a mockery out of your business, then?" he said drily.

A snatch of pain at the edge of my fingernail.

"No," I conceded, rolling my eyes. "But if I leave Jess alone much longer, he might."

Ciaran watched me as the room fell silent around us.

Boy, it's warm in here.

"So, thirty?" I gulped, trying to keep cool.

Ciaran moved around the desserts.

How is the chocolate not melting?

My chest started to rise and fall more than it should do. I held my breath to steady it. Ciaran said nothing, a wolf stalking towards a doe.

My eyes plummeted to the floor. "Why didn't you say it was your party?" I asked in a small voice, watching his shiny old-fashioned dress shoes close in on me. They halted a few inches from where my toes peeped back at them through patent Diors. The shininess of our footwear made for a his-and-hers effect. It was almost funny.

"Because I wasn't sure that you'd come," he whispered, leaning in close, too close.

The shiny blackness fell away, leaving brown the dominant colour. An endless umber I didn't know I liked.

"Ciaran. We have a situation in the bar." The ice maiden's brusqueness pulled me back to where I stood, the butterflies dissipating from my chest. She glared at me while Ciaran moved closer to her. I tried to push away the mental image of Jesse body-popping all over Aleta Delgado, and cringed at what was coming next.

"What situation?" Ciaran asked.

Here it comes…

"The Freddy situation, Ciaran. You need to get him out of here. He's already offended Dickie's wife and security don't know what you want to do with him."

Ciaran turned serious eyes back towards me, his brow furrowed with thought. He looked predatory when he concentrated, and I felt like the doe again.

"I'll find you again, if that's all right?" he asked, forcing his eyes to soften. I didn't risk a reply but played it safe with an almost indecipherable nod.

I watched his shiny shoes disappear through the partition, leaving me alone—with the snow queen. She sauntered over to where I was still pulling myself together, and ran a long nail the colour of new blood over the contours of Jess's cake. I could try for small talk, but I didn't think she'd reciprocate the effort.

"I love your shoes," she purred, "but they're less shapely than I thought."

It occurred to me then whose feet the Diors had been destined for. For the barest second, I nearly let her intimidate me, but I'd met women like her before and I was not my mother. This bombshell had nothing I'd want for myself.

"And they're better suited to platinum."

"Sorry?" I asked.

"Oh, don't be." She smiled sweetly. "Dirty blonde *can* be a good look. Sometimes. Best kept to beach shoes, though, not Diors." She laughed.

Dirty blonde. It was a new slight, and almost, *almost* enough.

"Well, you'll have to excuse me, Marilyn. Your shoes are starting to pinch." I started for the gaps between the panels, pleading that now was not the time I stumbled. Anytime but now.

"You won't keep him, you know," she said, her derision stopping me dead.

I stood fast, taking a deep breath. "Why do you care, Penny? You're knocking his father off." I tried to see if my words had stung her, the way she was trying to sting me.

"Not always," she simpered. "There's more than one apple on the family tree."

I needed at least one more deep breath. I couldn't *stand* women like her, women who chose their men for shoes and big houses.

"Well, Penny, I'm not looking for anything. Apples or otherwise." I smiled.

"I'm only trying to be kind." She smiled coyly. "I've seen it before with Ciaran. Women, like yourself, maybe not used to the flattery, falling for those seductive brown eyes of his." I held my smile, but all sentiment behind it had gone. "Don't feel bad, Holly. You aren't the first and you won't be the last. Women are like sport to Ciaran. He tries them out for a while, then when he gets bored, he moves on to something more fun."

"Is that right?" I asked quietly. She could take it as defeat if she wanted to.

"Ciaran's had every type of woman there is, Holly," she said, nibbling on something of microscopic proportions. "Some more than once, some together, but I don't believe I've ever seen him with a dowdy little shop girl."

Ouch. That one stung. My smile had already abandoned me.

"But you should definitely try him out—" she grinned "—I can vouch for that, *personally*."

chapter 15

At least no one had closed the partitions or my big exit would have been an epic fail.

Penny had a thing for Ciaran and I *knew* there'd been something between them. Well, he'd have to find himself some other *dowdy* shop girl. This one was going home.

More people were enjoying the pool as I walked back out towards the bar, hunting for my only ally in the place, the venom of Penny's words ringing in my ears.

Sport.

Maybe she was lying. Maybe I was just lying to myself.

I tried not to dissect why I felt this way, like I'd just been kicked in the stomach. But the undeniable reality was that at someone else's party, wearing someone else's shoes, there was only so long I could fool myself.

Jesse, on the other hand, was the epitome of cool, out on the terrace, trousers rolled up to his knees. Aleta Delgado and her gazelle-like friends had all slipped from their shoes, too, heads thrown back in laughter at Jess's joke.

Why can't they all be like you, Jess? I puffed away the thought.

"Holly!" Nat's familiar red updo was snaking through the bodies towards me. "The buffet's about to open, then I'll introduce you both to Aleta."

I looked back out onto the roof terrace. "I think Jesse's already got that covered."

Nat stood next to me silently observing. "It's a good job Modesto isn't here. He can be quite the jealous boyfriend. If security thought Freddy Ludlow was a handful, they'd have no chance of containing Modesto."

"They kicked Freddy Ludlow out?" I asked, surprised.

"Not kicked, exactly. He's always the same—swaggers into a party, full of it. Drinks too much, throws his weight around and inevitably pisses someone off. I don't know why Ciaran invites him. He's too nice." I had the impression Nat was going for some sort of solidarity-amongst-colleagues vibe.

I saw an opportunity to probe. "He seems nice," I said, immediately wanting to take it back again.

"Oh, he *is*. Don't you think? And *so* hot with it. Between us girls, I've been throwing pheromones his way for a while now."

The images were back again. I scanned through them for one featuring Ciaran with a redhead.

"But, he hasn't bitten…*yet*."

Nat was pretty when she smiled, and less innocent. Leaving the probing there seemed a waste now. It felt a lot more acceptable when the *probee* was willing.

"I heard he's a bit of a player," I fished.

"A player? He *was*. Ciaran used to leave parties with a girl on each arm, and one for later. He still plays up to the press but we all know Fergal gets more action than him these days."

Jesse had all four women exploring the soft fuzz of his hair.

"What about Penny?" I asked.

"What *about* Penny? Penny's a bitch."

"Yeah, I got that."

"She doesn't like any women working near Ciaran. She's been trying to bag him for years, on the side. But Fergie's the one with all the money. He sits at the head of the company, so Penny stays where the going is good. I'd rather play Buckaroo with Junior myself."

"Heroes and villains!" came the boom of a microphone. *"If you would like to help yourselves to a glass of our finest, from any of the waiters eagerly awaiting to serve your every need, we can make our way through to the buffet for a rousing rendition of 'Happy Birthday'!"*

A few gentle whoops and claps and maybe half of the congregation gradually made their way to the food. The rest stayed put, and drank on. I knew which half I'd rather be in, but I was driving. It had nearly been an hour now; I'd be good to drive. Ciaran looked over the head of the brunette accompanying him that way. I tried not to watch him as they went.

"Are you coming?" Nat asked, and, before I could answer, "Come on, this is your part," she said, pulling at my arm.

I hung back from the thick of the crowd in the buffet room, while the brunette blended in with at least a dozen more beautiful women all watching Ciaran readying himself to address us. Nat had pushed her way closer, too. Marilyn Monroe was right up top with Ciaran.

If she sings "Happy Birthday," I'm going to throw her shoes at her.

I could barely hear Ciaran from here, and was thinking of leaving when an arm slipped around my waist and pulled me in.

"Hey. Been having fun?" Jesse's grin said it all.

"Do we still have an engagement-cake order?" I asked him, grimacing at the pink drink he offered me.

"So far." He grinned, clinking his glass against mine. "But I'm working on it. Come on, let's watch them hack our cake to bits then I'll introduce you to Aleta."

It was easier moving through this crowd—women's frames take up less room on average, and it was mainly women in here. "Happy Birthday" sounded more tuneful, too.

Slender hands were still clapping the air when Penny presented Ciaran with a big wodge of whisky-and-ginger cake. He held it aloft and nodded across the crowd of women at Jess standing next to me. Jess returned a raised glass.

The crowd delighted as Ciaran took an overemphatic bite. Lemon buttercream clung to his nose. One of the women seized her chance and reached to dab it from him.

Ciaran took the napkin from her, letting her kiss his cheek before finishing the job himself. The tiniest bit remained, just above his mouth. Another birthday kiss, and another on the other cheek. I waited for that tiny morsel of sweetness to be transferred to one of the women's faces but it was hanging on in there, just over his mouth.

"You're watching the frosting on his face, right?" Jess asked, homing in on the same.

"Oh, yeah—" I smiled "—any kiss now."

Any kiss now.

We both watched her lean in towards him, her hand reaching up to his neck. A strange pang bit down in my stomach. Penny wasn't going in for a peck on the cheek. She was marking her territory again.

Maybe Ciaran wasn't expecting it, but there was nothing that said he didn't. Her mouth worried at his long enough that I knew no buttercream made in our bakery was going to survive. By the time they broke for breath, I was out of there.

"Hol, where are you going?" Jess asked, skipping along beside me.

"Home, Jess. I'm tired."

"Tired? It's only half-ten."

What the hell was I doing? This wasn't like me—this whole place, him—none of it was me.

"Well, I am."

"Hol! Slow down. That came on a bit sudden, didn't it?" Jess's face was serious, so I couldn't look at it. "You haven't even met Aleta yet."

"Aleta doesn't need to meet me, Jess. You've already nailed her down. I can see that."

"What's the matter with you, Hol? Loosen up a bit. Have a good time."

"We were going to be leaving separately anyway, Jess. I was never going to last as long as you. You stay, enjoy the night. These aren't my kind of people."

"I'm your kind of people," he said, and I knew he wanted me to stay. And maybe more for me than for him. His look made me soften a little.

"Jesse Ray. Within the hour that 'fro is going to be in that pool, probably chasing an A-list actress in her bikini. You don't need me here, Jess, but I appreciate you asking." I handed him back the drink I hadn't touched. "So can I have the van keys?"

Jesse dug around in his pocket.

"You haven't had more than one, have you, Hol?"

"Of course not. I only had the bubbly you handed me."

Jess encased me with strong arms, and planted a chaste kiss firmly on my cheek.

He almost watched me the whole way to the lifts before going to find the complimentary swimwear.

chapter 16

Security weren't so fussed about escorting anyone *down* from the party. Well, not an unknown such as myself. I even got to punch the buttons. It was going to be cold outside, but the van was right next to the exit and it would kinda warm up, eventually. Familiar pieces of art on familiar walls led me quickly back from Narnia to the wardrobe door, marked Fire Exit.

Please, don't let the alarm go....

Bloody hell!

If I had set the alarms off, I couldn't hear them over the instant protest of chattering teeth. I automatically grabbed my arms, forfeiting the chance to change my mind as the door clattered shut behind me.

I was at the van in seconds, trying to force uncontrollable hands to be still just long enough to sink the key home. *Finally.*

Unexpectedly—unbelievably—the engine choked into action, and I let it run, waiting for the screen to clear while every muscle in my body jerked in spasm. I wasn't cold; I was *petri-freezing.*

Through the film of condensation, Narnia still shone glee-fully at the top of the tower. It was hard to believe that Jesse was probably swimming up there, right now, Aleta Delgado probably holding his towel.

A trickle cut a wet track through the condensation on the window. It reminded me of the glass of bubbly Ciaran had given me.

Crap. How had I forgotten that? I'd had *two* glasses, not one…. I'd be over the limit. *Holly…you idiot.* I'd had no intention of drinking tonight. That had worked out bloody fantas-tically. I drummed my fingers on the wheel. *Think. Think…*

The contents of the glovebox felt sharper against cold skin, so I tried to root more gently around in there. When you drive a vehicle that's older than you are, it's always prudent to plan ahead. The emergency twenty-pound note I kept in the sunglasses case was my version of planning ahead. It would get me a taxi about as far as Martha's, a little shy of halfway home. At least she'd be pleased that I'd been out. And in heels.

Or I could just call Rob, forget the taxi.

The phone I'd left in the glovebox for the night had slipped into a cold-induced state of inertia. Nothing registered. Well, that was useful. Taxi it was.

I really needed Martha and Rob not to be at the hospital when I got there.

The service yard was even bleaker now, as I clip-clopped across the smooth concrete. It wasn't that late. There would be people around on the street out front. If I couldn't get a cab, I could at least get back into the building.

The sound of my heels scuffing along the floor echoed off the rise of the buildings boxing me in. I walked quickly to the last place I had watched Jesse before the dark of the building had swallowed him up. It seemed you had to go down, before you could come up again, like one of those horrendous exercises the army made people do in troughs of water.

The night felt suffocating here, but ahead there were the beginnings of light, real light, holding ground down there.

In the near darkness, a grunt froze me to the spot.

I held my footsteps still, waiting for a repeat of the sound that had stemmed from my right. From the darkness, a faint pattering—a leaking pipe maybe—was the only sound coming from there now. But my heart was already on guard, thumping away dramatically, feeding adrenaline around my system.

The pattering slowed to a trickle, and another gruntlike noise was enough to make me slip out to barefoot. The light of the car park? Or the enclosure of the van?

These were my choices.

The glow of a cigarette, sucked on by the grunter, danced around in the dark.

Thump. Thump. Thump.

I was the doe again. Frozen in headlights like those on the forest roads—the deer Charlie would track when they'd fled after a collision, to spare them their drawn-out death.

I wished Charlie were here.

A man zipping his fly staggered into view.

"Hurry up, Fred, there's a couple of tasty pieces waiting for a cab. They might let us give them a lift," a second man said, striding up the ramp from the car park.

The taxis were this way.

I began walking again, towards where the second guy had come from. I was irrelevant here and it relaxed me.

"Hello, beautiful," mumbled the voice behind me. "What are *you* doing back here?"

Beyond the bobbing cigarette, the van wasn't as close as I thought. I pressed on, as though oblivious. The taxis wouldn't be far. I could hear the road from here.

"Don't be shy. We just met," the voice called, a harmless tone to his banter.

I stayed calm. He was the only one of the two being over-friendly, and I was nearly past his friend. There was an unspoken rule about being a woman finding herself alone in unfamiliar surroundings. Head for people, head for light, and wherever you head, look like you know where the hell you're going.

I stopped hugging myself against the sharp air, to try to look more at ease as I began the gentle descent into the car park. There was no confirmed threat here, I reminded myself, not yet.

Without warning, the second guy stepped out in front of me.

"You look cold, sweetheart. Do you want warming up?"

The pulse in my throat began to jump again. He'd startled me, but I stepped out to walk around him.

He stepped out, too, and grinned lazily. I knew then. I was in trouble.

"I could warm you up, sweetheart." He leered, the smell of cigarettes growing stronger.

I could see the brightly lit lift shaft at the far end of the car park, beckoning me to safety. The shoes were already off. I could probably outrun him, *probably*. If he were drunker than he was.

"She's Ciaran's bit," said the other voice behind, its owner now free of the shadow. I hadn't wanted to be in Freddy Ludlow's company in a crowded room; I really didn't want to be in it here. I wasn't sure if I felt more threatened it was him or less so.

"He hasn't asked you to leave, too, has he, sweetheart?"

"I was just saying, Fred, she looks like she wants warming up. What do you reckon?"

Freddy had pushed the hair back from his eyes. There was nothing handsome about him now.

"She's already started to get undressed." Freddy smirked, yanking the shoes from my hands. I felt the twenty-pound note fall with them and watched as he sent the shoes bouncing along the floor. I felt dizzy with the thumping of blood rushing to my head.

"Now, about that dress…" It was the last thing I heard before he lunged at me.

He'd moved so quickly, I was pushing out against him with feeble arms before I knew what had happened.

I heard the other man's footsteps running over the concrete before I screamed as loud as I could into Ludlow's ear. I thought I'd hurt him, somehow, and I was glad. He hesitated, pulling away with his hand at the back of his head. Someone took a swing at him, sinking a fist home in Ludlow's left side before yanking his bulky frame away from me. He groaned as his torso struggled to take the impact, sending him flailing to the ground.

The friend hadn't left as I'd thought. He was laying into a third man I hadn't seen arrive. They were scuffling like dogs, the dull slapping thuds of fists on faces.

"I was playing with her, Argyll!" Freddy screeched on the floor. The fight broke as soon as Freddy had spoken, his partner holding on to the kick he was readying for delivery.

Ciaran was enraged, eyes wide, panting like a crazed animal as he took the other man at his neck. "You haven't heard the last of this," he snarled, teeth inches from the other man's face.

Ciaran shook him free, sending him bouncing across the ground like my shoes. Immediately, the other man took on a whole other persona. It didn't make me any less scared of him. "Argyll, I'm…I'm sorry. I—"

"Move," Ciaran growled, stalking back to Freddy, who was

feebly making it to his feet. I'd automatically stepped back from them all. Ciaran looked fiercely at me. His shirt was clinging to its collar on one side. The other sleeve had been torn clean away, taking half of the material and leaving the cummerbund saving what it could.

He scooped the shoes up and led me without discussion away from the men.

His hand was shaking around mine.

We were across the car park before he spoke, his voice uneven with anger.

"Are you all right?" he asked, waiting by the door next to the lifts. He laid the shoes down. "Do you want to put these back on? Or we can sit for a minute?"

He was asking me too many things at once. I shook my head as he tried to straighten what was left of his shirt. The blood streaking from his eyebrow had already reached his jaw. I'd seen enough of Charlie's blood to know when stitches were needed.

"Are you hurt?" he asked me for the second time tonight. His nose was bloodied, too.

"No," I managed. A little shaken maybe, but more astounded at how quickly things could get out of hand.

Ciaran led us up a set of steps, where the scents of the street outside—sweet herby Italian food and exhaust fumes—came to meet us.

"Do you need to get checked out at the hospital? Do you want to involve the police?"

I shook my head. Ciaran had given more than he'd got; I didn't think he needed to go to the police station covered in blood. And I believed him when he implied that he'd deal with them later on. They'd believed it, too.

"Can I take you somewhere, then, Holly?" he asked.

I couldn't go to Martha's—she'd freak. "I need to go home," I said.

"I'll take you. I can't go back inside like this."

"But it's your party," I said.

He smiled crookedly. "Very few of those people are here for me."

He eyed the line of waiting cars. "Do you want to share a ride? I can drop you off on the way."

"I don't live in Hunterstone."

"I know," he said, taking me by the hand again.

Sat between two black cabs, the Bentley looked as though it were trying to blend in with its poorer cousins. Ciaran tapped on the glass and it slid down, and the same guy who had paid for Fergal's cake peered out.

"Freddy's lending me the car," Ciaran said.

The driver nipped out to hold the door open for us. I climbed in the back, while Ciaran skipped round to let himself in the other side.

"What happened to you?" the driver asked.

Ciaran leaned forward, the blood streaking over his eye. "Isn't it about time you came and worked for me, Toby?" he asked as we pulled out into the traffic.

chapter 17

Under the last lights of Hunterstone a red slick glared angrily against what was left of Ciaran's shirt. It hadn't got much larger since we'd left the city, but it was conspicuous enough. Almost as conspicuous as the silence in the back.

"I think somebody should take a look at that. Before we leave the town," I tried. The hospital was only ten minutes from here, and that eye needed something doing.

"I'll see to it when I get home," Ciaran reassured me.

I didn't believe him. Toby punched my address into the GPS as Ciaran dictated it, then silence reigned once more.

The light of my porch fending desperately against the dark was Toby's only point of reference when home finally drew into sight.

I popped the car door open before anyone else felt the need to do it for me, and stepped tender feet onto the cool earth. Toby's phone interrupted my attempts to thank him and Ciaran left him to take the call while the lantern drew us nearer like moths.

"Will Mary be at the manor?" I asked.

Ciaran swayed slightly on his feet.

"No, she went home at five." Ciaran's footsteps steadied, giving way to a snuffling under the door.

"Are you all right?" I asked him, a silly question for a man who looked like he'd been run over.

"Yeah, I just need a few aspirin. Too much champagne."

"Ciaran, does your head hurt? I think you should go and get looked at."

"I'll be fine. Are *you* okay? Is there someone here to look after you?"

"Ciaran?" Toby called across the yard. "I've got to get this car back, sharpish."

"Hang on, Toby," he called back.

Dave started to growl at the foreign voices.

"Shh," I said, "don't wake my neighbour."

Toby dashed over to us and thrust some money into Ciaran's hand. "You'll have to get a cab from here, mate. I've got to get back before they have me done for theft. You'd better have a job lined up for me, mate."

I still had a ready supply of first aid good enough to serve a forester in the kitchen cupboard. Ciaran had gained his injuries on my behalf—patching him up was the least I could do. Another growled warning slipped under the door.

"What have you got in there?" he asked as the pebbles skittered across the yard.

"A man-eater. Just relax and he'll leave you alone, once he's patted you down. You might want to lose your gun," I whispered.

Ciaran smiled at the joke.

Warmth welcomed us into the cottage. Dave ignored me completely and went straight for Ciaran's groin.

"Whoa, boy," Ciaran yelped, under Dave's close scrutiny.

Bravely, Ciaran pushed past him, following me through to the kitchen.

"Nice kitchen. Did you do this?" he asked, surveying his surroundings.

The bandage box hadn't been used in a while, but it was stocked with Steri-Strips and antiseptic swabs. I headed for the sink and knocked the tap on. Reflected in the black glass before me, Ciaran was already releasing the remaining buttons of his ragged shirt. My skin screamed as the water suddenly scalded.

I pulled a stool over from the breakfast bar and sat it next to the sink for him.

"We should bathe your eye."

I busied myself with cotton buds while he took his place, the cummerbund nicely hiding any additional distractions. A large cut glistened with newly clotting blood, gently giving under dampened cotton swabs. I could smell the effort on him, where the sweetness of his aftershave had given way to blood and sweat as he'd fought.

He turned tired eyes up to me. I hadn't squeezed hard enough this time. My arm tickled as a pink droplet chased down to my elbow. I watched another topple onto his collarbone.

"Your neck isn't red anymore," he said, watching my face as I worked.

The cut was about an inch long over his right eye, and gaping with the swelling.

"I'm just going to put a few butterfly stitches on there." I swallowed.

"Do you always blush around men?"

These packets were a bugger to get open. "Only the ones who make me uncomfortable," I answered.

"You're not uncomfortable now."

I tried not to hurt him as I pulled closed the mouth of the

cut, and stuck it there. It helped that he didn't flinch, but he'd still have a scar for his trouble.

"No," I said, "not now. Thank you, for getting me out of a pickle." Had his lower lip been hurt, too? It looked not swollen, but full.

"Don't mention it." His aftershave was fighting back against the scent of injury, until I broke the antiseptic out for the grazes on his knuckles.

"I'll be okay. I'll just wash them off," he said. Good. I hated the smell of antiseptic. Too much like hospitals.

Dave nudged me over to rest his head on Ciaran's lap.

"Security?" he asked, shoulders relaxing with a deep exhalation.

"Company."

Ciaran dabbed a towel to his neck. "It's customary for a rescued maiden to reward her dashing hero."

"Sorry, I'm all out of embroidered hankies," I said, watching him.

"I'd settle for a drink?"

I was so out of practice, I hadn't even thought about that. "Sorry. Tea? Coffee?"

"I was thinking more a glass of the red?"

I flicked on the kettle. "Coffee, then?"

"Perfect." He grinned.

The swelling over his eye looked sore, giving me at least some protection against the butterflies when I looked at him.

"Would you like an ice pack? Well, a bag of peas?"

"No, thank you. James Bond doesn't *do peas*." His smile was crooked again.

I set two cups down on the bar and stole a glimpse of his back as he turned to wander the kitchen. It was only supposed to be a glimpse, but I was caught off guard by the large image governing his left shoulder. The kettle clicked, unsnagging my attention from the young woman, tattooed in wistful portraiture. I fought the temptation of another look. I didn't think I'd hold off for long.

"I'm just going to grab you a shirt," I said, disappearing upstairs.

I dusted off one of the simple navy shirts Charlie had kept for council meetings. Better to lose one of those.

Ciaran had made himself comfortable in the window seat, the cummerbund discarded next to him. He seemed bigger, athletic, without morning tiredness to relax wide squared shoulders. Strands of the woman's hair peeped over his collar, just into view. His hands cradled one of the two steaming mugs I'd left on the breakfast bar. The other was on the coffee table in front of him.

"I'm not sure how well this will fit. It may be a bit big."

Ciaran stood, taking the shirt from me.

"Thanks. I'm sure it will be fine."

I watched one brown arm disappear into a sleeve and turned my attention to the other mug.

"So whose shirt am I stealing?" he asked, buttoning up. It was a closer fit than I'd expected.

"Charlie's. It's one of Charlie's shirts."

"Charlie…brother? Or Charlie, ex?" he asked, raising his eyebrows light-heartedly. It felt so good to say his name. It was on the tip of my tongue, all the time, but my lips missed the feel of it. I tried it out again.

"Charlie, husband."

Uncertainty wasn't a look I'd seen Ciaran wear. I threw him a smile to take the edge off.

"Sooo, where is *Charlie* now?" he asked, his still uncertain eyes checking the room.

"At St Nicholas's churchyard, in the village," I said, nodding at the truth of it. "Charlie died. Nearly two years ago now." My hand patted against the forearm it lay over. "So, you can relax. No one's about to come charging through the door with a shotgun."

Ciaran didn't look relaxed, but strangely I felt a lot more at ease now that I knew it wasn't going to creep up on me.

"I'm sorry, Holly. If I'm making you feel uncomfortable by being—"

"Actually—" my lungs filled with air "—without sounding like some crazy widow, it feels good to talk about him. People avoid the subject, and I know that they mean well. It's just, sometimes, it's like he never existed.... But he did."

If he was going to bolt, he'd probably do it now. Make some excuse about the toilet and get out of Dodge.

"How long were you married?" he asked, patting down the shirt he felt less than comfortable in.

"Six months."

"Six months?" His lips parted to allow an expulsion of breath. "That's...rough."

I almost laughed at the understatement.

"Yep. Quite rough. We'd been together since our teens. I got to keep him for ten years." I smiled.

Ciaran's eyes narrowed the way I'd seen them do before. "Still not enough, though," he said.

"No. Still not enough." The first burn of unexpected tears stirred behind my eyes. Just in case I was about to be rushed, I hid my face in the mug, gulping down the last of my drink and any notions of blubbing along with it. All better.

"So, Mr Bond." A quick regain of composure. "I hear you're quite a hit with the ladies?"

His face softened as we moved to a more manageable subject. He stifled a laugh, looking down to the floor between his knees.

"Why would you think that? I'm single."

"Call it female intuition." *That, and the power of vision.*

"Well, you have to look, right? To find *The One*."

I wondered what all of those women had thought of the tattooed image of *The One* girl who had literally made it under his skin. She must have been special to him.

"Haven't you ever been in love?" I asked, probing. Again.

"No," he said, giving nothing away. "But I like looking." He shrugged.

"Did Charlie do the work on the kitchen?" he asked, taking in the features that didn't belong to a hundred-year-old farmhouse.

"Mostly. His friends helped out, too. The only time we ever had full occupation at that table." Ciaran followed my eyes to the banqueting table surrounded by a quantity of chairs no normal-sized family would need.

"They weren't dwarves, were they?" It was enough for a smile. How refreshing to talk about this stuff. "What did he do? For work, I mean. Builder? I'm guessing something manual to give him wrists this wide." Ciaran held up a hand to show the only place Charlie's shirt came up big on him.

"He did have big wrists." I smiled, happy that he'd noticed it. These things never found their way in to conversation now. "And huge hands. Which was good because he did a lot of work with chainsaws, heavy equipment. That sort of thing." My wedding band was always slipping inside Charlie's where they hung on my chain.

"Ah, a woodsman?"

"Yep. And forest manager. It was his job to make sure the *dwarves* didn't chop too many trees down." I smiled, looking at the table where I'd kept them all in cooked breakfasts. Dwarves would have been cheaper to feed.

"I work in construction, mainly. And we have the health-and-safety boys on our backs all the time. But I remember reading somewhere that the rate of fatalities and serious accidents is something like sixty times the national average for forestry workers."

It was an understandable assumption. Charlie, flattened by a tree.

When I'd taken the call from the commission office that morning, and heard the urgency in her voice, it was the first thing that had gone through my mind, too. A fall. A load breaking free. A serious cut.

"Charlie didn't have an accident at work. I was always fussing at the things he did, the risks...but it wasn't the forest that cost Charlie his life. It was the driver who smashed into him on his way there."

I couldn't remember the last time I'd spoken about Charlie without the weight of sympathetic eyes or the looming threat of a change in subject. Ciaran didn't shy away while I talked, telling him things he didn't need to know about my life. With those pressures lifted, I was free to bring Charlie home, to talk him back to being something more than a ghost.

"What happened to the other man? Was he prosecuted?"

The mug was already cool in my hand.

"Do you want another coffee?" I assumed he wanted another and took his cup with mine. "No, he wasn't prosecuted, not that that would have changed anything. He died from his injuries, too. When they released the report, they said he probably shouldn't have even been driving. For some reason, when you hit seventy you have to apply to renew your licence." The weight of the kettle saved a refill. "But it's self-certified. No one actually tests you to make sure you can still see."

"So he didn't *see* Charlie?"

"He didn't see the kerb. When he clipped it, it was enough to send his car spinning out of control and Charlie was in the wrong place. No greater reason than that. No act of heroism, no nobility. Just gone." Because sometimes, that's just what happens.

Ciaran listened as I told him all about the plans we'd had. Of trying our hands at living off the land here and making the house more environmentally friendly, the amazing things Charlie was going to achieve for the local kids if he could just talk the commission around to his ideas. It was a brave new world for Ciaran, and a world I enjoyed revisiting, but as the hours rolled by coffee eventually took too long to make, replaced with the much smaller effort of pouring the red.

I quickly relaxed around my new friend. Dave was here, and Ciaran wasn't stupid. Besides, women chased him, not the other way round. I was safe as houses, enjoying the fun of exchanging snippets of lives the other had no feel of.

"So you've *never* been to Hollywood?" he asked, emptying his glass.

"Ha! No! Is that in America? Oh, yeah. I have a theory about America. Do you wanna hear it?" My mother had always said that a woman should never drink to the point of slurring.

"A theory?"

"Yeeeep…" I lost my trail of thought.

"You were saying?" Oh, Lordy, another smile.

"Yes. America! I don't think it exists." I chortled. "I don't! I think it could be a trick, on the TV. I've only seen it on TV!"

"It exists." Ciaran smiled, moving around me to the sink again. "If it doesn't, I want my money back."

"Have you been?" I asked. The yip in my voice seemed loud even to me.

"I took a girl there once," he said, rinsing the mugs. Boo, I didn't want to go back to *coffee*. "She was in a girl group, if I remember correctly."

"Oh, that's so romantic!" I cooed.

"She was desperate to see the sights. I was desperate to get into her Agent Provocateurs," he said, wiggling his eyebrows.

Dave jerked awake when my cackle burst like a firecracker through the kitchen.

"But, women throw themselves at you! Why did you do that?" The spent bottle on the side was moving all by itself. It was like a star in the sky—the more I tried to look at it, the less focused it became.

"Not all women. She was a particularly hard nut to crack."

"And did you…*crack it*? Was she impressed with the sights in…in…?" *Where did he say again?* Closed eyes aided concentration. "Hollywood?" It had got very dark. Ah, no. Eyes open.

"It did the trick. Wouldn't that impress you?" Something steamy and milky appeared in front of me. *Ugh*. I pushed it away.

"I can't see me going to Hollywood anytime soon." I laughed. "*If* it actually exists. Ooh, I could build a plane! Out of cake, and Jesse would help me. Ciaran, do customs check for food at Hollywood airport?"

"I think they might notice if you arrived in a cake."

"Oh. Well, *Holly*wood…will just have to come…to meee!" A clatter of wood and the floor jumped up at me hard enough to throw the laugh from my mouth. It was still funny, until warm wet slobbers brought on a wave of nausea. Someone was helping me up. *I didn't know you had arms, Dave!*

My stomach lurched as I jarred back onto my feet.

"I think you've hit a wall" came that gentle nearly Scottish voice. *Was that a wall?* "Do I have your permission to take you to bed?"

Another jolt and the nausea was building.

"I don't want to go to bed. I want to talk about hot tubs and…and your lay-dees who love you, Ciaran Argyll!" Giggles met with creaking floorboards and Dave ran up the stairs in front of me.

"Do you see this newel post? That is supposed to be…an owl!" Small sniggers grew into a great whooping laugh. "An owl! But it looks like a peanut!" The creaking continued.

"Lead the way, Dave," said Ciaran as he moved us along.

The soft embrace of something delightful gave me a cushion of softness to wriggle my shoulder blades into. Oh, this was comfy! Like really comfy! I swatted at the hair on my face.

A soft stroke I didn't think was me, and my hair wasn't annoying me.

"Good night, Holly," I heard him say as sleep pulled at me.

"No, wait! I want to talk about your girlfriend. The girl on your back. You must have loved that one," I murmured, trying to fight the heaviness in my head. "Was she the only girl you ever loved, Mr Bond?" I could still giggle but my eyes weren't opening for anyone.

The door creaked, and I could smell Dave close by.

Then a whisper, quietly slipping away.

"Only girl who ever loved me back."

chapter 18

Gnats drifted on the same warm summer breeze that saw colourful paper lanterns swaying on their strings. Lily of the valley filled jam jars at each table, but sweet peas had won out in the battle to fragrance the evening air.

Mum was fussing somewhere, probably in the marquee with most of the guests, still trying to come to terms with a wedding in a *war zone*. It was a good job the weather had been so kind, or she'd be nibbling vol-au-vents indoors, with seventy friends and family all trying to keep the stench of turps from their nostrils.

The sweet peas preferred it up there by the cottage, their perfume dying away the closer we moved to the water. The air was different down here, cooler, less giving to the advances of delicate blooms.

"I love you, Mrs Jefferson." His eyes sparkled like the waters, the stars only catching on them a little here and there while the moon tried its best to cast everything into ethereal shades of blue.

"I love you, too, Mr Jefferson. Now shut up and kiss me."

Hands spanning the breadth of my back pulled me closer, and the taste of him invaded my mouth as he pressed himself in. He was tasting me, too, his tongue delicately greeting mine. My lips closed in around him to hold him there. I loved the way Charlie kissed me, gentle and urgent, building until kissing alone wasn't enough.

I could feel the contours of his back through wheat-coloured cotton, the added warmth of his forearms where sleeves had been rolled back to elbows. His twill sandy waistcoat had set him aside from the rest of the forest boys in their shirts to match and casual braces, but I wished he'd left it up there with them.

Hard brown buttons made fiddly work for my eager fingers, trying to hurry without ruining the threads.

Oops. A worthy casualty.

Charlie's shoulders were cavernous over me as I finally discovered him inside his waistcoat. I pulled his shirt up, out of my way, to run impatient hands over the ripple of his stomach before reacquainting them with the expanse of his chest. I wanted to feel his skin against mine, but the dress would only hitch to the waist and we didn't have any more time to waste, not before someone noticed us gone.

A second to savour the view, then I allowed hungry lips to feel of him what my stiffened breasts were unable to, to find him where the May evening air hadn't, and paint all that warmth in wet eager kisses. The skin was hotter here, smoother, softly defending his nipple. I took it between my teeth, and promised it my tongue, but I'd made him wait too long.

Charlie arched away from me, to come at me on his terms. He grabbed me certainly at my waist, where light floaty fabric became heavier under the weight of pretty lace, and lifted me as if I weighed nothing. My legs instinctively rose to lock around him, to help him carry me quickly to the gently sloping bank near the water's edge. I held myself there as he walked us, freeing his hand for it to explore as I knew it would. I trembled when he found me under my gown, knocking away already slackened wellington boots to take in the softness of me from ankle to hip. His hand rounded on me, investigating the trim of panties he hadn't seen yet. A low guttural appreciation escaped his chest.

So close. Just a little closer…

"I want you, Charlie," I whispered. "I want to feel you inside me." My mouth was dry with desperation, to feel him plunge into me for the first time as his wife. To see if he felt the same.

A strained gasp at my ear, the tiniest scratch of his whiskers and Charlie's scent began to ride over his cologne.

"I love that I excite you," I whispered between teeth nibbling at his neck.

"I love that you excite me, too." And his mouth was on me again.

Cool grassy earth made an unlikely cushion, perfectly angled for such trysts in the moonlight when Mrs Hedley was safely tucked up in bed, or wedding guests were preoccupied with music and merriment.

So much heavy lace. I scrambled to pull it all away, to liberate my legs and offer him haven. The pale of his shirt flittered to the ground like a towel thrown in a boxing ring, but there was no surrender here, not yet. The frantic tinker of a buckle and dark trousers slumped to reveal strong thighs tinged blue by the moon. The shadows hid from me what it was I wanted the most, his thick warm length so nearly here, *nearly in reach*, nearly laying its kiss against my softest part.

Charlie crawled over me, nuzzling breasts he couldn't reach and then panties pulled aside as the first slip of a finger found its line and gently, surely, slipped inside. Charlie was testing my readiness. I knew I was ready. The hot throbbing down there was calling for him, aching to be touched. Pleading, for all that slick sensation to be satiated.

Charlie growled into my neck, "Mrs Jefferson, do you know what you do to me?"

I loved that it drove him wild, to slip and slide so easily over the most throbbing beacon of all, before dipping his fingers into me again.

The air had been cool between my thighs, but I felt the warmth now, radiating from his skin, the beast still hiding in the shadows. A glancing touch, and then warmth and delectable smoothness pressed at my opening. I wriggled into it, to spread the sensation around, before he sank down hard into me.

The torment of steady slides was relieved by the urgency of thrusts, and in the cool blue night, hot and hard and trembling, Charlie bucked and rocked me to climax. I gripped at the grass behind me as I rode out the aftershocks. He was close, too. Faster and harder he thundered until finally, my fingers hanging on desperately at the back of his neck, he exploded into rapturous release.

"I want to stay here," I whispered over his panting body. "We've been up there all night."

"But it's not enough," he answered, familiarity in his words.

His voice sounded strange, laboured maybe, but I was distracted by the noises of the party above us. Melodious fronds of violins and guitar had come looking for us where we lay, recovering, trying to marry mismatching rhythms of heartbeats and breaths.

Under his weight, I kissed the crest of his shoulder, just a few more times, before he'd get up and make us rejoin the group.

The moon shone on his back, throwing indifferent light and shadows onto his skin.

"Charlie?" I whispered, tracing my finger over the darkened shapes there. I strained to see better in the light, to make out the defined lines of something that couldn't be shadow... flowing lines, rolling over one another like reeds in a current.

"Charlie, you have someth—"

The shapes started to pull together, to make sense. Not reeds, hair...on the wind, long sinuous tresses of a woman's hair, tattooed into Charlie's back.

A rush of saliva filled my mouth.

Nausea had been traded for a very immediate need to get to the bathroom. A short spell of thudding and a changing landscape of soft carpet to threadbare rug to cold tile told me I was nearly there. *Nearly there.*

The toilet seat clattered back against the cistern with an angry slap and the nastiness erupted on cue. I recognised the acrid bitterness and remembered it tasting a lot less offensive when I drank it.

I wiped the bitter residue from my lips.

The sink made for a good grab-rail, but the mirror didn't do much for me. I looked like death—death in an LBD.

Downstairs, a cough broke the stillness of the house. It hadn't come from me.

By the loo, I'd been at around a one on the sobriety barometer. One misplaced sound and I was now at about a five and a half.

No. Oh, no, he was *not* still here? My head throbbed against my efforts to force a little clarity. I couldn't believe it. He couldn't be.

With the stealth of a toddler, I tiptoed downstairs. I couldn't remember climbing them. I could remember the sounds of a man sleeping on the sofa in the man-cave, though, but it was a worn memory.

I followed the muffled noises of soft breathing, and found Ciaran had settled for the couch, Dave contentedly snoozing on the floor beside him.

Traitor.

In the light of the hallway behind me, I could see just a sliver of him. He looked softer in sleep. Gentle. On the table next to the settee, his mobile phone silently cried for attention. The green glow throbbed in the picture frame there, showing Charlie holding me like a log over his shoulder while I clung to my posy of flowers.

Dave wasn't the only traitor around here.

chapter 19

At least I hadn't thrown up in bed.

Under the bedclothes, something dug in my ribs as I stretched against the morning. A dreamcatcher was one thing, but a photo frame made for an unusual talisman.

The vibration of a kitchen chair grinding across flagstones had me up onto my elbows. Before I'd even heard Mrs Hedley's unmistakable drawl, I knew who she'd be chatting to. Downstairs. In my kitchen.

I jumped out of bed, checking I'd found myself a pair of shorts last night, and content with my modest nightwear made a silent dash for the bathroom. Whatever humiliation was waiting for me down there, I wasn't going to meet it with morning breath and Alice Cooper eyes.

I *never* woke to voices in the house and knowing whose voices they were made the occurrence even more unsettling.

"Holly doesn't usually have breakfast. But I've tried telling her, it's important when you're on the go as she is all the time." Mrs Hedley spoke in short sharp syllables. Dave was both extremely fond, and frightened to death of her. Sentiments Charlie and I had shared.

At the door the smell of toast and boiled eggs hit me as I locked sights on the sinks. Someone had washed the wine glasses and had left them to drain there. I could see two glasses, two mugs, and had absolutely no idea how to walk into my own kitchen right now.

Feign illness? Hide until he leaves?

Don't be such a baby.

A deep breath, and then confidently, nonchalantly even, I stepped out onto the flagstones and made a beeline for the kettle.

"Speak of the devil," Mrs Hedley said. "I thought you'd like some eggs bringing, in case you were running short."

In a week Dave and I hadn't made it through the last pile we'd had from her, most of which were still sat in the bowl next to the toaster, buzzing and glowing with its next consignment. She wasn't here to make breakfast.

An acknowledging look for Mrs Hedley bought me the quickest of glances at Ciaran. For someone who had probably been interrogated already, he looked more than at home sat back into his chair, casually dipping a sliver of toast into an egg.

Nope, I couldn't look at him before coffee any more than I could look at the several buttery rounds on standby in front of him.

The floor was freezing as I tiptoed over it to the fridge, buying myself a few more moments of obscurity behind its open door.

I needed coffee, fast, if I was going to be on my toes this morning, and as far as my house guest was concerned, well, I wasn't sure there was a drink for that.

I shuffled back to the sink, tying my hair on top of my

head. I wasn't completely convinced it had escaped unscathed last night while I touched base with the loo.

I grabbed a new mug—inscribed with Paddle Faster, I Hear Banjos!—from the cupboard. Jesse had given it to me last Christmas. I wondered how his night had turned out.

"Ciaran here was just telling me that he got so tipsy at his party he went toppling over. I told him he was lucky he didn't knock himself senseless." Mrs Hedley tutted, wiping the crumbs from around him. He flashed her a smile for her efforts and I swear I saw Mrs Hedley swoon a little.

"Cora, that was the best breakfast I've had in weeks. Thank you." Ciaran smiled, rising from the table.

Cora? Did he say Cora? I never knew Mrs Hedley even had a first name. She was like Brindley's Nook's very own Boudica. I hid in my coffee mug, a little surprised by the love affair unfolding over egg and soldiers down at the other end of the kitchen.

Mrs. Hedley's eyes followed as he brought his dishes over to the sink next to me. The leaves had started settling on the ground in the garden and I concentrated on their colours, trying to keep at least one foot warm by standing it atop the other.

Dishes clinked in the sink, another forced sip from my mug, and the unexpected touch of a hand gently at my lower back.

"Good morning," he said, softly.

I mistimed the next anxious gulp and had to contract my throat to stop from spluttering. There was a smile on his lips when he walked away again.

"So you were saying, Cora, about the benefits of a green-house?"

Mrs. Hedley sat at the chair facing him, topping up his cup with a pot of tea I wasn't sure she hadn't brought from her house. They were about as far removed as any two people could be, yet sounded like old friends on a park bench.

When the image of water showering down a tattooed back made a circuit around my head, it was time to take back my house. I would not keep on being some blushing little princess; I would be Boudica! And return my home to normal. With a confirmative slam of coffee cup on worktop, I turned to face the enemy square on.

"I'm going to jump in the shower, and then I'm going to get a lift to my van. You might want to call a taxi." There. Not too curt, not too friendly—just right.

"You don't need to do that. It's taken care of," Ciaran called over, before resuming talks of tomatoes and compost with Mrs Hedley.

"Taken care of? How?"

"The van's already been moved," he answered.

"Moved? Moved where? I have the keys here!"

Dave was barking in the yard outside. Ciaran checked his watch.

The barking intensified as a pickup truck rolled up carrying a familiar burgundy van on its back.

"Did you do this?" I asked Ciaran, already knowing the answer.

"I'd better go say hello. I don't think he'll get out while Dave's there."

Mrs. Hedley and I exchanged a look. She raised her eyebrows and smiled as if to suggest we were both in on the same secret—whatever it was it was news to me. I tiptoed back out into the hallway and pulled on my wellies and clumped into the yard.

"You didn't have to do this, you know," I said, finding myself next to him, again.

"That's okay. It's the least I can do after bed and board. Of sorts." He turned and reminded me of the weight of those richly brown eyes. I found them exhausting in even the tiniest increments—he was probably used to that. "I didn't think you'd be in a rush to go back there anyway."

I wasn't—he was right—but not because two drunken idiots overvalued their charm.

"Ciaran, how much do I owe you for this?"

"It's fine. We have an account with these guys."

"Ciaran, I can't let your father's company pay for my inability to count drinks."

He drew in a deep breath beside me then let it out slowly. "Holly, it's fine."

I wasn't used to hearing my name in that voice, so balanced in assertion and gentleness.

Another puff of brown dust swept up into the air over the hedgerow. A few seconds later, another shiny black car I hadn't seen before bobbled towards us over the track before crunching to a halt. Mrs Hedley came to stand with us, waiting to see who this was. Ciaran was less interested.

She looked even more sullen this morning, marching without hesitation over the unevenness of the yard to where I stood, in nightshirt and wellies, possibly with a little sick in my hair.

"What the hell happened to you last night?" she snapped over my shoulder. Ciaran stood casually behind me, Mrs Hedley firmly attached to one arm.

How could she look this good again already? It was inhuman.

"Good morning, Penny. This is Cora, and you know Holly."

Mrs. Hedley looked as impressed as I was, but the ice maiden didn't care. She was too busy scrutinizing my morning outfit.

"Everyone was asking after you last night, Ciaran. And your face. That's going to go down well in the boardroom."

"I'm sure everyone enjoyed themselves nonetheless," he replied, eyes narrowing again.

"Ciaran, people don't attend an Argyll birthday at an Argyll location and expect there to be *no* Argyll. I didn't know what to tell them."

"And that's okay, Penny. If you were my personal assistant, you would need to know these things, but as it is, you only need to be familiar with Fergal's diary."

Penny's eyes tightened, too. "I did offer to take care of your diary, Ciaran," she said, preening herself. "Now your father keeps my hands full." She smiled. She had the smile of an asp and I was fast starting to think there might be nothing I could ever like about this woman.

Dave ambled over, his massive round head fixed on the killer legs he hadn't smelled before.

Penny stiffened. "If that touches me, you'll be getting the dry-cleaning bill."

Dave did touch her, but only just grazing her skirt with one slobbery globule. He could tell she was mean, and saved his affections for elsewhere. I didn't see a need to alert her to the trail of goo he'd left for her to find later, but I would absolutely be giving him a treat for it.

"Cora, thank you for such an interesting morning," Ciaran said, planting a welcome kiss on Mrs Hedley's cheek.

The ice maiden had her elbows in her hands, glaring at me as though I'd been sick in *her* hair last night.

Ciaran came to stand between us, and the asp was at least out of view. "And thank you, Holly, for such an interesting night."

I'd been too transfixed by his mouth as he spoke to notice the hand slipping its way over my hip. I did my best not to react how Mrs Hedley had as I felt the delicate press of his lips just centimetres from my own.

"I'll return the clothes," he called, serious once more.

I tried not to watch him as he stepped into her car. We both watched as they rolled off down the track.

With Ciaran gone, I turned my talent for avoiding eye contact on Mrs Hedley, hoping she'd return to her own door and not mine. The dust pluming over the track made its way closer to the road. I half watched the pickup driver leave, too, before trudging back for more coffee.

It tasted like consolatory coffee. I didn't know why, but it did.

"I'll have two sugars in mine," Mrs Hedley said, settling back at the table.

I'd never been questioned by the police, but as Mrs Hedley poured milk into both of our cups, taking a sip before she started getting down to business, the only thing missing was a swinging light bulb and a tape deck.

"You never got to meet George, did you?" she said, settling into her chair.

Mrs. Hedley had never spoken about her husband other than when his name was dropped into a recollection, and on those few occasions, she always referred to him as Mr Hedley.

"Um, no. I didn't."

"You must have seen him, though, before he died? It was only a month or so after you moved your things in, but he was always out on the field feeding the geese, right up until that blasted stroke of his."

"Oh, you mean the gentleman from the farm over the reservoir?" I asked, realising my mistake. "Didn't he come by one afternoon with some lovely tulips for you, Mrs Hedley?"

"Yes, that was George, the old rascal. He knew I loved tulips, but I prefer them growing in the ground, not cut off in their prime."

"Sounds like you had an admirer, Mrs Hedley, or do you

prefer Cora?" I was teasing, on both counts, but she didn't seem to pick up on it.

"George was often bringing me things, little offerings or gifts if you want to call them that. He'd been a widower for longer than I'd been a widow. We'd met at church once or twice, and he was always kind enough to share his service sheet with me. Over the years, we became friends. Good friends, I'd have said. He'd come over with a basketful of shirts for me to press for him, and I'd get to have my pick of his allotment for my trouble."

"Ah, that sounds lovely, Mrs Hedley. It must have been a nice friendship for you both."

"Oh, it was. And I was happy with how things were that way, with a chat on Sundays and a nice visit in the week. He was lovely company, George. He was a cheeky old bugger, but kind… Took good care of his farm and his animals. A real winner. He should have found himself another woman to love him."

Mrs. Hedley had popped in for chats many times in the last two years, but we'd never strayed outside the parameters of polite conversation.

"So why didn't he find a wife? Sounds like he was a catch," I said.

"He was. He'd have made any woman a good husband. You see, Holly, George was accepting of his circumstances. He could see that there was more happiness to find before his time was up. It was a terrible shame when he died, with no one to comfort him in that big house of his."

I could see the house Mrs Hedley was speaking of from the window. It seemed to stir something in her to look at it now.

"Are you all right, Mrs Hedley?" I asked, taken aback by the softness in her face.

"Poor old George. I do miss our talks. I should have been

there with him, to take care of him. Instead of being a coward. But, I couldn't leave the house, you see."

"What do you mean, Mrs Hedley? You sound like you
were a good friend."

Mrs. Hedley's grey eyes warmed with whatever emotion
they were holding on to. Her white hair fell around her face
as she shook her head to herself.

"And I couldn't face the thought of George coming to live
with me. Not with Mr Hedley's things all around me. This was
his home, too. It wasn't right. And I couldn't just leave him to
go and live over the water. You see, George, he got this idea
that we might become man and wife, you see. Live out our
days together feeding the animals and eating our meals at the
same table. He took it quite badly when I told him I couldn't
be his wife. I just couldn't. I thought it was an impossibility."

When she looked at me then, the loss in her was like a blow
to my stomach. If she felt this way, why hadn't she accepted
his offer? Instead of living so many years alone?

"But why? Why was it an impossibility?" I asked her, trying to offer her the comfort of my hand on hers.

"For the same reasons you're going to find for keeping that
nice young man from coming back here again." Her other
hand found its way on top of mine. She held me with eyes
that knew the pain of love, the unrelenting weight of its cost
around your neck.

I swallowed past the lump forming in my throat. "I don't
know what you mean, Mrs Hedley. Last night wasn't what
you think. He was only here be—"

"He was here for one reason, girl. Because he wanted to be
here. And in some small way that you probably won't agree
to, you wanted him to be here, too."

It wasn't true. Last night wasn't planned; it was just coincidence. Knowing that a man is attractive doesn't give them an open door into your life. It...it just *doesn't*.

Wrinkled hands clasped down harder around mine and for the umpteenth time in weeks I felt my neck beginning to flush. I bet she thought I didn't love Charlie—that I'd forgotten him as soon as some flash chap with money to burn had looked my way.

"Really, Mrs Hedley. You have the completely wrong idea."

"No, I had the completely wrong idea when George brought me those tulips. I thought that they were enough. More than a silly old woman like me should even hope for. But those tulips were like the moments I shared with him—a lovely burst of colour in my day, but they were always temporary, girl. That man would have done anything for me, and I watched him live out his days from that window, because I was too much the coward to let life take me on another adventure."

"But, Mrs Hedley, George died."

And there it was.

Mrs. Hedley got up from her chair and stepped quietly to the window overlooking the little white farm on the hillside.

"When I lost Albert I thought that was the very worst thing that could happen to a person. To lose the one they loved more than anything. More than themselves. But when George didn't go out to the geese one morning, and I realised, there was a different grief came to seek me out. The very worst kind because it could have been avoided." Mrs Hedley's chest rose with one heaving breath before she sighed at the windowpane. "I'd have grieved for George either way, but I'd have never regretted it. Not like now. Don't be a fool, girl. Don't be afraid of unexpected joy. Don't find yourself grieving for an opportunity wasted, because no matter how much you love the ghosts, they don't keep you warm."

I could feel the burn again of tears about to run over, unsure of who it was I wanted to cry for. She was wrong. There was no worse kind of grief—there couldn't be. Not even aching regret would make me accept that.

"That boy likes you, girl. He didn't think I saw how he watched you this morning, the way he kept looking at your feet because he knew they were cold. All right, so he's a brawler. I didn't buy that cock and bull—but, Holly, think of it this way. All the pain Charlie left you with, all the unbearably long nights waiting for the dawn to chase the nightmares away, all the looks that made you want to curl up and die, the clinging on by the nails to a world that doesn't know what to do with you, just to try and see if the next day holds any more hope—even after all that Charlie left you to deal with, you wouldn't go back and not marry him, would you? If you had the chance to meet someone else, and save your poor heart, would you take it?"

A hot stream fell over my cheek, and I knew it would be seconds before the other followed suit. I shook my head to answer her.

"That's the difference, girl. Of having no regret."

chapter 20

"The baby's coming! The baby's coming!" Rob shrieked from the earpiece.

"Okay, I'm on my way. I'm coming now!" I stammered through the thick black dark pressing out against the walls of my bedroom.

"Okay, we're just getting parked. We'll see you here soon. And don't forget the aromatherapy pack!" Rob hung up, leaving me confronted with the double-pronged enigma of how long it was before dawn, and why the hell hadn't I bought the aromatherapy set I was supposed to have. Within twenty minutes I was out of bed, teeth brushed, and wrapped up against the cold waiting for me inside the van.

Martha was going to kick my ass for not providing the essential oils. I hadn't been given many responsibilities as the second ranking "birthing partner"—namely don't forget the oils and don't faint. I wasn't off to a good start. Luckily for me, two chaotic hours later and a grovelling text to Jess asking that he cover for me while I recouped a few hours' sleep, and I was back at home with a second chance to buy the oils.

The orange light of dawn was bleeding across the sky when Mrs Hedley opened her door to greet me. There was something different about her this morning, some small indecipherable change I hadn't seen before. Perhaps it was that she hadn't piled her hair neatly up onto the back of her head yet, or the prettiness of the delicate flowers patterned on her shirt not yet hidden beneath the green quilted waistcoat she always wore. Most likely, though, it was the subtle smile she was wearing as she held out the parcel for me.

There was nothing exceptional about the brown papered item Mrs Hedley passed to me, other than the fact that there was no address on it and so someone had taken the trouble to deliver it all the way out here by hand.

No address, just *Holly* written in black ink.

Mrs. Hedley gave nothing away as I examined my delivery. "I wasn't expecting you back so soon. I assumed you'd been called out for the little 'un's arrival," she said, rubbing the chill from her arms.

"False alarm." I smiled. "Something called Braxton Hicks?"

"Well, it won't be long, then. She'll be getting impatient, I expect?"

Impatient wasn't the word for it. Three days overdue and the baby was not following Martha's schedule. After catching a glimpse of the words *serene* and *drug-free* in her birth plans, I tried to ignore what other oversights Martha might have in store. I didn't know that much about childbirth, but I knew enough that Martha couldn't have read the same texts I had on the subject. I'd had a book once on the whole shebang, a comedy wedding gift from one of Charlie's lads.

After moving from conception to the labour and delivery section, and seeing nothing that even remotely made me think *serene* or *drug-free*, Charlie said the book was more like a contraceptive device than a field guide. It was one of the few things I'd had no problem throwing out in the early days. I didn't like to look at it before, and couldn't bear to look at it after. I didn't begrudge Martha her impatience. She knew what a luxury it was.

"You could say that, Mrs Hedley. So who brought this?" I said, weighing the soft package in my hand.

"Ciaran." Another twist in my stomach. "He dropped it off for you, about half an hour ago. He said he was on his way to work."

"Oh. On his way to work?"

"He didn't stay long. I just happened to catch him as he was leaving it on your doorstep."

Yep. That figured. He could have just mailed it back to me. He probably wanted to make sure there was no room for error, no reason for me to turn up one day looking for the shirt that hadn't arrived in the post.

He wanted to tie up any loose ends he might think there were between us. No one wanted loose ends with a widow, especially not when the particular widow in question was both a bumbling mess when sober and a rambling mess when drunk. He probably couldn't get Charlie's shirt back to me quickly enough. And I couldn't blame him for it.

Mrs. Hedley was already closing her door behind her.

I was slumped on my bed, the package still in my hand. I knew what was inside, but found a few moments' interest in inspecting the handwriting I took to be his. Five letters spelt a world of difference between Ciaran's school days and Charlie's. I wondered if Ciaran had ever had the burden of heavy secrets, like the inability to read without stammering, or writing his letters the correct way around. Charlie could have achieved so much with the right opportunities. If he'd had a powerhouse like Argyll Inc. behind him, he'd have had a forest school set up in every county. Even without that kind of backing, he'd have fought for it until they gave in.

Now the forest was slipping from all our fingers, soon to be the next site of two-bed starter homes and streets named nostalgically after the woodlands they usurped.

Stiff paper crinkled scratchily under my hands and soft blue cotton ironed to perfection slipped from its wrapping. It was going to look out of place next to its dusty brothers, neatly folded and smelling of someone else's washing powder. A slip of white paper peeped from inside the spent packaging.

Holly,

Thank you for your hospitality this weekend, and for your enlightening geographical views. I enjoyed our conversations, but your geography needs work.

I was hoping we could discuss this further sometime soon, over coffee, or red wine if you prefer?

You're busy, so I'll call you in the week when you've had chance to check your schedule.

Yours,

Ciaran

P.S. The eye hurts like hell.

The letters were raised against the paper, the mark of a fountain pen with not a blemish of ink out of place. I ran my finger over them again.

Hoping. Soon. Yours.

The sensation of someone tasering me scared me half to death. I dug around in my jean pocket for the frenzied buzz of my phone.

"Hello?"

"I wanted to catch you before you went back to bed or showered or... Can you talk?"

Looking at his writing and hearing his voice all at the same time threw me.

"I passed you on your way out of Hunterstone. You're hard to miss, Holly."

"Erm…"

"Were you singing? You looked like you were singing."

"Er…"

"Did you get my note?"

"Er…no! Erm…no…I…er…" *Damn it, Holly! Pull yourself together!*

"Oh. I was just wondering if you'd like to come for lunch with me this week? I thought we could finish our conversation maybe, over a bite?"

"What conversation?" *He's asking you to dinner. Who cares!*

"The conversation we were enjoying Saturday night, just before you fell off your stool."

I closed my eyes at the image he'd just painted. "Oh, I did, did I? I must have forgotten about that." *Really cool, Hol.*

"Yes. You did. And then I picked you up, and asked your permission to carry you to bed, which I did, and then you said—"

"Lunch sounds nice!" I blurted, cutting him off. It seemed the best measure to stop him from relaying whatever cringe-inducing one-liner I might have said to him in my drunken stupor.

"Great. I was thinking tomorrow, around one-thirty?"

I hadn't expected him to keep coming with more propositions I needed responses for.

"Tomorrow? I, er…I have to work. All week actually."

"But you leave early some days. Is that right?"

"Yes, but not one-thirty early." This was so weird, it was like haggling with one of the suppliers.

"Okay, well, you tell me a time that's good for you, then."

The supplier had just asked me to name a price. I was notoriously bad at this kind of conversation.

"Well, Sunday's really my only guaranteed day off."

"All right, well, how about Sunday at one-thirty? I could pick you up, or we could meet there?"

"Meet where?"

"I was thinking Atlas. Seems appropriate for someone unsure of the existence of whole continents."

Atlas was one of the most established eateries in the city. Even I'd heard of it, which said a lot as to the kind of reputation the place had earned itself. It was just the kind of restaurant I could see Ciaran in, enjoying fine foods I probably couldn't spell let alone identify, and drinking wine so expensive it must have been bottled somewhere near the fountain of youth. Just the kind of place I would never have gone to with Charlie. Just the kind of place I would never have set foot into with anyone, actually. I didn't want to go to Atlas. I needed something that resembled a comfort zone if this, whatever this was, was going to happen. *What would Boudica do?*

I can't believe I just asked myself that. I am officially going nuts.

"I know a place. It's closer than Atlas, and the views are better, too." Finally, cohesion. Talking to Ciaran was like being lost in the fog, trying not to lose focus on the glow of distant light. Finally taking some degree of charge over a conversation with him was like finding a flashlight in my pocket. "If you don't mind me choosing?"

The phone went quiet. He was thinking.

"Sure. You choose, I pay?"

"You're offering to pay before you even know where I'm suggesting?"

"It can't be more expensive than Atlas. Nowhere in the city is."

"Actually, it's not in the city. But you're right—it won't be as eye-wateringly overpriced as Atlas."

"You don't like Atlas?"

"I don't know. But no food costs that much to make."

"No, you're right. But it's not just the food you're paying for—it's the surroundings, the experience of dining there. I think you'd like it, Holly."

My name sounded softer when he spoke it and it made the tiny hairs on my neck react. I breathed the sensation away. He was probably right about Atlas, but it would only be the spectacle of it that I enjoyed. And that wouldn't last.

"I'm sure I would, but I happen to know somewhere whose surroundings can't be topped. And I think you'd quite like the experience of dining *there*." I wasn't actually convinced he'd like it at all. In fact, he'd probably hate it, but there was no point in pretending to be something I had never been or would never be, and Atlas was all about the pretence.

"So, are you going to tell me where this fantastic restaurant is, or are you going to surprise me?"

I hadn't thought very far into my own plan. "I think a surprise would be better."

"Then I'll need to pick you up?" I hadn't thought that far ahead, either. "Shall we stick with one-thirty, then? Your place?"

I was thinking on my feet. "Make it eleven-thirty. It can be difficult to get to. We don't want to leave it too late...in case we lose our reservation." If we left at one-thirty, we wouldn't be eating until after three.

"It must be good. I'm intrigued. Do I need to worry about a dress code?"

"It's better than good. There's nowhere else like it around here. But the best seats are alfresco, so remember your coat."

"My coat?"

"Yeah, and wear something comfortable." I knew exactly where I was going to take him, and couldn't help but smile as I remembered how much I loved it there.

chapter 21

The adrenaline rush at making the morning's mad dash to Hunterstone General had peaked and crashed on the journey home, yet there I was after our conversation, lying on my bed unable to relax into sleep.

By eight-thirty, I'd given up altogether and opted for a shower and work instead.

Ciaran was right—I had been singing. Loud and wildly with blissful abandon.

Under the hot pattering of the shower, I found myself singing again. Normally, I wouldn't have bothered again so soon, but smoothing my legs off with the razor, I reminded myself of my mother's words of wisdom. Always wear clean knickers and have cleanly shaven legs; you never knew when you might be knocked down by a bus. There weren't many buses around Brindley's Nook, but lately I'd found that you couldn't be too careful with the unexpected coming your way.

Jesse was singing, too, banging out Bill Withers's "Lovely Day" when I let myself into the shop half an hour earlier than I would have done normally. Jesse wasn't ready to accept what my garden already showed, singing his way to a more summery state of mind. Even Jess wasn't usually this chirpy on Mondays. Saturday night must have set him up for the week.

"Hey," I said, dumping my things on the side.

"Hey yourself," he said, casting expectant eyes on me.

"What?"

"What?" he mimicked, shrugging shoulders that didn't fool me.

"What?"

Jesse threw me the same look I'd seen his mother throw him. The don't-give-me-that look.

"Well, I could start with the reason-you've-come-in-to-work news but I'm going to cut straight to the what-happened-to-you-Saturday-night news instead." Whatever information Jess thought he had, I was about to stick a pin in it.

I rolled my eyes at him. "I'm in because I can't sleep, and you know what happened to me Saturday. I said goodbye to you and then went home." Which was all true.

"And?"

"And what?"

"That's it? You just went home? Nothing to tell?"

"Nothing to tell about what, Jess?" I could already feel my cheeks reddening.

"You're really going to play it this way? I tell you that Aleta dragged me into the ladies' room with her and showed me just how high those legs of hers go, and you're keeping your secrets to yourself? That's cold, Hol."

"You didn't! You did not have sex with our client in the loos. Tell me you didn't, Jess."

"I didn't, not in the conventional sense. But you could say that we've been properly introduced now." Jesse's face said it all. I didn't need to know what they'd got up to, and neither did Modesto Benini.

"What were you thinking, Jess? Modesto will go crazy if he finds out, and what about the work? Cinder Events won't touch us if Nat hears about it."

"Nat knows," Jesse said, grinning those perfect teeth of his at me.

"What? Nice one, Jess. That's that door closed, then."

"Relax, Hol. The only door that's been closed was the door to the powder room. And both the lovely Aleta and Natalia were on the same side of it with me."

I looked at Jess and realised what had put him in a good mood. "Both of them?" I asked. "At once?"

"Yeah, right? They hadn't got *that* down in the papers about Aleta. To be fair, Aleta wasn't all that surprising, but Nat?" Jess whistled at the surprises she'd shared with him. "Now that girl's a dark horse. We'll be getting a lot of work through Nat in the future."

"Don't tell me any more," I said, walking past him with my fingers in my ears. He was making cut-out hearts from a layer of rolled hot-pink fondant. "Have you washed your hands this morning?" I asked him.

"Clean as a whistle, boss."

"Wash them again, dirty boy."

Jess started chortling in that throaty way men do.

"So, anyway, boss. How clean are *your* hands?" He wasn't making chit-chat; he'd turned and braced his arms behind himself on the ledge of the counter.

I felt my eyes narrow.

"Spotless. Thanks." Jess's eyebrows rose, inviting me to convince him further. "Perfectly spotless. Why?"

His bottom lip arched up then, questioning my honesty.

"A little bird told me that Penny flipped out after you left. Something about a certain super-fly double agent ditching his own party and taking you *all* the way home?"

"Well, you shouldn't trust little birds, Jess. They might not have their songs straight."

"Trust me, when a woman is in the position Nat was in when she told me why Penny had sent her looking for me, I'm telling you she had her song straight. She was too preoccupied for anything else."

"Penny sent Nat after you? To find out where Ciaran had got to?"

"Yeah, man. Nat busted us big-time. I thought I was in for the sack, until she started peeling herself out of her knickers. Man, that was some party." The giggle was back.

I just shook my head. It had been a long time for me. I couldn't imagine walking into a room with anyone and just dropping my knickers. I wasn't sure I even owned any nice knickers anymore. I wasn't sure about a lot of things.

Jess was enraged when I told him what had happened after I'd left the club. He was a different creature when he'd digested the behaviour of Ludlow and his friend, so much so that I sped into the ins and outs of Ciaran's time at the cottage just to calm him down. It seemed to appease Jess, to know that Ciaran had stayed the night, despite there being no knicker-dropping involved.

I told him about the lunch I'd agreed to, and, strangely, Jess didn't give me any of the hoo-ha I'd expected him to.

The week trundled by without any fuss and, come closing time Saturday, Jess simply told me to have a good day. Jess seemed to know how to play me, always. For his sake he'd better be as good at keeping Nat and Aleta on side.

It didn't matter how good Jess was, though—once we'd broke for the weekend and I was back at the cottage, there was nothing to chase away the butterflies from my stomach.

I was going to make everything fresh in the morning, but

my fingers were tempted to send Ciaran a coward's text, telling him my excuses for cancelling on him, so I put them to work on the food instead.

Dave sat turning his head from side to side like a dysfunctional pendulum, watching as I chopped and bagged my way through a cucumber, a bunch of celery, cheeses, tomatoes, peppers, before making a start on my long-forgotten pièce de résistance, home-made coleslaw.

It was late by the time I set everything in the fridge to chill before tomorrow's picnic. Everything was done, bar the quiche and bread rolls, which I'd finish baking in the morning. Dave had lost interest, leaving me to survey the pile of food I'd created spanning nearly the entire breadth of the breakfast bar.

I fell back onto the same stool I'd fallen off last weekend, and in one huge surge all of the butterflies suddenly materialized again, only this time they were wearing steel boots.

My head felt hot in my hands as I sat staring at the small area of breakfast bar between my elbows. I'd spent nearly two hours making enough food to feed the forest lads, and all for one man who was used to dining at Atlas. A man who was going to hate my idea of a pleasant Sunday afternoon. A man who had been documented enjoying more women more times than I'd enjoyed home-made coleslaw. This was ridiculous. I was being ridiculous. What the hell was I hoping for here? What could possibly happen? I slid my phone open and pulled his number up on my text screen. A mail symbol flashed silently in the corner of the display. *Please be Martha. The baby's coming and she needs me there tomorrow. All day.*

No such luck. Jesse had messaged me. I touched the icon to open the text. His text was simple and concise: Don't cancel. Have fun.

I let my head bump off the breakfast bar, groaning all the

way down as I went. "What are you doing Holly?" I whispered to myself, the left side of my face squished against the cool wooden surface. "Ciaran Argyll is a player."

chapter 22

Four changes of clothes and things were getting out of hand. I'd already smashed a glass in the sink, snapped at Martha because she didn't need me over and trodden on Dave's paw. Now I had the insurmountable task of picking out which of three sweaters I was going to wear hidden under my jacket all day, where no one was even going to see it.

This was ridiculous.

Stones skittered across the yard outside and my time was up. Eleven-thirty on the nose.

He'd come.

The voile drapes turned out to be good for something. It wasn't spying when it was your property, was it? No, I wasn't spying on Ciaran Argyll as he strode across the yard to my front path. He had sunglasses on, and I realised what a beautifully sunny November morning it was. His hair looked blonder in this light, but it was a trick. I knew it was more brown than blond. He looked up at the window before disappearing from view under the porch.

The knocker rapped against the door and a battalion of

butterflies skipped down the stairs with me to open it. Even in the shade of the porch, the sunlight still clung to his hair.

"Morning." He smiled, cocking his head to one side. "Nice sweater." He nodded towards the very boring berry-red sweater I'd just pulled over my checked shirt.

"Hi. Thanks." We stood for a moment, appraising one another's outfits. I should've realised that Ciaran's idea of *comfortable* was going to be sharp enough to attend a job interview.

"Am I, er, a little overdressed?" he asked, taking in my jeans and polka-dot socks. He looked awkward, which immediately relaxed me.

"No, you look great. It's just that tailored trousers might get a bit messed up. It's my fault. I should have been more specific." I'd already cocked up. He couldn't wear brogues where we were going. We were going to end up at Atlas. I knew it.

"Well, I have a change of clothes in the car. Mary suggested it. I have jeans and I think she threw some boots in there, too."

Hold the phone.... We weren't at Atlas yet.

"That sounds ideal. Do you want to get changed while I finish packing the lunch?" I asked. I hadn't even invited him in yet.

"Sure, give me a minute." And he was already walking back to his car.

"Just come on in. Dave's out back," I called after him, then nipped back to the mirror sat over the console table in the hallway and quickly smoothed back the wisps of hair I'd disrupted with my sweater. A nervous sweat was trying to break out as I made it back to the breakfast bar to put the last few items of food into the top of the cool bag.

"A picnic, then?" came that soft Celtic lilt from the doorway. "You should have said. I make a decent asparagus-and-prosciutto sandwich."

I stopped packing the cherry tomatoes. "Asparagus-and-prosciutto sandwiches?"

He pulled the sunglasses from his face, revealing the still very sore-looking cut over his right eye. I felt my breath catch.

"Sure. But only when the Marmite's run out." He grinned.

"Well, no Marmite, I'm afraid, or asparagus. I have ham and mustard, though?"

"Ham and mustard is my favourite." He was still smiling as he moved over to help me put the last two foiled packages and plastic cups into the bag. His hand showed a few grazes now, just over the knuckles. "Anyway, I thought we'd agreed I was paying for lunch. You must have been working all morning on this."

I zipped up the bag and tapped the top of it. "You are going to be paying for it…. You're carrying it."

"So do you mind if I go and change?" he said. "Or I could just whip my things off here while you finish up?"

"No! You can go upstairs!"

It was plenty hot enough in here without Ciaran whipping off anything. I listened as he creaked upstairs and into the bathroom, not bothering to close the door behind him. A few moments of rustling later and the stairs were creaking under heavier shoes. I pretended to be busy when he appeared in the doorway again.

"Is this more suitable?" he asked.

Ciaran looked good in a suit, but I liked him even more so in his casual gear. Heavy dark blue denim sat over battered brown leather boots, and a cream cable-knit sweater rode high over his neck to greet the lower edges of his hair.

"Much better." I smiled, hoisting up the bag off the side. Ciaran automatically reached to take it from me, and I was hit by the fronds of his aftershave, sweet and fresh as the morning.

Despite his change in clothes, I looked no less plain beside him when we walked out to the car. I looked plainer still when he opened the door for me to slip into the front passenger seat. It was hard not to be wowed by the luxurious interior of the car, a paler cream than Ciaran's sweater and every bit as immaculate. Behind my head, the wings of Aston Martin's logo were stitched, probably by vestal virgins, into the headrests of the seats. It was like sitting in the cockpit of a very nice spaceship.

Ciaran slumped the boot closed with a cushioned thud and came around to the driver's door. *Please don't let anything leak in his boot*, I wished as he got in beside me.

"So, where to?" he asked, sliding his glasses back onto his nose. Every time he moved, a waft of his cologne teased my nose.

"Do you know Ellard's Covert? On the far west road of the forest?"

"Sure I do. My mother used to take me riding there when I was a kid."

"You've ridden? Well, that's going to save time, then."

"Are we going to the old trekking centre?" he said, breaking into a grin. "I didn't realise it was still there!"

"Is that okay? I thought we could take the trail up onto the ridge and have lunch up there?"

The car growled to life underneath us and Ciaran seemed to take on a new eagerness to get on with the day.

"That sounds great. I haven't ridden for years, though. I can't guarantee the safety of the ham sandwiches."

Ciaran rolled the car out of the yard. Just past him I could see Mrs Hedley, placing an empty glass vase back in her front window. She smiled and gave a small nod as we passed. My hands felt clammy as Ciaran negotiated us through the rotten wooden gateposts and over the potholes in the track. Rob had warned me of people suing owners of private property for damage incurred on ill-maintained paths. I wondered how many cakes an Aston Martin claim would set me back.

"Me neither," I said. "They won't let anyone take the horses out without a buddy."

"So what? You haven't got any buddies? I find that hard to believe."

"I talked Jess into it once, but it wasn't really his thing. He complained about the saddle sore for nearly two weeks afterwards, so I didn't make him come with me again."

"What about your sister? You mentioned a sister the other night. Martha, was it?"

I couldn't actually remember talking about Martha.

"That's right. Martha loves to ride, but she's allergic. And her husband, Rob, is a little out of shape. They're both busy at the moment anyway. They're expecting a baby any day now."

"So you're going to be an aunt? Congratulations." He smiled. "That must be exciting? I always thought I'd make a good uncle, but being an only child kind of puts paid to that." Ciaran touched the accelerator and the car pounced fluidly into a speed my van could only dream of.

"So no brothers or sisters? You must have friends with children?" I asked.

Waves of warmth started to permeate my backside. *Was this a heated chair? Holy—*

"Not really. I don't actually have that many people I'd count as friends, if I'm honest. Although the ones who do have children seem to be more trustworthy on the whole. Less cut-throat."

"Cut-throat? They're not all like Freddy Ludlow, are they?"

"Just for the record, Freddy Ludlow has *never* been a friend of mine. Fergie couldn't have got himself caught out soon enough. It won't be long before all ties between me and Freddy will be severed altogether. I won't be sad to see the back of that prat."

Well, we were off to a good start. We did have some things in common after all.

"Martha can be high-maintenance sometimes, but she's great. I couldn't stand having someone like Freddy Ludlow as my step-anything." I sighed.

"Well, he's not usually short on women, that's for sure," Ciaran said.

"Well, it can't be his winning personality that they're after. The man's a moron."

"I think it has something to do with an inheritance esti-mated somewhere between the one-forty and one-sixty mark."

"One-sixty what?" I asked.

"Million."

"One hundred and sixty million pounds? You *are* kidding?" His face said he wasn't kidding. "Maybe I should have been a bit more receptive."

Ciaran looked at me to check my expression.

"I'm obviously joking. But one hundred and sixty million pounds! All that money and not a bit of charisma. They do say money can't buy everything."

"No, it can't. But it can buy an awful lot," Ciaran added.

"What would you even do with that kind of money? I can't even comprehend how much that is."

He grinned again. "I like shiny new things. I'm sure I could think of a few ways to spend it."

"Like flying pop starlets out to Hollywood motels?"

"Let me assure you, that was no motel I took her to. That trip cost me a fortune." He laughed.

"Hmm. Money well spent, was it?"

Ciaran shrugged. "What would you spend that kind of money on? If you had it?" he asked.

"Me? Blimey, I don't have a clue. I could say something lame, like finishing my house, but that kind of money could make some serious differences, to lots of people. I'd have to think about that one. I'd probably start with a very tall wall, though, to keep the likes of Freddy out of my hair."

"Believe it or not, Freddy's okay until he has a drink. He's been overindulged by his mother for too long—he doesn't have a brake system in place for his behaviour."

"How nice for Freddy. I think he's a lot like his mother. The rest of us don't have their luxury."

"Do you think that's a luxury?" Ciaran asked, turning to face me. "I think it's a handicap. One you're far better off for not having."

"I never said it was a luxury I wanted for myself. It just seems a wasteful use of their resources. They should put their good fortune to better use. There's got to be more in their lives than flash cars and decadent parties."

As soon as I said it, I cringed. I had completely forgotten myself already. I sneaked a sideways glance at Ciaran, focused on the road ahead. I couldn't see his eyes but there was the shadow of a smile at the edge of his mouth. "Sorry, Ciaran. I didn't mean—"

"Don't be sorry. You're not like most of the women I've met. Your views are…refreshing. If a little judgemental."

"You think I'm judgemental?" I was shocked. One of the perks of my life was that no one, bar my mother, ever said anything inflammatory to me anymore, for fear of me imploding or something.

"Well…an expensive car doesn't necessarily mean the driver's a self-obsessed egomaniac any more than a battered old bicycle means its rider is of limited finesse. You wouldn't disagree with that, would you?"

Was I judgemental? I didn't like to think of myself that way.

"No. I wouldn't disagree with that." Damn it, I *was* judgemental. And he'd pulled me up on it. I mentally subtracted one of the brownie points I'd previously awarded him.

Outside, grassy embankments were already merging into ever-thickening woodland as Ciaran's car glided easily over the road. Autumn didn't reach here, where evergreen Corsican and Scots pine held their ground against the changing months.

"So they're not all like Freddy, your circle of *non*-friends?"

Ciaran laughed lightly. "No, there are a few good men, so to speak. But my father's company has had its prolific ups and downs. When people think they know everything about your family's business interests, it's not the Freddys you have to watch out for." Ciaran swung a right onto the first road that would intersect the forests.

"The Pennys, then?"

He smiled again. "No, not the Pennys. Penny would be one to be wary of if she had any clout. But Penny's like most people, happy enough to look the part even if the substance is lacking."

I gave him back the brownie point.

"Who do you have to watch out for, then, if not people like them?"

"In my world? Everyone who comes at you with a smile."

We sat for a while, quietly, while Ciaran took in the surroundings of the forest. We were nearly at the point the road forked off to the commission offices and visitor centre.

"We should get off soon and take the long route. There have been a few incidents involving deer on this stretch of road."

It was true, there had. The forest was some fifteen miles wide but it was shrinking over on the east side, pushing the herds further this way. There had been plenty of near misses reported between the fork in the road and Charlie's old office. It was difficult enough to concentrate on the road down there without five hundred pounds of stag running over your bonnet.

"Are you sure? The trekking centre is just down past the visitor centre, right?"

"Yes, but we can double back on ourselves from the other end. Trust me, it will be quicker." Now that bit was not so truthful. This was the same road Ciaran would have used to cross the forest during the week, but he didn't argue the point. In this car, the difference would be negligible anyway.

"So do you still come here? To the forest, I mean. I know that you said Charlie worked here. That must have its difficulties."

"Not so much. I do miss it, though."

Outside, our detour was taking us into the beech woodlands, where the brown earth crept beneath a carpet of brightly coloured leaves, scattered like confetti at a wedding reception. Evergreen turned to yellows, then burnt oranges and eventually hot reds before the beech leaves finally flittered to the ground.

"I'd forgotten how beautiful it was here," Ciaran said as we headed through the riot of colour around us. "I don't see this on the other road."

"Like I said, can't be topped."

chapter 23

The trekking centre hadn't changed since I'd watched Jess waddling his way out of it more than a year ago. The girls there were new, young perky horsey types who couldn't get enough of Ciaran and his car.

We saddled up and packed most of the food into the saddlebags on each of the horses, and left for the tranquility of the trail. Ciaran waited for me to pass before following on. He must have smiled back at the girls because they both slipped into a fit of stifled giggles behind us.

I got it. Even a helmet did little to knock him far down the barometer of sexy. Well, I wasn't here for that. I just wanted to ride the trail, and Ciaran had given me the opportunity. If anything, I was taking advantage of him.

"Like riding a bike," he called as he cantered to catch me up.

"Just take it easy. I don't know CPR, so don't fall off!"

He flashed me one of those smiles that affected every part of his face, and I fought everything not to giggle like the girls.

The forests were like a dreamscape over this side. The colours were incredible around us as the gentle sounds of hooves thudded home into the spongy forest floor.

"So you never said why it is you don't have anyone to come trekking with."

I felt comfortable around Ciaran, enough to take his question without feeling like a total loser.

"I do have friends. It wouldn't be fair to them to say that I didn't. But after the accident I didn't want them around me. I didn't want anyone but him." I was talking about Charlie again, not a drop of alcohol and still at ease.

"That's understandable," he said, bobbing along beside me. "Unfortunate, but understandable. So weren't they supportive?"

"No, they were. They tried, but it wasn't their fault. After you've pushed people away enough times, eventually they stop calling."

"And do you regret that now? Pushing them away," he asked, swatting at a bug.

"I do—for them, anyway. I didn't let them do the only thing they could for me, and that was hard for them. But I think that life is easier this way. I don't want to go clubbing or drinking my cares away. What's the point when they're still there in the morning?"

"That's exactly what I tried to tell my old man, you know? That the drinking didn't make anything better. But he couldn't cope with the pain of my mother's death. So he drank to numb himself to it."

A gentle tug on the reins was enough to stop my animal.

"Ciaran, I'm sorry. I'd thought that maybe your parents were divorced." Ciaran stopped his horse, too. "When did she die?"

He smiled, but I knew that smile, knew what it was for. "A long time ago now. I was seventeen when my mother died. A very sudden onset of cancer. She was only ill for a few months, and she suffered every minute of them."

"I'm sorry, Ciaran."

"If you're not going to go off the rails at seventeen, when are you, eh?" he said jokily.

"Which cancer did she have?"

"Cervical. By the time we knew, it was everywhere. At least she died at home. She was the typical homebody, y'know? Even when Fergal built the business up, Mum never bothered with shopping sprees and health spas. She just carried on as she always had, keeping the home fires burning while my dad worked his arse off to secure a stable future for us. He was all hard graft and vision back then, the old lad. My mother's death changed all that for him."

Ciaran urged his horse on and called for mine to follow.

"It sounds like they were a good unit?" I tried.

"They were. Too good. I think if it had been Fergal who'd gone first, my mother would have been heartbroken, but she'd have kept it together better. But Fergal just wasn't as strong as she was. He couldn't get through the day without sleeping for most of it. We nearly lost the business to his grief."

"But he's okay now, isn't he? He's doing well again. You must be relieved?"

"Oh, yes, he's okay other than the odd lapse in judgement and having his head turned by a gold-digging tart. Other than that, he's grand!"

I made a mental note to cut Fergal a lot more slack if our paths ever crossed again.

The ride onto the ridge line overlooking the northwest side of the forest had been about as beautiful as it could have been in the low November sun.

The horses were left to graze and most of the food had survived the journey. I enjoyed watching Ciaran getting covered in coleslaw while I did my best to eat daintily.

"So how long were your folks married?" I asked him, intrigued to hear more of Fergal.

"Oh, I don't know...twenty-five years, give or take. They grew up on the same tiny street, played together while my grandmothers scrubbed the front steps. Fell in love, married young, had me. Great coleslaw, by the way."

"So they both came from modest backgrounds?" I asked.

"Very. Fergal was destined to work on the trawlers like everyone else he grew up with, but he was the only son of Arbroath born without sea legs. So he got himself a job cleaning bricks and worked his way up from there. My father always said that he was the machine, but my mother was the engine driving everything along. He said that's how he came to do so well for himself, because of her. The love of a good woman and all that."

I hadn't got any of that from my encounters with Fergal.

"And what about you? Did you always want to follow your dad into the family business?"

"Carrying a brick hod around freezing building sites? Not exactly. I wanted to be an architect. Seven years at university then a job at the warmer end of the building trade."

"But I thought Argyll Inc. was already up and running by then?"

"It was, but Fergal's working class down to his bones. He made sure all the lads without letters after their names learned the business from the footings up. I was no exception."

"Sounds like a good enough reason to get yourself to university." I smiled, remembering the splits Charlie used to have all over his hands from working in the cold. He only had to make a fist and the skin would crack open, spotting the bedsheets with blood each winter.

"When my mother was dying, my dad spent much of her last months trying to explore different avenues for her treatment, trying to make the money work for her. The sad reality was, the money couldn't help us. Nothing could. Fergal invested every minute he had trying to find a new treatment or medicine, and I spent the time nursing her through her last months. I knew she was slipping away from us. I could feel the time running out of her with every heartbeat."

Something tensed in Ciaran's jaw as he remembered.

"And you were just seventeen? Ciaran. That must have been horrendous for you."

He smiled the tension away.

"By the time she died, I'd missed out enough of my college studies that it threw my progression to university off for at least a year. My old man had thrown himself into work and that seemed to occupy him. So I thought I'd do the same, while I got my college work back on track. Working at the company, though, it soon became obvious…Dad was struggling. He'd fallen into a depression or something. Some black hole he couldn't climb back out of."

I knew that hole. For the last two years I'd been clinging on to the edge of it. It seemed okay to acknowledge that now, now that I knew it had claimed others, too. People who, like me, were still walking and talking and breathing.

"So you never went to university?" I asked.

"When the time came, there was no way I could leave him to live alone. So I stayed, learned the ropes. Tried to figure out what to do about the effect my mother's death had on him." Ciaran took a deep breath. "She was like the linchpin that held us all together. Everything started to slide pretty soon after she went."

"And your dad started drinking?"

"At work, at home. Before lunchtime, before the morning

meetings. Fergal was drinking more unabashedly with every passing week. Relations within the company were becoming more fractious and over time Argyll Inc. started to slip. Everything they'd worked for going down the pan."

Ciaran poured us both a small plastic cup of coffee.

"But, weren't there protocols in place to protect the company? Didn't anyone try to help your father through it?"

"Like your friends tried to help you? It's not that simple, is it? Fergal had a good inner circle at the company, but money is like blood in the water. Soon enough the sharks start to circle. A lot of people took advantage of us while our eyes were off the ball. People who have made a lot of money off investments they were never supposed to have a shot at. They nearly cost us everything."

He was clenching his jaw again, all the softness gone from his face.

"But you must be back on track now? I mean, nice cars, nice home. Your dad must be getting there?" I hoped he was; so many years on, it would be beyond cruel to hear that Fergal was still suffering like a dog in the street. Ciaran knocked back his coffee. And jumped to his feet.

"Yeah, we're back on track. Fergie got his act together and it's all worked out in the end." He held his hand out for me, and I was still mulling over our conversation when I took his hand without thinking. "Come on, let's get our money's worth out of our four-legged friends," he said, pulling me to my feet.

Back down on the trail, our luck was beginning to thin, as great globules of cool rain were sploshing onto my hat and soaking into my shoulders.

"Head further into the woods," Ciaran called over, "it'll be drier there." He'd already picked up his pace when I called an okay back to him. He definitely hadn't forgotten much from his riding days as I watched him picking his way through the trees. He'd been quiet since we'd packed up the picnic, but I'd run through the conversation twice now and couldn't think what I'd said to offend him.

I fell into my stride and began to canter through the woods, gradually gaining on Ciaran. I was watching him as he took his horse deeper into the beech trees, where the ground swept away spaciously between each of the neighbouring trunks. I'd been so busy watching him, trying to keep up with him, that I hadn't noticed the reaching branch at head height.

A sudden hot searing lash tore across my face and my horse whinnied beneath me as I cried out. I grabbed at whatever felt embedded in my eye, finding nothing to pull away.

"Holly!" Ciaran shouted.

I was panicking; I couldn't see. Had I hurt myself? As in *badly*?

Hooves thudded into the ground next to me.

"Holly? What happened?" I was trying to rub the grinding ache from my eyes, and felt the soreness cutting a trail across my cheek. "Holly, talk to me!"

I felt my horse pulled suddenly over towards Ciaran's voice, then his hands finding their way to the clasp under my chin. I tried to blink against the sting but my eyes wouldn't open. The hat was pulled free of my head, and the weight of my displaced ponytail slumped against the back of my neck. A cool hand, either side of my face, and then the patter of rain-drops on my skin.

"I think it was a thin branch. I didn't see," I said, trying to blink away what felt like a lump of wood stuck in my left eye.

"You're not cut. Just relax. Keep blinking. If you've scratched your eyes, it's going to feel uncomfortable for a while but you'll be okay."

I could feel the water already streaming from my eye as my body mechanisms swung into action, trying to rinse any debris from in there. I could tell now that it was mainly my left, with the right eye just doing that solidarity thing that eyes tended to do.

"That's it—just keep batting those lashes."

I could feel his breath on my cheek. Ciaran still had hold of me, holding my face up to the cooling sensation of rain against my eyelids. Finally, the left blinked open through eyelashes thick with salt water. He was looking straight into them, examining them for damage, and, as the stinging slowly ebbed away, I began to take full advantage of my own chance to look right back into his.

"That's it," he whispered. "I can't see anything that shouldn't be there."

A familiar warmth began under the spot where his hands still lay against my cheeks, fanning out to where his fingers reached into my hair. Another wave of stinging behind my eye and I shut them tight before it could worsen. I held them like that for a moment, until the burn subsided and the taste of Ciaran's breath danced over my lips.

I felt my breathing quicken, then a new warmth moved in against me, delicately pressing a gentle kiss to my mouth.

I responded to him.

The tiniest movement, but it was enough, enough to tell him it was okay. Ciaran responded, too, slowly working his lips over mine so that I could taste every edge of them, every softness they had to offer. In the distance, something neighed and shifted under me, and like that, we were broken. Before I opened my eyes again, his fingers slipped from my hair, and the rain began to fall on my face again. Perhaps it had never stopped.

"I'm sorry," he said softly as I peeled my eyes open. "I should have asked."

I felt myself nodding. My body answering him before my brain had caught up.

He looked at me, unsure, and then again he pulled my horse closer before his hand found its place again at the back of my neck. He sat there, holding me that way, giving me a fighting chance to say *no*, but I was ready for him this time, I knew what to do. I leaned into his hand, this time finding the back of his neck, too, slipping my fingers through the hair there and breathing in every drop of the aftershave that clung to him. I saw him lean in this time, watching him draw all the way in before I let him kiss me again. Slowly, sweetly, as though he were opening his favourite present.

And I kissed him right back.

Neither of us said anything as Ciaran led us slowly through the woods. My eye was still streaming, but that wasn't the part of my body bothering me. Everything was tingling.

I know I blushed every single time he checked back on me, but what could I do about that?

I hadn't even noticed where we were until Ciaran's hushed voice broke the sounds of the horses moving through the leaves.

"Son of a bitch!" he growled.

chapter 24

The dense copse of holly right over on the north side of the forest had been Charlie's favourite area of woodland on account of the holly trees here. Of course, there hadn't been an enormous Sold sign nailed into one of them when I'd last been there.

"No! They can't have sold this off, not yet!" All thoughts of kissing left me as I jumped down from my horse. Even Ciaran looking at me couldn't curb my sudden need to cry. "They can't! This was where Charlie wanted to set up the school, so the kids could see the mistle thrushes guarding the berries!" I said, fighting to hold back the tears.

Ciaran booted a rock on the ground, sending it bouldering angrily over the path. For a property developer, I was surprised by his reaction as he stood glaring at the second sign. Sawyers' Developments stood boldly in white against its stark teal background. It was an ugly sign.

"I'm sorry, Holly," he said, touching my elbow. "Sawyers have a nose for deals like this."

"You know them?" I asked, looking at their name again.

"I know them. No shark grew fatter off us than James Sawyer."

"What do they develop? Please don't say houses."

Ciaran blew a large breath away and seemed to look for another rock to kick.

"I'm sorry, Holly. But there will probably be houses on here within the next few months."

I kicked a rock of my own.

For two years I'd had my head stuck up my own ass, ignoring what was going on around me. I'd done nothing to support the action group campaigning against the sell-offs and now I had absolutely no right to whine about it.

For the entire journey home, all I could think of was the cost of my long-standing inaction in the woods, interrupted only by my more recent actions in them.

I'd have felt more awkward had Ciaran not seemed so pissed off next to me.

"Did Charlie enjoy his work?" he asked, breaking the twenty minutes of silence we'd just shared.

Ciaran made the turn and we crunched up the track to the farmhouse, wet and fed up.

"He loved it. Loved everything about it. That's why we never got round to finishing this place off. We were either disagreeing on paint colours all the time, or working." So much time wasted.

"I take it you'd have finished it if you'd had the chance, then?" he said, looking over the steering wheel at our beautiful cottage.

Even my house had a brave face. Looking at it from out here, no one would ever guess the turmoil the place was in on the inside.

"I'd need to take a few weeks off to even make a dent on it. I'll get round to it, one day. The structure's all sound now. It just needs someone with more of an idea than I have to come up with a decor that works. Would you like to come in for coffee?" I asked, but even to me it sounded paltry.

"No, thanks. I've got to get back. Check Fergal's not up to mischief." I smiled at his joke, uncertain of how we should part ways. "I'm sorry about the woodland, Holly. I was having a good time until then. Well, I'm sorry about the branch, too, but what I mean is that there were parts I really enjoyed today."

I was fixed by brown eyes again.

"Me, too." There, I said it. I had enjoyed today, had enjoyed feeling that way again. "I'm sorry I'm such hard work, Ciaran. I'm just…not used to this. It doesn't come easily to me."

"Shall we have another crack at it? Maybe somewhere less… wooded? Seeing as *trees* seemed to be our main stumbling block today." He was smiling, and I couldn't help mimicking him.

"That sounds nice, Ciaran. Thanks." How had I not sent him running yet?

"Okay, but it's my turn to choose, right?" he asked.

"Seems fair." I winced. "Where were you thinking?"

"Leave it with me. I'll call you." He jumped out of the car and shot round to open my door before running the remnants of the picnic to the house for me. He didn't make a big deal of the goodbye, which I appreciated.

"I'll call you," he repeated, hovering at my door. A lingering peck on the cheek and he was out of there.

It was strange how the mere act of closing your eyes could help you to see something more clearly. The contours of a person's mouth, for example, the tender parting of lips. I reached a hand up to feel where those lips had been just an hour ago, to remind my own of the sensation, and was hit by the pungent aroma of horse.

No wonder Dave had sniffed me to death. I'd thought he was after the food bag. Ugh. I'd leave the coffee until after I'd showered. As soon as I crossed the hall, I could hear the muffled buzz of my mobile where I'd left it on the bed this morning. *Oh, no!* Today was going to be the day I was about to find out that my poor sister had delivered her own baby on the front lawn because she couldn't get hold of me!

I flew up the stairs and into the bedroom, tossing the sweaters aside to see *Martha* flashing angrily on the screen.

"Hello? Martha? Hello!"

"Where the hell have you been? I've been calling you all day!"

"What's happened? Are you okay? Have you had the baby?"

"No, you lunatic. But good to know you're on hand, Hol." I started to breathe again. This baby was already giving me heart attacks and it wasn't even born yet! "Anyway, back to my original question. Where the hell have you been?"

"Nowhere. Just out," I panted.

"Don't lie to me, Holly Jefferson. I know you're keeping something from me, and I'm not getting off the phone until you come clean." I didn't want to set Martha off on some big misunderstanding about my friendship with Ciaran, a friendship I didn't understand myself. "How long have you been sneaking around with *Ciaran Argyll*?"

His name was sharp in my ear.

"What? I'm not sneaking around with him. Have you been talking to Jesse?"

"Oh, so Jesse knows? The whole of the county knows, but I have to guess?"

"Martha, calm down. The whole of the county does not *know* anything. There's nothing *to* know!"

"Well, they do now. As of this morning, your picture has been through every letterbox courtesy of the *Sunday Journal*."

"What? The *Sunday Journal*? What picture?"

"The picture of you, my sister, slipping into a limo with those *Diors* in your hands, followed by *Ciaran Argyll*! That is you, isn't it? It didn't look like you at first, wearing a dress, but the shoes in your hands gave you away."

"Oh, no, no. Martha, hang on to that paper. We don't get the *Journal* here. I'm having a shower then I'll be over."

"Forget that. I've been stuck in this house counting stretch marks for weeks. I'll be there in half an hour." The phone clicked dead. Twelve calls I'd missed from her. Twelve! I dreaded what the article said. The *Journal* covered the whole of Hunterstone, and the city—where most of my customers came from.

I spent most of the time in the shower running through the pictures I'd seen of Ciaran on the Net. Ciaran with a blonde, Ciaran with twins, Ciaran covered in blood with a barefoot woman. I was a statistic. I hadn't so much as—well, done *more* than kissed the guy, and I was already the latest in a long line.

I'd only just stepped from the cubicle when Martha screeched into the yard. She must have been flat out all the way here. She wasn't even supposed to be driving. I hurried into my room for a quick change, watching Martha waddle comically across the yard like a little plump duck.

The front door swung open. "Hellooo? Come out, come out wherever you are, lady."

I threw on my joggers and an old baseball tee over still wet hair.

"Hey," I shouted, bracing myself.

"Don't you 'hey' me. Who's been keeping secrets?"

I walked to the landing and looked down the stairs. She stood in the hallway, one hand on where her hip used to be and the other holding up the paper. "Not now, Dave!" she snapped as I trudged down the stairs. Dave was outsized, and he knew it.

Opened out to page four, Martha held aloft the half page devoted to a picture seemingly showing two people, mid-escape from some sort of rampage. The headline shouted Prodigal Son on the Verge of Losing Argyll's Bidding War! And already I had a feeling it wasn't going to say kind things.

"You look like Bonnie and Clyde, Hol! What's going on?"

I took the paper from her and walked through to the kitchen with it, skimming over the caption beneath the photo.

"Put the kettle on, Martha."

Playboy lout beats hasty retreat with latest squeeze.

"You're going to want something stronger than coffee," Martha uttered.

"Shhh!"

The only son of property tycoon Fergal Argyll has plunged Argyll Inc. into yet more hot water after failing to behave himself at his own birthday celebrations. Argyll, who turned thirty last week, was seen leaving the Gold Block, a prestigious Argyll Inc. development in the heart of the city, sporting facial injuries after an altercation with an unidentified bystander. Argyll was reported to have then commandeered a fellow guest's limo before fleeing the scene with an unknown woman in a state of undress...

"'A state of undress'! I was holding my shoes!"

This comes just weeks after Argyll Inc. were warned in no uncertain terms that their bid on five hundred acres of prime development land was at risk of refusal if the company courted any more bad publicity. The Lux

Foundation, current owners of the land situated in close proximity to the government's latest proposed high-speed rail route, are notoriously thorough in their vetting of potential investors.

Argyll Inc.'s chief competitor, Sawyers' Developments, must be ecstatic at Argyll's latest blunder, which could only serve to strengthen Sawyers' position in the bidding war. Fiery relations have long been documented between the two rival powerhouses, said to have started when Clara Sawyer, James Sawyer's daughter, broke off her engagement to the hotheaded Argyll heir. Judging by this photo, we doubt it's a decision she regrets.

I was dumbstruck.

"That's not right. That's not…fair," I said, as Martha sat our mugs between us. "He didn't do anything wrong that night. He was a complete gentleman." Martha said nothing. "How can they write that kind of thing when they don't know?"

"So he *wasn't* involved in a fight?"

"It wasn't like that, Martha. There were these guys and—" Martha didn't need to know this crap. "They were fighting, and he tried to break them up. That's all. He wasn't fleeing from anything. He just said that he couldn't go back inside the party looking like he did—it would court attention."

"He's already done that. What were you doing there in the first place? And dressed to kill, Holly!"

I told Martha how I'd come to find myself at the Gold Rooms, skirting around any incidence of my interaction with Ciaran. It was pointless not telling her that he'd stayed over, though. She'd hear it from Jesse at some point. As soon as I'd told her, she didn't stop grinning.

"Didn't you see that you were being photographed?" she

asked, still utterly thrilled that Ciaran had been sat at this very breakfast bar.

"No, I didn't have a clue. I'd have put the shoes back on." I smiled.

"They sound like they've really got it in for him, the papers. And to splash it around that he was dumped by the Sawyer girl. That's harsh."

"You're a fan, Martha. Did you know that he was engaged once?"

"Not since he's been on my radar—" she grinned salaciously "—but I only follow the more spirited ones. If he was engaged he must have been a lot quieter back then. Ooh, let's look her up on Google. What was her name? Cara? Clara?"

"No! We're not doing that, Martha. It's none of our business. The guy's got enough people poking around in his life."

Martha watched me carefully with richly hazel eyes, made prettier still by the length of her lashes.

"You like him," she said, burning me with the same look Mum had.

"No, I don't!" I retorted. It was possibly the most childish response I could have offered.

"Fibber. Your cheeks are a dead giveaway." She smiled. "You're as red as a berry, Holly. Even your eye is turning pink."

"Actually, I poked it on a twig." I slid from my stool and started to unpack the bag of picnic food on the other side. "Don't you have a long painful labour to get to, Martha? Don't let me keep you."

She ignored me, moving over to pick at the food as I took it from the bag.

"So what's with all the food? You made coleslaw! Uh-oh, and *two* cups! You've been out with someone, haven't you? You've been on a *date*! Was it him? Was it Ciaran?"

This was exactly why I didn't say anything. Because Martha was going to get carried away and then when it all came tumbling down I'd have to avoid dewy eyes and conversations with her.

"Look, Martha. You know me…. You know that all this isn't me. I don't know what I'm doing! I don't belong in this world," I said, waving at the paper.

"Don't belong in what world, Hol? Picnics with a drop-dead gorgeous millionaire who's taken an interest in you?"

"Not the picnics. Being photographed as a *latest squeeze*. And he's not a millionaire, Martha, before you get carried away. He just works for his father."

"All right, Hol. If you say so. Does it matter anyway? Any of it? If you're having a good time. Lord knows you're about due for one."

"I enjoy myself," I said, more defensively than was necessary.

"Oh, you do? At work? Or Saturday nights watching movies at ours? Or do you mean enjoying your time here, with half a ton of dog slobber for company? Because as far as I'm aware, you don't get out much, Hol." Martha didn't look like Mum then. She looked like my big sister, who'd always taken care of me.

"But what can he possibly see in me, Martha? I'm nothing like all the other women he's used to. He said as much!"

Martha shook her head. "You've always been the same, Hol, even when we were kids, playing in the dirt while the rest of us braided each other's hair, shirking pretty dresses for hideous hand-me-downs. Even then you couldn't see the boys watching you. I'm just going to throw this one out there, but maybe it's because you're *not* like all the other women he's used to."

"He doesn't know what I'm like, Martha. I'm not what he

thinks." I wasn't what anyone thought; I'd spent most of the last two years hiding it.

"Who's to say he's what *you* think? Why are you holding back, Hol? If you like him?"

"I don't want to be another conquest! You've seen yourself how many women he's had—I haven't been kissed for *two years*!" Up until today, in the forest. My stomach flipped at the memory.

"We've just ascertained that the papers are unreliable, Holly. You said yourself that they don't know what's going on with him! How much of your hang-ups about him are based on other people's opinions? You can't judge him fairly on that and you bloody know it. That article has done you a favour— now you know it's all bullshit." She smiled. Martha didn't usually swear.

"It can't all be, Martha. I've seen how women react to him. They're like sharks around—" It was Ciaran's analogy that tripped off my tongue.

"Sharks around what? Blood? Well, then no wonder, Hol," she said, laying her hand over her swollen tummy.

"No wonder what?"

"No wonder he acts like an emotionally impenetrable playboy. He's been burned by that Clara and now he's hiding. Something the two of you have in common."

"I don't hide," I said, busying myself away from her.

"I know you like him. You're hiding from that. And you're also hiding behind all this rubbish you don't really believe about his character, it's an excuse to avoid the real issue here."

"Okay, Martha, you know best." I wasn't going to fight with an emotionally volatile pregnant woman.

"I know you, Hol, and I know that to let him get this far inside your city walls, he must mean something to you. And

I also know that there's only one reason you can't admit it to yourself."

"Oh, yeah?" I said, giving up altogether.

"Yeah—Charlie."

chapter 25

The rest of Sunday had been about trying to blot my sister's voice from my head. We weren't kids anymore. She didn't always know best. Martha's trouble was that she still bought in to the whole fairy-tale thing, but she'd never been burned by the dragon.

Monday had mostly held a sense of relief that he hadn't called. Tuesday brought with it niggling questions, understanding, then confirmation of the obvious. I'd said I was unsuited to him. I'd known it since first seeing him that night under the manor entrance with Penny, Queen of Ice. Then Wednesday had arrived, bringing with it resignation.

"What's eating you, Hol? I don't think I've ever seen you… mope." I was not moping.

"I am not moping. Have you finished those cookie favours yet?"

"Touchy touchy… Yeah, they're nearly finished. All the outlines are piped. They're just drying off and then we can flood-ice them. D'ya want a cuppa?"

I shook my head. I was not moping.

"I'm going over to the golden girls for a smoothie. I think I need a vitamin C boost or something. Do you want anything?" I asked.

"You're ending the boycott? You must need a boost." He chuckled softly.

"I haven't ended it. I'm just taking an interval. Do you want anything?"

"Nah, I'm good, ta."

I didn't bother answering the phone on my way past it to the door.

"Get that, Jess?" I yelled back over my shoulder. I didn't wait to check he'd heard.

Standing in line listening to the golden girls flirt with each of the two men either side of me, I could see Jess through the shop window across the street, elbows on the counter, laughing into the phone.

"Next?" I bet it was one of his girlfriends, calling him up for a chat. Aleta Delgado probably. *"Next?"* The suit behind me touched my elbow while golden girl A waited for my order. Her eyebrows reached over leathery brown skin to a perfectly set mousy bouffant.

"Just a mango-and-pineapple smoothie, please." I shouldn't have bothered with the "please"—the guy in front had got an extra dollop of clotted cream on his scones, the guy behind a compliment on his tie. All I'd got was "next?"

"Small or large?"

"Small, please." Damn it, *please* had fallen out again.

"Eat in or out?"

"Drink out." Point for me. Golden girl B, almost the negative version of her co-worker with dark bouffant and pale skin, raised her eyebrows as she rang it through the till. I went back to watching Jess, still gassing.

"You work over the road, don't you, love? With that lovely brown fella?" The darker of the two threw her thumb over her shoulder towards the window.

"Jesse?" I asked.

"That's it, Jesse. Would you give him this? We haven't seen him all week."

I watched as she moved brightly painted talons over the Chelsea buns before slipping the largest into a paper bag.

"Will do." I sighed, trying to avoid touching the nails. Golden girl A passed me my smoothie, charging me a small fortune for it.

"That's all fresh fruit in there. Might cheer you up a bit." She smiled with lips coloured to match her own talons. "Tell Jesse we miss him."

I waited until I was outside before taking my first slurp of fruity goodness.

Damn, that tastes good, I thought, gulping my way across the street.

Jess radiated with glee as I shambled back into Cake. Now I knew he was talking to a girl. I moved around the counter for the bakery. Jess's arm shot out to the facing wall, blocking me.

"Yes, mate, no problem at all. D'ya want to speak to her? She's just walked in."

Rob? I mouthed. Jess shook his head.

"Yeah, I'll tell her. Nine a.m., her place, get Mrs H. to feed Dave. Got it. I'll tell her now. Cheers, mate…. Yeah…see ya."

"Who was that?"

Jess cocked an eyebrow. "The name's Bond, Ciaran Bond. He's picking you up in the morning."

"That was Ciaran?" My voice nearly caught on his name.

"Yeah, man, and he's got a surprise for you tomorrow."

"But tomorrow's Thursday…. I have work!"

"Not anymore. It's all sorted. I'm gonna cover you tomorrow and he's going to let me use his box at the footy this Sunday."

A mixture of excitement and dread began rising through my chest. I gulped down more smoothie to wash the sensation away.

"Well, what did he say, Jess? Where's he taking me?"

"I don't know, but he said wear whatever you like, casual, and that you'll be gone until late afternoon." Jess lent over the counter, trying a look of innocence that had never suited his face. In a matter of seconds it had broken into a wide-reaching smile.

"What smoothie did you get, Hol?" he asked coyly. "Whatever it is, it seems to have given you that boost."

I didn't like surprises. Even ones that involved casual clothing. It was easier when I'd had a picnic to prepare, but too much time waiting around had led to too many cups of coffee, and now I was jittery with nothing to keep my mind off the clock other than bothering at my stubby nails.

I watched eight-forty-five become eight-forty-six. By eight-forty-seven I was calling over the back fence to Mrs Hedley. "Morning, Mrs Hedley."

"Good morning."

"What are you up to, feeding the chickens?"

"I'm just having a potter. A few of these pots need attention." In her arms she cradled some sort of plant, way past the point of attention.

"Oh, that one looks destined for the compost heap," I said empathetically.

"Don't you believe it."

I watched as she poured no more than an egg-cupful of water over the dead brown leaves, then shoved the shriveled plant into my arms. "Where there's life, there's hope. Some things just need a chance to grow. Put it on your windowsill."

Great. These crispy brown leaves were never going to be green again, and now I had to find space for it for enough weeks before justifying its journey to the bin.

"Thanks," I said. "I'm going out shortly. Dave's shut up in the kitchen, but could you feed him for me? In case I'm late?"

"Off anywhere nice, are we?" she asked.

"I don't know yet." I shrugged. "I'll let you know."

Dave's barking saw Mrs Hedley break a smile.

"Enjoy yourselves."

I'd watched Ciaran walk towards me enough times now that *surely* it shouldn't affect the rhythm of my breathing, but then, this was my first time after being featured in a newspaper with him, after feeling his fingers through my hair, after tasting his mouth on mine.

"Hello," he said, stopping just short of the doorway.

"Hi. Casual, then?" I nodded at his outfit, the same leather boots he'd worn trekking, heavy mustard trousers and chunky grey hoody zipped over a white tee.

"Absolutely no posh restaurants today, I promise." He grinned. The tapes over his eye had come free, and the bruising was little more than a tinge under his skin now. "Are you ready?"

"Yeah, I just need to grab my keys."

"I'll get them for you. Go and jump in the car. Is Dave in the kitchen?" Ciaran shuffled past me into the hallway and found my keys on the table there.

"Yes, I've shut the doors, haven't I?"

"I've got it." Ciaran checked the kitchen door was closed and then followed me out, locking the front. Next to us, Mrs Hedley peeped her head around her own front door.

"Good morning, young man. How's that eye of yours?" she called, stepping onto the path.

"Fine, thank you, Cora. You're looking ravishing this morning!"

Mrs. Hedley cackled at that. "Go on with you, you cheeky boy."

Ciaran reminded me of Jesse in some ways.

"I won't be a minute," he whispered into my ear, before nipping over to her. He whispered something to her, too, before joining me at the car.

"So where are we going?" I asked, climbing in.

"Today, I am taking you for the Argyll experience. How's your aim?" he asked, starting the car.

"My aim?"

"Yes. Your aim."

It was easy with him. Comfortable. Too comfortable, if anything. I was at ease by the time we were into the forest, Ciaran having me in near hysterics with a tale involving Fergal mistaking a boardroom water cooler for a urinal.

I was relaxed enough that I hadn't thought about the route past the visitor centre until Ciaran had taken the same turning at the fork. I was glad he had. I didn't have another excuse for us not to go down there.

I'd needled him for a rough outline of the day ahead. He'd convinced me on the fishing, but after a little bartering Ciaran agreed to substitute the partridges with clay pigeons instead.

"Hello, dear! So nice to have you back." Mary was the perfect welcome for any house.

"Hi, Mary. Nice to see you, too." I smiled.

Mary seemed pleased that I'd remembered her name. "Can I get you both a pot of tea? Or some breakfast? You didn't eat this morning, Ciaran."

"Don't worry about any of that, Mary. I'm going to be taking care of Holly today. Just so she knows I can tie my own shoelaces."

"Oh, all right." She smiled. "Your father's in the kitchen."

"Keep him in there, would you, Mary? We're taking the shotguns out later. I wouldn't want Holly to mistake him for a wild boar. I might be getting my inheritance earlier than I'd hoped." Mary was too polite to laugh, but it was nice to hear Ciaran loosening up. He always had a tension about him, a coiled spring that could ping off at any time. At Hawkeswood, he was at ease.

The morning's fishing was…interesting. Ciaran had to do the maggot thing, though, which was gross, and when he hauled an eel out of the water, I was ready to play with the guns.

Fergal joined us, and sat back into one of the stone chairs overlooking the river, which swallowed every single clay disc Ciaran blew from the air.

"My arms are aching. Would you like to take my spot?" I asked, sitting beside Fergal on the stone bench.

He reached to take the gun from my hands, passing me the little wooden duck he'd been shaping with his penknife.

"That's pretty," I said, turning it in my hands, admiring the symmetry he'd achieved with such a simple tool. "I wanted to do woodwork at school, but my mother said it wasn't a pursuit for girls."

"And would your mother consider *shooting* a pursuit for her wee girl?" he asked.

My mother would have considered any pursuit acceptable on an estate like this. Another reason I didn't want them to know about Ciaran.

"I guess that would depend on what I was shooting at." I smiled.

Fergal laughed to himself. "Oh, aye, there're a few beggars I could line my barrels on, I can tell ye. James Sawyer bein' ma fust choice."

"Careful, Fergie. You don't want Holly appraising your craftsmanship. She's quite the artist," Ciaran said, nodding to the carving in my hands.

"Aye, I could see tha' when she served me ma balls on a plate, lad!" Fergal handed me his knife. "Have a go, lass. Just take a little off the top there."

"Oh, no, I'll ruin it. Wood's harder to shape than it looks, literally," I said.

"So you did try woodcarving in the end?" he asked.

"Oh, no, not me. But I watched my husband make a pig's ear out of a newel post once."

"Aye, Ciaran told me about your man—Charlie was his name? Aye, lass, that's a terrible burden on anyone so young. I was sorry to hear of it."

"A burden at any age, Mr Argyll. But I was lucky to have him." Maybe it was inappropriate, but for Charlie I had to speak his name here.

"Call me Fergal. Was your Charlie no much good with practical work?" Fergal asked, undeterred.

"No, he was very handy, actually. He did most of the work converting our home."

"He did a good job, too. It would have been a lot of work for one man," Ciaran added. I was glad he'd joined the conversation.

"Well, he didn't do all of it. We bought half a farmhouse on the understanding we divided it into two separate homes. To save money, Charlie did most of the work himself, but the boys at the timber yard helped with the stairway and things."

"Which timber yard is that? No' Beckitts?" Fergal asked.

"Yes, that's right, Beckitts. A lot of the Beckitts lads worked up at the forestry commission with Charlie. Do you know them?"

"We do a lot of work with Beckitts," Ciaran said.

"Aye, they're a good bunch of lads," Fergal agreed.

"Yeah, they are." I smiled. "I remember them all killing themselves with laughter when Charlie proudly unveiled his finishing statement on the stairs. He'd tried for an owl as the first thing people would see walking into our home, but ended up with a monkey nut."

"So you made him replace it?" Fergal asked, smiling back at me.

"No, thank goodness. It's still exactly as it was, and I'm glad. It reminds me of him every time I walk through the door." It hadn't felt that way at first. At first it was just one more thing I had to navigate myself around. I'd retrained my hands to resist grabbing on to it each time I passed by, because I could still make out the tiny pencil marks he'd made. Where he'd tried to work out how to pull a discernible shape from the wood. I was frightened to death of rubbing Charlie's marks away.

"Would you excuse me, Holly? I'll be right back." Ciaran started at a gentle jog back towards the house.

Fergal moved to rise from his seat and then thought better of it.

"Oh, I canny be bothered," he rumbled, taking a hip-flask from his jacket. He unscrewed the cap and offered it to me. The whisky was sharp as it raced down my throat, but the warming effect was instant. Fergal took a nip, too.

"It's no' like ma son to talk to me of women, least of all lovely young ladies like yourself, with their own husbands to love." Fergal's eyes were like black ice under the seriousness of his eyebrows. "You do love your husband, don't you, lass?"

I held Fergal's eyes with my own. "Every day," I replied.

Fergal nodded. "Aye. That's what I thought. It hurts, no?" he asked, offering me another nip.

"Every day." I smiled.

"Well, be glad, lass. Some poor beggars go their whole lives not knowing what love feels like. We might never find it again, but at least we know what to look for."

I sat back next to him and looked out onto the water. It was so quiet here—not quite as calm as the hillside back home, though. The waters were still there.

"And does Ciaran know what to look for?" The question fell from my mouth.

"He thought he did. He was engaged to a lass we all thought loved him. But all Clara ever taught Ciaran was what *not* to look for."

"What *not* to look for? As in nutcases, widows…?"

"As in women who are only interested in what they can gain from him. Women who will turn their back on him as soon as something better calls. Women who will parade themselves as the genuine article while they squeeze him for information they can pass on to Daddy."

"I'm sorry, Fergal. That must have been hurtful for him," I said quietly.

"Well, she had us all fooled. It wasn't really her fault. Some girls are raised to think of men that way, like a selection in a vending machine. They're trained to love the money before the man who earns it. But Clara ruined my boy. Changed the way he looked at women, until he forgot how wonderful they could be."

Fergal turned as Ciaran reached the bench. "Sorry, Holly. I had to make a call. I hope he hasn't been boring you to death?"

"No, no. We were just taking in the views," I said.

"Are you cold out here? Mary's cleared the kitchen, so I thought I'd show off my sandwich-making skills?"

Fergal was watching me but Ciaran couldn't see it. The smallest nod, and we had an understanding.

"Okay, chef, but I draw the line at eel." I laughed.

The rest of the day was more than enjoyable. We spoke about everything—school days, childhood memories, favourite films, embarrassing parents. As the day wore on, the distance between us grew narrower in every way. There had been lots of opportunities for Ciaran to see if I was as ready to be kissed as I had been in the forest. All day we traded subtle touches and knowing looks, accompanied with a hankering for *just one* of them to flourish into another elusive kiss.

But nothing happened.

And that's how the day went until much later. As we walked across the silent courtyard towards Ciaran's car, his fingers finally slipped deftly through mine.

I stopped. I couldn't help it, and looked up at him, at the hair in every shade of brown falling forward in that same place, at the cut healing over solemn brows, and the abyssal brown eyes watching me taking it all in. This was it—he was going to kiss me again. My heart quickened, my breathing became shallow and then—

Boom!

Ciaran crouched as I did the same, my hands shooting up over my ears. Overhead a flock of birds shot screeching from the trees around us and an alarm somewhere on the property started to wail.

"Bloody hell, Fergal!" Ciaran cried.

"What was that?" I asked, not daring to move.

"It's all right. Sounds like Fergal's got the elephant gun out."

"Elephant gun?"

A ripple of nervous laughter rumbled through me. Ciaran

joined in, too. He had a good laugh, a laugh that reached right down into my tummy and filled me up. "Come on," he said, "I have a surprise for you."

chapter 26

Ciaran's laughter had resonated to new heights on the way home. Fergal's eccentricity had kicked off some childlike thread of amusement between us that seemed to pick up pace with every snicker and rasp we traded with each other. We laughed so much that he was going to have to pull over if we didn't get it together soon. It felt good.

My eyes were still streaming when I popped the car door open outside the cottage.

"Are you coming in?" I said with an assumptive smile.

"You go on ahead. I just need to make a call." He smiled back.

"Okay. I'll put the kettle on," I said, digging the keys from my pocket, feeling for the right one for the door. When I fed it into the keyhole, it wouldn't turn over. I tried it the other way and felt the lock click into place. Dave was going crazy in the kitchen as I fumbled my way into the cottage, scratching forcefully at the kitchen door.

"Dave, what's the matter?"

Dave shunted past me, sniffing and snorting the hallway

floor. I didn't register what had set him off at first. He left the hall for the main lounge while I realised what it was that had changed.

I let my eyes move slowly, but still I couldn't understand what they told me.

The hallway was blue.

From the lounge, Dave woofed and sniffed, ignoring me as I walked slowly in after him. My lounge, that had this morning been a cold stark storeroom of furniture, looked like…someone else's house. The oak timber over the fireplace had been lightened. Vases I hadn't seen since our flat sat on top, their reflection held in the large unfamiliar mirror hanging there.

The tan chesterfield had moved, now sitting central to the room on top of a rug I'd never bought. A new coffee table tied in with the oak mantel, and my mother's tall dresser was in a new place along the far wall.

What the—?

The mock-antler heads Charlie had made out of sticks hung on either side of the fire over shelves stocked with my university books, and a chandelier of twigs hung over the coffee table.

Martha hadn't done this. She was good, but this was… I'd never seen a room so beautiful, so well suited to us. Everything tied in—the warm tones of timbers and leather, the soft greens of the cushions and the colours on the walls. The walls where Charlie's paint samples had been forever erased.

My chest tightened.

I ran through to his snug, where he'd slept when we'd fought, and found it untouched. But the relief was momentary.

Dave got under my feet as I scrambled back to the hall.

The timber looked unchanged, *but was it?* Or had it been ruined in some other way? I tried to slow my eyes enough to search the newel post thoroughly for the tiny pencil marks Charlie had left there, bursting into tears when I found them.

★ ★ ★

I sat there for a while, my face in my hands, sobbing at the unexplained invasion around me. Dave spent a few moments sniffing the new pinstriped carpet beneath me, before lending me his head to hold. He started to whimper. He'd been stuck here all day while strange people did strange things in the rooms next to him.

The saltiness of a tear made the gauntlet to my mouth. I sat there and sniffed against my feebleness. I traipsed through to the back doors, Dave slipping through them as soon as I opened them, and I followed him out into the cool air.

Orange leaves tumbled indifferently past me as I sat on the damp grass and looked out over the reservoir. How was it that a day could change so quickly? How was it that I was still surprised when they did?

He didn't mean to upset you, I told myself. But the words wouldn't bed down. I tried to will myself to be happier for what Ciaran had tried to do for me. To be *grateful*. But I wasn't ready for this. I wasn't ready.

Was he still even here? Or had he left…after he'd realised I wasn't coming—elated with my new home, liberated from its moroseness.

There was movement behind me.

"I wasn't sure green was your colour," he said uncertainly, holding back behind me, "but then, you loved the forests so much and…the designer said it was this year's colour, or something like that…." He trailed off.

I took a deep shuddering breath, fostered in me by the crying, and kept watching the movement of the leaves.

"I like green," I said quietly. "But you can't just come into my life and paper over the cracks, Ciaran."

He was only trying to do something good for me. I knew

that…but he'd just crossed the line. This was Charlie's territory. *I* was Charlie's territory.

"They haven't set foot further than the landing," he reassured me, coming to stand in front of me. "I thought I was helping you, Holly. That you didn't have the time to finish the work. You said that was the reason you hadn't." He was right; I had.

A deep sigh helped me collect my thoughts. "I know I led you to believe that. And I know you've tried to do something thoughtful for me, but… But I never thought that you'd come in here with a task force, Ciaran. This is our home."

"Was, Holly," he said gently. "It was yours and Charlie's home. Now you live here alone."

"Ciaran, don't. I don't want this conversation."

"I just wanted you to have somewhere warm to relax, Holly, instead of hiding in one corner of your house like some timid little mouse."

"I don't hide!" I said, my hackles rising.

"Don't you? I don't like to think of you like that," he said.

"So don't! Don't think of me like anything!" My voice was climbing.

"I can't help it, Holly," he whispered, his eyes darkening. "I can't stop thinking about you."

My chest was growing tighter again. What did he want from me? What did he want me to say?

"I…I…do not *hide* in my house, Ciaran." Yes. That's what I needed to say. I was sick of hearing that this week. "Normal people don't do a *DIY SOS* on someone else's home!"

"*Normal people?* And do normal people live alone in the house that time forgot, with only an obscenely scary-looking dog for company?" he said.

I was on my feet now, angry enough that I might just cry again, damn it.

"You still live with your father! At least I stand on my own two feet!" I snapped.

"You can't just bury your head in the sand, Holly, and expect the rest of the world to go away."

"And you can't just throw money at a problem, Ciaran, and expect *it* to go away!"

"That's not what I was trying to do, Holly. It was a gesture. A stupid gesture that I didn't think through."

I didn't know what to do. What to say to him! "I'm sorry, Ciaran. But I'd like you to leave."

He held his palms out to me. "Holly. Come on."

But it was too late.

"I wasn't sure what was happening here, Ciaran. New feelings I hadn't felt for a long time were…confusing me. I thought I could do this, but I'm sorry. I can't. I can't…betray him."

"*Betray* Charlie? No one's asking you to betray anyone."

"But that's what I'm *doing*, Ciaran! Pushing him to one side to make room for another."

A look of utter incredulity fell over him. "I haven't expected you to push Charlie anywhere. I've *never* made you feel that you couldn't include Charlie in conversation. I don't want you to feel that way." He was nearly shouting.

"I'm sorry, Ciaran. I can't. I love him."

I could feel myself shutting down. Folding in on myself until I was far away from the surface. Ciaran's hands found the tops of my arms.

"Of course you do. I know that, Holly. But did he love you?"

"What?"

"I said, did he love you, Holly?"

"Yes, he loved me!" *Do not cry. Do not cry.*

"And was he a good man?" Ciaran looked dark again, as he had in the back of the car, bruised and bleeding as we'd left the city. "Was he a good man?" he asked again, urgency in his voice.

"Yes. He was a good man. He was the best man I've ever known." The tears were burning, burning to run over like lava from a volcano.

"Then if he loved you, and if he was half the man you say he was, he would want you to be happy again, Holly!"

Too late. The heat coursed over my cheeks.

"I want you to be happy, Holly. I believe I could make you happy."

I watched through blurry eyes as Ciaran's face softened, but I was too far gone, tumbling back down into the black hole.

"How?" I smiled through feeble lips. "By keeping me in cake orders and decorating my house? How are you going to make me happy, Ciaran? You buy everything you have!" I loosened myself from his grasp and wiped my face on my sleeve. "I'm sorry…. I can't be bought."

"Holly! Where are you going?" he called after me.

"Work. Unless you've had the painters in there, too?" I snivelled.

"Holly. Please. The shop's closed now!" he yelled after me. "Holly!"

I carried on stalking through the house.

"You're running, Holly. Like a little mouse." The frustration in his voice bounced around the kitchen as he followed me.

I left the front door open behind me. It had been open all damned day anyway.

"You're being a coward, Holly," Ciaran said, falling behind as I stormed in furious silence to the van.

He lingered there, watchful in the dust, as I spluttered out of the yard.

Who did he think he was? Interfering with *my* home?

The van stuttered as I shifted the spindly gear stick into fourth. The engine groaned in protestation but it could shake to pieces around me for all I cared. The adrenaline was coursing through my veins. I hadn't shouted at anyone like that for a long time. I dismissed any thoughts that I'd been unfair to him, that his intentions were good. I wanted the anger, but an ache had started to grow in my head.

Just get to the shop. Get busy.

My breathing had begun to level out when a streamline shine of black appeared in my rear view.

I pushed down on the pedal, flat to the floor. Nothing changed. I was already flat out at just under fifty when Ciaran glided past me. I watched him slide back in front of me, then disappear off around the sweeping bend. By the time I'd driven around it, his car was already gone.

"Jerk. Your car's faster than mine—good for you," I muttered. And again, I ignored the whispers of unfairness.

When I screeched to a halt outside the shop, the last few pockets of activity on the high street were dwindling as all the stores were locking up for the day. Across the road, Ciaran stepped out of his space rocket. One of the golden girls was taking in the menu board from the pavement, and stood admiring him as he sauntered towards me. I turned my back to them all, digging at the lock.

"Did you take a detour?" he asked nonchalantly. He was goading me. Good. That would make things easier.

"We don't all have a rich dad, Ciaran. Some of us have to buy our own cars and we can't all have one of those."

He laughed next to me, but it was a hollow laugh.

"So you think Fergal pays my way?"

Over his shoulder both of the golden girls were brazenly watching us. I pushed into the shop.

"It doesn't really matter, Ciaran. You have enough women keeping an eye on you. Ask them what they think."

"I know what they think. I want to know what *you* think."

The truth was, I didn't know what I thought when I was around him. My brain didn't work properly. I turned at the counter and faced him, trying to uphold my umbrage. But he looked like he belonged on display somewhere, in a gallery where he could be gazed upon, striking with his dark features and fairer hair. So serious, so wounded. Wasted here with me.

"I think you're used to getting what you want." I swallowed.

"And what do I want, Holly?" he said quietly, closing the space between us. His hand moved over mine on the counter, and my breathing hitched again.

He came closer still, so that I could smell the sweetness of him.

"I don't know..." I muttered, searching. "To try something else? Something *dowdy*?" Penny's words sat heavy in my head, and I hated that I couldn't purge them.

"Dowdy? Holly...you're *beautiful*."

I swallowed again, and slipped my hand from under his.

"Holly," he said, behind me as I moved into the bakery, "would you stand still for a minute?"

"I can't, Ciaran!" I blurted. "Don't you understand? I just can't!"

Jess had made a start on the fondant roses, lined in rows of fuchsia pink, egg-yellow and clementine on the central worktop. They'd do. I'd make some of those. Ciaran watched as I heaved the tubs of colourant from the far shelf.

"Have you always been so stubborn? Or did you just find that you liked to wallow in self-pity when Charlie died?"

I stopped throwing the lids I'd ripped from the tubs on the side. "What did you say?"

"People experience tragedy every day, Holly. You aren't the only one. You're just one of the few who are prepared to take it lying down."

"Lying down! You don't know me! I get up every day and push on with it, Ciaran. Trying not to envy my parents for their long marriage, or…or *Jesse* for his rampant sex life, or my sister for the baby that kicks inside her!"

"So you want those things?" he asked, moving closer.

"Yes, I want them!" I turned back to start scooping globs of sticky pink paste onto the mound of fondant I'd opened.

I felt him behind me.

"But still you choose to live like Cora? To accept your loneliness," he said quietly.

I moved to the counter by Jess's roses. I knew I was going to cry again. I picked the nearest rose, and began to clumsily dust the edges of the petals with the blossom tints Jess had left there.

"You choose to live like your father!" I tried, but I already felt lost in the argument. "You'll probably end up just as… as…feral as he is!"

Ciaran seized my wrist, knocking the brush and rose from my hand.

He pulled me into him.

"Yes, I want to be like my father. To be driven *insane* by a woman because of how much I love her and how much she loves me. My father loved my mother since the day he first saw her playing in the street when he was eight years old, and every day since."

He leaned in, just a breath away from my mouth. I watched his lips as he spoke.

"I want to feel that, too, Holly, to be *maddened* by it. For it to be real."

A heartbeat after his words, and Ciaran's lips were on mine.

There was an urgency I hadn't tasted when he'd kissed me in the forest rain; it was enough to flavour this kiss unlike anything else. I was sinking into it, free-falling as he kissed me deeper still.

A yearning, gone neglected for so long now, raised its head.

I wanted him. I did. And as soon as I thought it, the levee broke, leaving me to drown in the crushing force of my need for him.

His lips parted and the tip of his tongue gently teased over mine. I tasted him and the force of the deluge around me exploded. His mouth moved adeptly over mine, moving hungrily along my jaw before lavishing gentler kisses at my ear. It made the hairs all along my body stand for him. I leaned away to give him access to it all, allowing his mouth to trail a line of caresses down to my collarbone.

My hands had remembered what to do. I grabbed at the waist of his jeans where the warmth of his skin found my own. His stomach was so soft under my fingers, the lines inside his hips calling me to follow them. I swallowed, watching dry-mouthed as Ciaran tore himself free of everything from the waist up.

He stood there for a moment, hair ruffed and half-naked while I concentrated on breathing. I saw him swallow, too, movement in the faint shadow of his neatly stubbled neck. I wanted to look at him, at his chest and the rippled torso my fingers had just stroked, but I couldn't break from the hunger in his eyes.

He moved closer, finding the hem of my shirt. His eyes held me while his fingers released the bottom button from its hole. Then the next. Then another. We said nothing as he unbuttoned me, sliding the shirt from my shoulders.

I knew, when he touched his lips to mine again, it was all over. I was right.

As soon as we touched, my body reacted. I felt myself raise for him, offering myself to him.

It had been so long.

Ciaran unclasped my bra, and the stiffness of my nipples betrayed the eagerness of my breasts to feel him against them. He cupped me, holding me firm in his hand before leaning over to take me in his mouth, gently kissing and pulling, first one and then the other. My breasts were on fire against his tongue, his saliva quickly chilling against the first. It made me want him to return there, to suck softly against me, to pull me into his mouth. He obliged and my need spiked.

I reached beneath him, to feel those lines, those delectable lines that would lead my hands to the hardness I'd already felt pressing on me. I pulled at his belt and it gave as easily as my bra had. He began to kick his boots away while I yanked at his fly.

He shrugged from his clothes then lifted me by my thighs onto the counter behind. My jeans tugged free, then his tongue buried into my mouth again.

He broke from me, and, at last, a sight that was enough to stop me dead.

Ciaran stood before me, hard and smooth and substantial. A thrill rushed through me to see his body, naked, perfect, ready. I looked at him, and swallowed again. He looked back at me, the wolf watching the doe, and all I felt was the need to be hunted.

He slipped my cotton panties from my hips, teasing them down my thighs and off my legs, one foot at a time. He stood and moved into me, pressing at that warm hardness gently against me. He pushed aside the tendrils of hair that had fallen in front of my face, and whispered against my lips.

"You're so beautiful, Holly. Is this what you want?" he asked.

I swallowed again, and nodded. It was. So much I didn't have the words. He laid me back against the cold steel counter, and my legs parted for him. He leaned down, the slightest touch and then he kissed me there, as he had my mouth, gently, slowly, deeply.

My body jerked with the instant pleasure of it. I held on until he lifted himself again. Our eyes met as he pressed his hardness against me, just touching me there. And then he pushed, hard and hot and sure....

A short sear of pain made the pleasure all the sweeter. He was home.

Cold steel felt good beneath me as he thrust himself again and again. I pulled myself up so I could hold his chest against mine, to taste his lips again while he made love to me. I slid when I lay back again, in the stickiness beside me.

"I've knocked something over," he groaned.

"It doesn't matter," I whispered. "Just, please...don't stop...."

Ciaran slipped his arms under me and, without withdrawing himself, moved us to the other worktop. I felt Jesse's roses squash under me.

"Shit!" he said, realising.

"It doesn't matter. Just—" Too late, we were on the move again.

He thrust me too hard against the metal racking and cornflour—I think—tumbled past us. A plume of white powder rose into the air and he started laughing then.

"Sorry. I'll clean up."

His smile was soft under my fingers, slickened by the purple goop I'd just smeared over him. I kissed the grin I'd watched so many times, hanging from his neck as I did, plunging my tongue into his mouth as he plunged himself right back into me.

The sex grew to furious proportions, hot and sweaty and

glorious, until at last, the dormant volcano in me erupted with Ciaran's. I felt his warmth spill into me, and held my thighs around him as he rode out his final twitches of release.

He held me there, trembling like a wild animal, held firm by the hunter—the rhythm of one heart thudding from one chest into the other.

The bakery was in chaos.

All of Jess's work, gone. Piles of colour where we'd knocked blossom tints flying, flour everywhere, a fortune in colourants seeping across the worktop.

Ciaran turned his head to kiss me again, and all thoughts of the mess fell away.

"Is that your phone?" he whispered against my mouth.

"Hmm?" I hadn't heard anything.

Through the rapture, a buzzing of jeans against the tiled floor, heralding the first stirrings of embarrassment.

Only Charlie had ever taken me like that.

I caught my breath, as his name sobered me. What had I just done?

I'd let lust take me over. Now the memory of it circled like a vulture over the bones of my fidelity.

Ciaran moved to pass me my phone but I took the jeans instead, quickly pulling them on. He waited while I turned away from him to fix my bra, sliding my shirt back on over sticky arms.

I took the phone from him, and the alarm of voicemail trilled in my hand. I hit the dial button.

"Holly, Holly, please get this! I can't get hold of Rob, and—" I listened to Martha panting into the phone. *"This isn't a false alarm, Hol! I'm scared. Please call me!"*

I speed-dialed her number, pleading for her to answer. The tone rang once, twice....

"Hello?"

"Martha, it's me!"

"Oh, Holly," she whimpered, "the baby's coming. Right now! And—" I heard a sharp intake of breath.

"I'm coming, Martha. I'll be right there.... Where are you?" I asked.

"I'm in the ambulance, going to Hunterstone General... Please hurry. I'm scared."

Ciaran was already pulling his clothes on.

"We'll take my car. It's faster," he said, passing me my boots.

"Martha, we're close. We'll be right there, honey. Just stay calm!"

chapter 27

I'd tried to get over my aversion to hospitals, and mostly I
had, but it was impossible here. It hadn't changed much—
the information desk was now a different pastel shade,
perhaps—but the thick choking smell of disinfectant hanging
heavy in the too-warm air was as stifling as ever.

Ciaran had dropped me out front while he went to park.
It was his idea. We'd made it in fifteen minutes, plenty long
enough for the remaining food colouring on our clothes to
ruin his leather interior. It was all over my jeans where he'd
picked them up, and everything else his hands had touched.

At least the film of flour in my nose was helping to stave off
the stench of antiseptic and illness, which was probably what
was getting up the receptionist's nose. She looked sternly at
me over purple-rimmed glasses.

"My sister, Martha Buckley—she's just been admitted by
ambulance. In labour."

"Maternity is ward eleven. Follow the green arrows," she
said, scrutinizing my appearance. My hair seemed to be of

particular interest, and I reached to feel what was there and a puff of cornflour fell about me. Great.

"Green arrows?" I asked.

The woman nodded at the wall, not wasting another word on me.

Right. I'd forgotten about the rainbow-of-arrows system, chasing around the maze of corridors. So green was for *new life*, whereas *no life* had been a misleading white. This system would really suck for my dad. He was colour-blind.

Two rights, and an absurdly long corridor later found me buzzing into a security intercom.

"Ward eleven?"

"Hi, yes. My sister, Martha Buckley—she's just been admitted."

"Is she expecting you?"

"Yes."

"Okay, the door's open."

I took a squirt of hand foam on my way in. It lathered purple where it lifted the food colouring. Into the ward, the smell was different—more talcum than bleach, where the soft bleating cries of tiny babies chased away my feelings of disquiet.

Martha is about to become a mother.

Another desk where two pretty nurses—one portly with a long blonde ponytail, the other a brunette choppy bob—sat staring into monitors.

"Hi," the brunette said, before her smile faltered. The blonde looked up and raised eyebrows in surprise. I resisted disturbing my hair again.

"I'm looking for Martha Buckley? She's…having a baby."

"You've come to the right place." The brunette smiled, already forgiving my appearance. She glanced at the wall chart behind her. "She's in delivery room three, just through the doors there."

"I'll take you," said the blonde, leaving her chair. "I'll show you where the bathroom is."

"Okay…thanks?" I think I needed a mirror.

"So, last-minute nursery decorating?" she asked, leading me past rooms of mothers beaming into clear plastic cribs.

"Yeah," I lied, as she showed me into the private room where Martha was on all fours on the bed, purple-faced and caked in sweat.

"Martha! Are you okay?"

"What the *hell* happened to y—? *Aghh!*"

"Just relax, Martha. Breathe, just breathe!"

Martha began panting like the Orient Express.

"The bathroom's across the hall," the blonde said, smiling, then she closed the door behind her.

"Relax? *Relax?* There's a person trying to squeeze through my vagina, Holly! *You relax!*" she snarled, groaning into the pillows in front of her.

Gingerly I began to rub her back.

"Not there!" she roared at me. *"Lower. Rub lower!"*

I made circles—quickly—over the back of her hips where I could feel something strapped around her middle.

"Shouldn't Rob be doing this?" I laughed softly, trying to hide the concern in my voice. It was probably more concern for my safety than hers.

"Rob's on his way back from London. He's stuck at Beckersley Station—the connecting train was cancelled. The next one's not for another *hoouurrr….*" Martha groaned again before more panting. On the back of her nightshirt, purple and orange stains had rubbed free from my palms. I needed to get cleaned up, properly.

"You need to get him here, Holly. He hasn't got any cash on him, the stupid sod. He can't get a cab!"

The door clicked open and the brunette slipped into the room.

"How are we doing, Martha?" she asked, looking over the printouts on the machine next to my sister. "Baby's heartbeat looks nice and steady." She smiled.

I smiled, too. Martha did not.

"We've examined her," the nurse said, turning to me. "She's eight centimetres dilated. She's moving along nicely. Martha, would you like any pain relief? How about we get you set up with the gas and air?"

Go for the gas and air, Martha, I willed her.

Martha nodded into her pillows.

"Nurse, her husband's at least two hours away," I said under my breath, following her to the door. "Will he be here in time?"

"He might be. But she's moving along quickly. You might want to hurry him up." She nodded, then abandoned us.

Martha began wailing.

"What can I do, Martha? Tell me what to do, honey."

Martha grabbed my hand and started to cry into the pillows. "Get Rob. I need him."

I left the room to try to call Rob when the nurses returned with Martha's relief. Outside in the corridor, I fed the payphone with twenties and punched out Rob's number.

"Rob?"

"Holly, are you with her?"

"Yes, we're at the hospital, Rob. She's good. She's doing well."

"Stay with her, Holly. Don't leave her!"

"I won't leave her, Rob. But you need to get here, fast."

"Holly, it's chaos here. The cashpoint's empty. I can't get a cab!"

"Right. Just stay where you are. I'll think of something. Just wait by the entrance to Beckersley Station, okay?"

"Yeah, okay, Holly. Thank you."

"You won't be able to get hold of me, Rob, so make sure you're there, okay?"

"I'll be here. Holly…tell her I love her."

There was something in Rob's voice that put a lump in my throat.

"I'll tell her. Don't worry. 'Bye"

I put the phone down and loaded more coins into the slot. Jesse had a habit of not answering withheld phone numbers and I was guessing this one wouldn't show.

Damn it.

Martha screamed from inside the room and I forgot the phone. The midwife had her legs apart under the sheet and was peering up there when I walked in. Martha had the gas tube clamped fast between her teeth.

"It's all right, Martha. Just keep doing what you're doing and Baby will be here soon." The midwife lowered Martha's legs again and smiled serenely at me. A rap on the door and the blonde popped her head around.

"I've just found him wandering the corridors. I knew you belonged together as soon as I saw him." She smiled, stepping aside for Ciaran.

It suddenly hit me just how much of a mess we'd made in the bakery. He had an angry purple smear across his mouth and cheek, and another much more dramatic deep orange stain reaching from his cheek beneath his T-shirt, which was also stained. His hair looked like he'd been talcum-powdered by an overzealous mum on his way through the ward.

He looked at me, and I knew he was unsure.

Behind me, Martha had stopped sucking for dear life on the plastic nozzle, and had propped herself up on her elbows. Finally, the gas was working…. In fact, she was grinning.

"Hi!" she rasped. "Come on in."

Martha and the two nurses all threw Ciaran warm eyes as he edged into the room.

"They've been decorating the nursery." The blonde nurse giggled. Ciaran looked at me with his hands in his back pockets. I looked at Martha, who was burning a smile back our way.

"Did you manage to get any paint on the walls?" the midwife asked.

"You could do with a change of clothes!" the blonde said, making cow eyes at him.

"You can borrow one of Rob's shirts, in the bag over there," Martha managed to say, before puffing on her fix.

"Oh, no. That's okay," he said.

Martha's grin widened. She loved an accent. So did the other two, it seemed.

"No, I insist. I packed extras for Robert in case he spilt anything down himself in the canteen. Hol, dig Ciaran a T-shirt out of the top of that bag."

Ciaran shrugged and I moved over to Martha's travel case.

"This one?" I asked, holding a plain yellow polo shirt up. Martha nodded.

Ciaran took the shirt. "I'll just go and, er…"

"Oh, you can't use the toilet. It's in use. And the bathroom's for women only. Ward policy." Blondie shrugged.

"I'll just…here, then?" Ciaran said, waving his finger at the floor.

They all watched him shamelessly as he wriggled out of his T-shirt. Martha's eyes widened at his torso, feasting them on him. For someone about to pay the waiter, she sure hadn't been put off admiring the menu.

Then three things happened at once.

Ciaran turned for the shirt. Martha sucked on her tube. The nurses and I gasped like hooked fish.

Ciaran's back was covered in handprints—some perfect,

most smeared, all in shades of fuchsia, yellow and clementine. The three women turned and looked at my hands.

But even that was a small humiliation in comparison to the gut-wrenching reminder I'd just had. I'd forgotten the woman with the flaxen hair, inked forevermore into his back. The woman who had ruined him, Fergal had said.

I'd forgotten that Ciaran had been someone's territory, too. And probably always would be.

"*Oooh!* Holly, get Rob!"

Ciaran followed me outside. "Where's her husband?" he asked.

"Stuck at Beckersley Station," I said, trying not to look at him. "He's not going to make it. He's going to miss the birth of his first child, and my mother is going to hold it against him for the rest of his life."

"I'll get him," Ciaran said, reaching for my arm. "Don't worry. What does he look like?"

Two more nurses on the desk were watching us, smiling. I couldn't let him go for Rob. The lines had already been blurred. I needed to undo this before it went any further. Before any more feelings grew.

Another gargled scream from Martha's room.

Think, Holly, think.

"Holly, what does he look like?" Ciaran repeated.

The nurses were still listening in to us. Ciaran was oblivious, staring at me.

Rob cannot miss their baby being born.

"Holly?" he said.

Martha cried out again.

I was all out of ideas.

"A little taller than you, short neat brown hair, big build. Look of panic on his face. He'll be stood at the entrance to the station."

The midwife left Martha's room, leaving the door swinging slowly closed behind her. From her bed, Martha was allowed just enough of a sight line to see Ciaran kiss me goodbye.

chapter 28

An hour and nine minutes, two centimetres and a broken sac of amniotic fluid later—at least I think that's what they called it—and Martha was finally breaking Rob's hand, and no longer mine.

I'd thanked Ciaran briefly at the door and said goodbye to him, resuming my cheerleading duties. He was a problem for another day. Today was for Martha now. Martha and her little family.

"That's it, Martha. Little pushes, little pushes! And, now... *pant*! Pant, Martha," the midwife instructed.

"Pant, Martha!" Rob and I uselessly chorused, following the midwife's lead. Rob was on the frontline, while I hung back on the periphery.

Martha's expression turned from pained to panicked. "Have I pooed?"

What?

Martha's voice elevated. "Oh, no, I think have! *Holly...* Have I *pooed*, Holly?"

The second midwife who had joined the melee took a small

neatly wrapped package away with her. I didn't think it was the baby. I looked at Martha, her scarlet chin buried into her chest, and shrugged, cluelessly. Uselessly. Again.

Martha squealed a new squeal that made my skin go cold.

"Well *done*, Martha!" came the midwife's sing-song voice. "Now I can see Baby's head. Look, Daddy, can you see?"

I was curious then, closing in just enough to see a shock of dark hair.

"Martha! He's got hair!" I yelped. Martha didn't care if he had horns.

The midwife geared up again. "Just another push, Martha, and… That's it, push down into your bottom. Keep pushing, keep pushing.…"

My sister's last guttural scream broke, and from under it a faint but unmistakable newborn cry. I felt the ecstasy fill me up, as if a switch had been flipped and all the fear had been blown out of the room.

"It's a girl! Our little girl. Martha, it's a girl!" Rob sobbed, showering his wife with a storm of relieved kisses.

It wasn't the relief I felt for my sister, or my new niece even, that saw me start blubbing like a big girl, but the pride in Rob's voice as he presented his wife with their tiny daughter. I peered over his shoulder and gazed at the beautiful bundle on her mother's chest. Rob was still crying, Martha just looked wasted and the little girl lay wide-eyed at her mummy.

"Well done, guys," I managed between tears. "She's *perfect*. Absolutely perfect."

After all fingers and toes had been counted, I left them alone. Partly to let them solidify their new unit, and partly so I didn't have to watch Martha being stitched.

Out in the hall, a pair of familiar boots stretched out from the chair where Ciaran had been waiting.

"Hey," he said, getting to his feet.

"Hi. I thought you'd gone home." I didn't want to feel glad that he was still here.

"I thought I'd stick around, make sure you could get home okay. Is everyone…well?"

"Everyone's…wonderful." I smiled.

The door opened.

"Ciaran! I'm a father!" Rob declared, bursting with pride.

"Congratulations, Rob. I'm thrilled for you, pal," Ciaran said, shaking Rob's hand. "Give her my best." He grinned.

"Come and have a look! She's beautiful!" Rob said, thumping Ciaran's back.

Ciaran looked at me—for guidance, I think.

"Rob, I think Martha's being…"

"Not for a minute. Come on in! You haven't held her yet, Hol." Rob ushered us both back in, where Martha looked a lot more with it, proudly gazing at her swaddled daughter.

"Hey, girl," I said softly. "Can I have a squidge?"

Martha looked radiant, awash with something new. She smiled at Ciaran as he came to stand next to me, but it wasn't for him; it was all for the little one.

Rob couldn't take his eyes off her, either. "Ciaran, Holly, I'd like to introduce you to our daughter, Daisy Grace."

"Daisy! Baby Daisy." I tried it out on my tongue. "I love it, guys. It suits her." I smiled, gently rocking my delightful new niece in my arms.

"What do you think, Ciaran? You know, for the *man vote?*" Rob asked, certain of his approval.

Ciaran's thumb had found its way under the fragile clasp of Daisy's minute fingers.

"My mother was named Grace. It's an excellent choice, my friend."

"Oh!" Martha smiled. "That's lovely! I'm hoping she'll live up to it, for her nanny's sake."

"Well," Ciaran replied, "it worked for my mother, the most gracious woman I ever met. She'd have made an excellent grandmother."

"You never know, mate—there's still time," Rob added, slapping Ciaran on the back.

Ciaran carried on running his enormous fingers over Daisy's.

"Ciaran's mother passed away," I said, saving Rob from digging any deeper.

"Oh…that's too bad, mate. I'm sorry," Rob said, slapping gentler this time.

Ciaran smiled at Daisy. "I keep her close. She was a beauty, like this wee one here. I always worried that I might forget how beautiful she was, y'know? Over the years. So I had my favourite picture of her tattooed on my shoulder."

The midwife entered the room carrying a small dish of very unpleasant-looking implements. "Right then, everybody who isn't a Buckley, out you go."

I kissed Daisy and gave her one last look before reluctantly handing her back to Dad. "I'll see you guys later," I said, kissing them all.

Rob and Ciaran shook hands. Ciaran gave Martha a kiss. The happiness in the room was tangible, as if you could swing a butterfly net around and take some home with you.

Ciaran and I walked through the door and into the corridor together. Today had been a good day. I felt…happy. Full up. I was trying to think of something to say to him when Martha yelled from the other side of the closed door.

"Holly Jefferson! You've got *food colouring* on my baby!"

chapter 29

Daisy Grace Buckley had entered into the world last night at 11:18 p.m., Thursday November seventh, weighing in at a tiny six pounds, eight ounces.

Six pounds, eight ounces of promise, purity and an incontrovertible sentiment of new beginnings. In nine months Martha and Rob had changed the course of their lives forever, a thought I'd turned over throughout the last four hours as I'd blitzed the bakery and made a start at replacing Jesse's demolished roses.

Ciaran had offered to help when he'd dropped me back here last night, but he'd already done enough, and I wasn't sure I'd be able to face the embarrassment of seeing it all with him. He had some important meeting to get ready for today but said we'd catch up either Saturday or Sunday.

I'd given Jess the morning off to compensate for yesterday, and also so he wouldn't bust me hiding the evidence of what had happened here. Ciaran was all around me now. At the house I'd returned to last night, made beautiful again, and here at the bakery, in the chaos I'd scurried to put right.

Somehow, unexpectedly, I'd held it together at both. A phenomenon I now regarded as the Daisy effect.

When Jess walked in, headphones clamped to his head, I'd
nearly replaced all of the roses.

"All right, Hol?" he asked, eyeing what I was doing.

"Yes, thanks. You?"

"Yesss… What's up, you look shifty. Do you know you've
got purple food colouring around your mouth?"

Yes, I knew. A lengthy spell in the shower hadn't done
much about that. Luckily, I had the ultimate curveball to
throw him off.

"Do I look like an aunt?"

Jess's face shone. "No way! Martha finally had a visit from
the stork? Nice one, Hol," he said, hugging me into his huge
frame. "What colour did she get?"

"Pink." I smiled. "Daisy Grace Buckley. Good enough to
eat!"

"What are you doing here, then? I can hold the fort. Go
coo over her, or whatever you girls do," Jess said, wriggling
from his backpack. "You're off now for the fortnight anyway.
A few more hours isn't going to make much difference."

On doctor's advice, I'd taken the same time off last year.

It would've been Charlie's twenty-ninth birthday on Sunday. Two days later his mother would be here to spend the
day in our home, along with Martha and Rob, and now my
parents, too, so we could all toast his memory and remind
ourselves what a crippling loss he was.

Last year had been horrific. I'd spent his birthday in bed,
much of the next day, too, until Martha had threatened me
with a call to Minorca. I wanted my parents to stay where they
were, so I'd limped through the following day like a zombie,
trying to blank out the sounds of Catherine's sobs, surfacing

at any given moment. Charlie was my world, but he was her child. I couldn't cope with her pain sat piggyback on my own.

But that was last year.

This year I couldn't avoid the inevitable. My parents were already trying to book tickets back to the UK to meet Daisy, but it wasn't enough to push me into the melancholy I'd barely survived last year. Nowhere near.

I was feeling okay about them coming, I think was feeling okay about the week ahead in general. There would be tears, a lot of tears, but I'd get through it; I knew I could. In fact, I would do more than get through it—I would do something useful, *positive*. Something Charlie would have spent *his* time doing, like starting a vegetable patch, or tidying the garden at least. Actually, I wasn't sure that it was the season for vegetable patches, but I could go to the garden centre, pick something out—a fruit tree maybe? We didn't have anything that blossomed.

"So? Are you going or what?" Jess asked.

"No, I'm staying. You've covered for me a lot lately, Mr Ray. Let's get through the rest of these roses. I'll miss you when I'm off."

Martha had taken to motherhood like a duck to water. I'd been at their place this morning when Rob had brought his two favourite girls home to a house festooned with pink helium balloons and flowers. I should get some flowers for the cottage, to brighten up the place when Catherine came on Tuesday. It had been months since we'd seen each other.

Driving back to Brindley's Nook, it was an unseasonably bright morning, perfect for a walk over the forest with Dave.

Mrs. Hedley let me borrow her truck, and Dave and I were off for a stint up the woods. The sun was notably lower with the passing weeks, throwing long reaching shadows across the road where it weaved between the trees.

I slowed a little on the approach to where the fork would take me either the long route around, or directly along the stretch where Charlie's accident had been.

New beginnings. I couldn't just keep waiting for my life to mend itself. I had to try, too, right? I watched the left-hand turn pass me by and followed the steep sweeping bend of the road to the forestry commission. There was a new speed-sensitive sign that told you how fast you were going, and several more deer warnings along the road. None of these signs would have made a difference to us, but I hoped they would make the difference for someone else.

When the road straightened off again, I found myself looking for what had greeted me that morning.

The glass had looked like ice at first, blending into the twinkling surface of the frosty road. The other car was the only spectacle of severity, while Charlie's truck had looked completely normal from the back. It wasn't until the ground began to crunch underneath my shoes that I really saw.

Someone had tied flowers to the tree afterwards. They already hung dying when I'd next driven through. I hadn't been down here since.

No glass this morning, no flowers. Just a full visitor car park heaving with families eager to enjoy the beautiful morning. Ciaran had said he would call this weekend. I hadn't told him about Charlie's birthday tomorrow. It would be weird including him in my plans.

But he might like to come with us *now*? I could keep driving and be there in another fifteen minutes anyway? The idea didn't seem that far-fetched, which had to be good, right?

Too late now, I'd passed the car park.

Mrs. Hedley's Land Rover made easy work of the cattle

grids running up to the manor. Ciaran's car was parked next to his father's. Penny's alongside that.

The gong of the doorbell thrummed from behind the heavy doors.

Mary stood, lovely as ever, behind them. "Hello, Holly! I wasn't expecting to see you today."

"Hi, Mary. How are you?" I asked.

"Oh, I'm fine. Would you like to come in?"

"Thanks, but my dog's in the jeep. I don't trust him. Is Ciaran here? I thought he might like to get some fresh air with us."

Mary's expression wilted a little. "I'm sorry, dear, but I don't think he's here." Dainty heels snapped sharply along the hall towards us. It was the first time I'd seen Penny in trousers, and—surprise, surprise—she rocked them.

"Oh, hello." She smiled sweetly. "Have you come to deliver a cake?" Penny pinched *cake* in her throat, making it sound almost offensive.

"No, Holly was calling on Ciaran but—"

"But Ciaran's not here." Penny smiled.

"I'm afraid I'm not sure where he is," Mary said. "He might be in the grounds somewhere…. You could try ringing him?"

"No point. His phone will be turned off," Penny said, still happily fixing sly eyes on mine. "He won't want to be disturbed, for the rest of the day, I shouldn't think. But you could try the restaurant, if you're desperate?"

"Restaurant?" Mary enquired. "Are you sure? His car's here."

Penny's smile hardened. "Yes, Toby ran them to Atlas about an hour ago…. Clara looked sensational."

My stomach felt like an old flannel, wrung out by Penny's spiteful words.

"We'll tell him you called, though, Holly. Is there a message?" Penny smirked.

There was an edge of pity in Mary's eyes that I couldn't stand to look at. Not this weekend. Not when I'd done so well.

"No. No message. Thanks, Mary." I smiled, and got the hell out of there.

It didn't matter, I told myself.

It didn't mean anything. He could do as he pleased. Who was I to even be interested in what, or who, Ciaran Argyll did? The bakery had been a…one-off. A momentary lapse, that's all. An itch, scratched. I'd wanted an excuse to apply the brakes, and now I had one.

Good.

I clung to my resolution for a positive weekend in celebration of Charlie's birthday. I was still clinging to it as I trudged over the forest, Dave dutifully behind me. But I hadn't factored in the inclusion of ten-foot-high security fencing.

Ciaran's estimation of Sawyers' development timescale of their newly acquired woodland had been generous. In six days they had barricaded the whole holly forest, banishing the prying eyes of people like me, foolish enough to have taken their infinite presence for granted.

Then it all began to slip.

chapter 30

Grey light filtered through the drapes, settling on the undisturbed pillow next to me. Charlie slept nearest to the door, so he didn't wake me if he had to go to the bathroom in the night. I slept this side now. It didn't make much difference where I slept—the bed was still half-empty.

Happy birthday, Charlie.

My phone rang out on the bedside table. *James Bond* flashed on the display.

Fine dining yesterday, today he fancied slumming it with a sandwich. I hit the reject button.

Seconds later it rang again.

"Hey, beautiful mamma," I said, smiling into the phone. I could already hear Daisy grunting next to Martha's face.

"Hello, beautiful Aunty Holly!" she replied, obviously for her daughter's benefit, too.

I smiled again. "How was your first night at home?" I asked.

"Good. She only woke me twice, which I think is good?"

"Don't ask me," I said, stretching. "I only know dogs and cakes."

"So what are you up to?" she asked, testing the water.

"I'm just finishing breakfast," I lied.

"Yeah? That's great! That you're up...and about. What are you doing after breakfast? You could come over here, help me work out the breast pump? Unless you have plans?" Martha was fishing. She hadn't had a chance to grill me on Ciaran yet.

"Sounds fun, but I have a full day planned. I'm going tree shopping, then I'm sorting the garden out." That should do it. For the sake of a quiet day, I let her assume Ciaran might be on the scene.

"Great! Okay, well, I'll let you go, then. Rob's picking Mum and Dad up from the airport late tomorrow evening, so we'll see you Tuesday, okay?"

"Yeah. Sure. Give them a kiss for me, okay? I've got to go," I lied.

"Okay, love you, 'bye."

It was already gone ten, and I had absolutely no intentions of leaving my room yet. My voicemail bleeped.

"Hi, it's me. I was wondering how you were? Any ideas how to get this colouring off skin?" He laughed, but his laughter didn't roll over me the same way as it had. *"It's raising a few eyebrows."* Whose? Clara's? I'll bet. *"Are you free—?"*

I deleted it before listening to any more.

The streaming patterns of rainwater spilling down the windowpanes danced over the pillow next to me. I watched them until they lulled me back to sleep.

The mysteries of Martha's breast pump had kept her nicely preoccupied. I'd dozed in and out of sleep all afternoon but the rain had fallen heavier into the early evening, making it harder to snooze. I hadn't eaten anything, and saw no reason to start cooking now. Screw it. I dragged myself downstairs to the sound of rainfall. The stairs didn't creak now, cushioned by a thick run of carpet. I dug a tub of pralines and cream from the freezer, wrapped it in a tea towel and walked through the picture-perfect lounge to Charlie's snug. The TV flickered to life as the first spoonful of ice cream began to melt on my tongue. What I needed was trash TV, and lots of it. I zapped through the channels looking for something good and low-brow to settle into.

Speed-dating TV. No. *Comic books that changed the world!* No. *Cravats: A History of.* How much did I pay for this gunk each month? Where were the empowered women kicking zombie ass? Or the programmes of promiscuous men having eye-wateringly invasive swabs taken from protuberances they should've kept zipped up?

A change of tack and I was jumping through the news channels. *Local, entertainment, business.* Business news? I let the channel sit as I considered how mind-numbingly boring the business news must be. For anyone.

"Argyll Inc. and Sawyers' Dev—"

The reporter's voice was interrupted as the TV sluggishly responded to my instructions at the remote. I hit the back button.

"—has reached its conclusion, with analysts across the city voicing their surprise at the outcome."

Footage of a sleek conference room, populated with suited men, appeared on screen before flashing to what looked to be Argyll Inc.'s head offices.

"Speculation had been rife that James Sawyer's rival bid was as good as accepted by well-known cancer support charity Lux Foundation, before sources claimed the board of trustees overseeing the sale had made a last-minute U-turn."

The footage led into Fergal shaking hands with suit after suit, Ciaran standing in the corner behind him, mouth smeared purple.

"Fergal Argyll, one of the city's more animated businessmen, is expected to release a statement confirming the reports tomorrow morning."

I hit the standby button. Fergal was every bit the charmer his son was. Ciaran must have taken Clara out to soften the blow for her. They were probably softening it all night in the hotel over Atlas.

He'd called me twice already.

Dave's great head lifted from where it had been lying on his front legs. I listened, too, but couldn't hear over the rain what it was that had caught his attention. He woofed, right as the knocker rapping against the front door echoed through the front of the cottage. If this was Rob with a breast pump, boy, had he come to the wrong house.

I ignored the smoothness of the floorboards Ciaran's posse had buffed to a polished shine in the hallway and held Dave's collar, as if that would help if ever he made a run for it.

In the glow of the porch light, rain dripped from his hair onto already sodden shoulders. Dave pulled free of me and went straight for his affections.

"Hey there, ugly!" Ciaran said, bothering Dave's jowls. He looked up at me. "I've been trying to get hold of you today, but I thought you might have left your phone somewhere again." Being caught in the candy-striped pyjama bottoms I'd had on since yesterday didn't bother me, but I could've done without the praline clinging to my vest.

"Are you ill?" he asked, straightening up. "It's not even eight. I thought we could go out to dinner?"

I took in a deep breath and exhaled slowly. "No, Ciaran. I'm not ill. Just sick. And more than tired. So I'm going to bed now. Good night." I tried to close the door, but Ciaran reached a hand to stop it.

"Hang on. What's the matter?" Ciaran asked, obviously unused to having doors closed on him.

Do not let him think you care, I warned myself.

"Nothing."

His eyes narrowed. "Well, don't you want Dave in there with you?" I looked at Dave sat staring up at Ciaran, his tail wagging with fervour.

"No, I think he'd rather be with you! He obviously knows where the grass is greener," I snapped.

"What?" He laughed, and it sent me up a notch.

"You're like the Pied Piper, Ciaran!" I rambled. "Personal assistants, ex-fiancées, *dogs*…" I said, throwing my hand at Dave. "They all just come running, don't they?" As soon as I'd finished my rant, I wanted to take every word back. To grab them all from the air and stuff them into my pyjama pocket. *Good job on the not showing him you care, Holly.*

Ciaran shifted on his feet, looking for his own words.

"Mary told me you came by yesterday, but I didn't get the message until this morning. I called you twice to make sure there weren't any misunderstandings, but you didn't return my calls."

"Misunderstandings? I understand, Ciaran…. You've had your fun. I get it."

"No, Holly. You don't. Look, you're pissed off. I'll call you tomorrow when you've calmed down. I'll take you for lunch, somewhere nice—"

"I don't *want* you to take me for a nice lunch, Ciaran! I don't need you spending your money on me, or buying my cakes or any of it! When was the last time you even managed to go a whole day without spending more than, than…a ten-pound note to get you through it?"

"What is your problem, Holly? Look, if it's my lunch with Clara, it was business-related. There's no need to be jealous—"

"Jealous? I'm not jealous, Ciaran. But I'm not stupid, either. I wonder, how many times has Fergal described his relationship with Penny as *business-related*?"

Ciaran's jaw clenched and the same sinuous lines flexed along his cheeks. I almost felt uncomfortable.

"Is there something else going on here, Holly? Because if there is, I need to know." He moved close enough that I could smell the rain wetting the aftershave on his skin. His voice dropped to a whisper. "I can't stop thinking about you, Holly. So if you've had some other…change of heart…"

I stepped back from him, clicking my fingers for Dave to heel.

"There's *nothing* going on here, Ciaran," I said, holding my new ground.

"Nothing?" he said quietly, watching me like a hawk. *"Nothing?"*

I knew what he was asking me. It was time to put all this to bed.

"Nothing," I said, closing my door, leaving Ciaran to the rain.

chapter 31

Catherine looked well when she stepped from the taxi outside the cottage. I could have picked her up from the station, but it was too long to spend in a closed environment trying to keep the conversation light. I knew this annual ritual was cathartic for her, but I couldn't just slide straight into memorializing Charlie. Not at 10:00 a.m.

"Holly my love, how are you?" she clucked fondly, hugging me in earnest.

"Hello, Catherine. You look lovely." Catherine had a penchant for flowery scarves, and was never lacking the colours I did.

"That's a pretty dress, Holly. Blue suits you."

It was a summer dress, really. Simply shaped, hanging just below the knee. A faint grey fleck allowed me to pair it with a grey cardigan and ballerina pumps, presentable enough for a walk down to the churchyard.

"Your hair has grown, too," she said warmly.

It had grown. It was loose today, in waves that now sat past my shoulders. Charlie liked it left down.

"Thanks, Catherine. Come on, Mum's looking forward to seeing you."

Inside the cottage, my mother was still marvelling at the lounge, while Martha sat on the sofa, feeding Daisy.

"Catherine, so good to see you. How was your journey?" Mum swung straight into hostess mode. Her skin was brown and weathered next to Catherine's milky complexion, bunching where her cleavage peeped above her polka-dot blouse.

"Hello, Pattie. My goodness, just look at this!" Catherine exclaimed.

Today was the first time this room had been used properly. Ever. "Yes, it's stunning, isn't it? I was just saying to Martha how glad I am that Holly finally let her work her magic."

Martha winked before turning back to Daisy, suckling away.

"I'll just go and put the kettle on," I said, beating a hasty retreat.

Mrs. Hedley had asked if she could join us today, and after a few rounds of tea and catch-ups and Dad's *pollo con manzanas* safely deposited in the oven, we all made our way on foot to St Nicholas's in the village.

Charlie and I had made this walk along the brambled footpath every Friday night down to the Dickens Inn for cold cider and hot toddies. I could feel my resolve buckling the nearer we got to the churchyard.

The weekend's mild temperature had carried over, but Sunday's rain had lingered on the grass as we stepped through the straggled edges of the path, leading us to where Charlie's simple headstone stood solid and unyielding.

Charles Alfred Jefferson,
Beloved Husband and Son
Died November 12th
Aged 27 Years

Twelve months had made the words no less offensive. I tried not to look at them while the wet seeped through to my toes. The women laid flowers. Dad said a few words. Mum held Catherine's hand as they wept quietly. Martha held mine as I didn't weep at all.

Mrs. Hedley rejoined our tribe, moving to stand with Rob and Daisy. I'd been watching her across the way, clearing old flowers from two graves of her own. I didn't bring flowers for Charlie. I preferred to leave him a pine cone from the forest. Not something short-lived, cut in its prime as Mrs Hedley had described, but a seed. The promise of something new, that might blow from where I left it and bed down into the earth, where it could grow strong and tall.

The scents of sizzling apples and garlic welcomed us home from church. Plates were clinking and cutlery chiming as the house rang heartily with the noises of family life.

I hadn't heard the knock, or seen Mum leave the table to answer it. I hadn't noticed her gone at all until Mrs Hedley swung around on her chair to see my mother in the kitchen doorway, Ciaran standing next to her, his sweater tied around his waist and a bunch of flaccid flowers in his hand.

The clinking of silverware quieted to nothing and all eyes followed mine.

"Holly?" my mother said, unclasping her hands. "You have a guest." Six pairs of eyes turned on me. The longer I took to respond, the thicker the air around me became. "Well, don't just sit there like a lemon, Holly. Where are your manners? Introduce us." Sometimes, Minorca was still too close.

Across the table Rob, my shining saviour, jumped to his feet and padded over the length of the kitchen. "Hello, Ciaran, good to see you again. Come on in," he called enthusiastically.

Mrs. Hedley patted my leg under the table. I darted eyes at

Martha sat next to her husband's vacant chair. She returned an encouraging smile. I stood as Rob led Ciaran over to the top corner of the dining table, where he waited, stood between my dad on the end and Mrs Hedley to my right. My mother maintained her proximity to him.

"Holly?" she pressed, expectantly. Dad turned in his seat to face our guest while Catherine leaned forward to peer around me at him.

"Everybody…this is Ciaran. Ciaran, my mother, Pattie. This is my dad, Phil…" I turned to face Catherine, patiently waiting her turn. "And this is Catherine, Charlie's mother."

"Oh, hello," Catherine said, smiling at Ciaran. "Are you a friend of Charlie's?" she asked hopefully. My knees felt weak under me.

"I'm afraid I didn't have the pleasure, Catherine. But I'm told he was a good man."

Catherine smiled in approval. I tried not to hyperventilate.

"Pleased to meet you, Ciaran," my dad said sincerely, standing to shake his hand. As he did, a few strands of grass fell from Ciaran's sleeve. His cream chinos were soaked up to his calves.

"Pleased to meet you, Phil," Ciaran said.

"And I'm Patricia. What a lovely accent you have," my mother cooed. Ciaran offered her his hand, but she ignored it, diving in for a kiss instead.

"Hello, Martha. Are you well?" Ciaran asked.

"Yes, thanks!" She smiled. "Would you like to join us?"

"Yes, come and have some food. Do you like chicken, son?" Dad insisted.

Everyone automatically took their chairs, Mum reluctantly so, leaving only the two of us still standing.

"Actually, I only came to give your daughter this," Ciaran said, moving around Mrs Hedley's chair to me.

"Oh, flowers," Catherine extolled. "Isn't that lovely?"

I looked at the white tulips choked in Ciaran's hand.

"I'm afraid the flowers aren't for Holly. They're for you, Cora, as a thank-you for breakfast here a couple of weeks ago."

My mother's eyebrows arched so high they were in danger of slipping off her face completely. I couldn't bear to see what Catherine's expression was behind me.

"Thank you, Ciaran," Mrs Hedley said. "Look, Holly. Tulips."

"They're a bit worse for wear, I'm afraid, Cora. They've been on quite a journey," Ciaran said.

"Oh, they'll be just fine with a drop of water." She smiled.

"And, Holly, I just wanted to give you this," he said softly.

We all watched as Ciaran dug around in his pocket. With the other hand, he gently took mine from my side and held it out between us.

He looked at me as if we were alone.

"I walked the five miles from the manor to the first bus stop I came to," he said, laying a small paper ticket on my palm. "It wouldn't bring me as far as Brindley village, so the fare was just four pounds seventy return." Coins slipped into my palm. "There's eighty-two pence there, from this morning's ten-pound note. There would have been more but I was thirsty when I passed the village shop just now.... Plus I had to buy an Elastoplast for my new blister. As for the flowers, I snuck them from Mary's display at home." He smiled, watching me closely.

"You've walked here?!" Martha asked. "That must have taken you all day!"

"Aye," Ciaran said, sounding more like his father than usual. My hand was still in his. "But it was worth it."

Mrs. Hedley gulped from her wine glass.

"Well, you have to stay, then!" my mother sang, skipping from her chair again. "Come and get your breath back, young man."

Ciaran touched my elbow lightly before being led to sit next to Catherine.

That I couldn't see him through the rest of lunch helped. I mostly managed to avoid looking at anyone for the remainder of my time at the table, but even I joined the tittering when Catherine relayed the story of the time she lost a four-year-old Charlie in a bathroom showroom, eventually finding him in the window display leaving a little brown present in one of the toilets there.

"I'm going to need to make a start back. Thank you all for your hospitality," Ciaran finally said, pushing his chair out from under him.

"Can Rob not give you a lift?" my dad asked. "You will, won't you, Robert?"

"Of course! I'll just get my keys," Rob said, devouring his last spoonful of pear crumble.

"No, you're all right, pal," Ciaran said, pulling his sweater on. "That would defeat my objective."

Ciaran exchanged his goodbyes with us all before my mother led him off to the front door. Martha's rosy post-pregnancy cheeks looked even chubbier when she grinned.

"Well, that was a nice surprise," Mum huffed, returning to the table.

"Yes, he was a lovely boy," Catherine agreed. "I hope his blisters don't bother him on his way home."

"He'll be all right, won't he, Hol?" Rob butted in, digging in for more crumble. "He'll just ring his chauffeur, won't he, Hol?"

Martha jabbed him in the ribs.

"What?"

"Chauffeur?" my mother exclaimed. "He has a *chauffeur*? And he's been having breakfast *here*?"

I could feel the ground, falling away at my feet.

"It's not what you think, Mum," I said, leaving the table with the dishes.

"How do you know what I think?" she replied.

I sighed, knowing there was no point going toe to toe with her. I began firing water into the sink. Mrs Hedley had been right—the near-dead plant of hers sitting in my window was already undeniably perkier. Martha followed my lead, bringing more dishes over.

"I'm only curious, Holly. I'd love to think that you're making new friends," my mother called, before sipping her wine. "He has a good job, I take it? What does he do? Where does he live?"

I was not talking about this now.

I hadn't looked at Catherine since Ciaran had first walked in.

"Don't spook her," Mrs Hedley said coolly to my mother.

"I beg your pardon?" Mum asked indignantly.

"Holly isn't interested in all that nonsense. She doesn't care for fancy pants and showboating. Don't *spook* her."

"I think I know my own daughter, Mrs Hedley. And I think I know what is and is not in her interests." My mother smiled coldly, before taking another sip. I plunged my hands into the hot suds, trying to blot them all out.

"Holly knows what's best for Holly. She's a clever girl," Mrs Hedley continued, calmly.

"This crumble is delicious, Pattie!" Rob tried desperately before he received any more jabs for starting it. "Or did you make this, Phil?"

"No, no!" Dad said, taking his cue. "Pattie's the dessert queen. I think her secret is cinnamon. It is cinnamon, isn't it, love?"

Rob and Dad carried on defusing the conversation and when Martha's soft voice joined in with theirs I hoped it would be enough to dissuade my mother. At least I hadn't cried today. Today of all days, and that had to be good, right?

The sinkhole slurped away the last few bubbles with a belch of air. A milky pale hand, more worn than mine, laid itself gently over my forearm.

"For what it's worth, Holly, I think he's a nice boy," Catherine said softly, "and I think that our Charlie would have liked him enormously."

chapter 32

The number of items Martha included in Daisy's day bag was inconceivable. The outfits alone nearly totalled double figures, leaving me slightly panicked that I'd misunderstood our conversation and Daisy was actually staying with me overnight.

Daisy was flapping silent arms around happily in her Moses basket while I lay next to her on the chesterfield reading. In the yard outside the window, headlights too sleek and too low for the profile of Rob's people carrier swung next to my van.

He hadn't called me since eating with us Tuesday. And I hadn't checked that he'd made it home, either. But I'd thought about him. Non-stop, actually.

I checked Daisy and got to the door before Ciaran's knocking could set Dave off.

"Hi," he said, slowly making the porch.

"Hi."

"I was just passing, and thought I might collect my eighty-two pence. Just so you didn't think I was throwing money around." The ghost of a smile on his lips.

"How are the blisters?" I asked.

"Better." He smiled. "So anyway, the last two times I've visited you, you haven't invited me in."

"You came in last time. And ate lunch with my family," I said, still surprised by it.

"Ah, but it wasn't you who invited me in," he said, dipping his head to one side. His smile faded with my quietness. "Holly, I don't want to go, but if you ask me to I will."

I hated that. Hated the way he always put me on the spot. Hated the way he made me feel when his lips pressed into a hard line under eyes grown guarded.

I didn't want him to leave.

I moved from the doorway, and let him in. Ciaran watched me close the door behind him. Minding my toes with his boots, he stepped forward and found my hand with his. A charge sparked through me.

"I need you to know, Holly, Clara was a lifetime ago. Our meeting wasn't whatever Penny implied it was." If there was a lie in his voice, I couldn't hear it.

I shook my head. "It was none of my business, Ciaran. I made a fool of myself," I said, knowing I should be fighting against his fingers, shouldn't like the feel of them so much.

"No, you didn't," he whispered. "I want it to be your business, Holly. I want you to care who I'm with. Because I care who you're with, and I don't want you to be doing this with anyone else." His other hand found its way around my back, and the feelings that had burst from nowhere in the bakery started to stir.

Don't let him kiss you. I knew what would happen if I did. I knew where it would end, knew that my body already remembered him and would override my brain, not that I was convinced it would put up much of a fight.

Ciaran leaned in towards my mouth.

"Don't kiss me, Ciaran, please." I trembled.

"But I want to kiss you, Holly," he whispered. I could taste his breath. "It's all I've wanted since I first saw you." He leaned in to test the resolve he knew wasn't there, and the stifled sound of gas, bubbling angrily from a little person's bowels, killed the moment dead. "What was that?" he whispered against my mouth.

"Daisy."

Ciaran stayed where he was while I slipped out from under him. Daisy's flapping had become more animated, and like the coward I was, I scooped her up and wielded her like a chastity shield. Ciaran followed me.

Daisy had made good on her threat.

"Oh, Daisy!" I whimpered, taking in the devastation leaching over her pretty white suit. "I'm just going to go and get us cleaned up," I said, carrying her past him. "Make yourself at home. You know where everything is." I laughed. He'd put it all there, after all.

"Good diversion, kiddo," I whispered, kissing Daisy's soft head.

Back downstairs, Ciaran had taken his jacket off, and was sitting looking over the book I'd left on the sofa. "A hardcore necromancer dating vampire masters and were animals?" he asked, shaking the book at me. "That sounds…*nice*."

"It's less far-fetched than tales of romance," I said, sitting, my human shield still firmly in my arms.

"So will Daisy be chaperoning all night?" he said, reaching over and stroking the soft down of her dark hair. "It's just that I wanted to invite you out, and I don't want this little lady to get jealous," he whispered.

"You still want to invite me out?"

"Well, I think you'll approve of this. It's a double event, really. We've just won a very big contract, so it's a chance to celebrate all the last year's work that's gone into pulling it all off. But primarily it's an annual fundraiser the company throws, in my mother's honour. We invite a lot of wealthy people to buy a table, and then raise as much money as we can for my mother's favourite charities. It's always a good event, black tie, so if you're wearing those wellies of yours—which I think you looked great in, by the way—you'd better have a long evening gown to cover them."

"That sounds like a great evening, Ciaran. When?" I asked, mentally scrambling through outfits I didn't own.

"A week tomorrow. I'd really like you to be there with me, Holly."

He was the perfect gentleman for the rest of the evening. Rob and Martha came back earlier than they'd thought after they both missed Daisy too much to stay away from her. They could have had coffee with us, but Martha was eager to get out of our way for some reason.

Ciaran would be driving, so we didn't drink anything that wasn't made with the kettle, and talked again into the late hours of the night.

"So your dad must be pleased, that you've successfully bought all that land? I caught it on the news," I said, watching Ciaran across the sofa.

"Yeah, I saw that." He laughed. "Sometimes the press do actually put across something good for his image—very rarely for mine, though."

"That must be good to see. Him making a turnaround?"

"It's good to see him comfortable in the boardroom again. At his worst, he couldn't be trusted anywhere near them. Even less so on-site. Working lunches became my obligation, with Fergal kept as often as possible either holed up with Mary at home, or on the golf course. It was the only pursuit he enjoyed for a while. Until he met Elsa, Ludlow's mother, at the country club."

"They don't seem like a very compatible pairing. Fergal's quite *fun*, and she seemed quite…"

"The bitch? Yeah, she can be, but she's not all bad. Fergal didn't marry her for her warm personality. He was worried about me. About my *behaviour*. Even through the semi-haze of drunkenness, he kept tabs on me. He thought I was becoming reckless. That I needed a mother. So, after seven years of drinking too much, nearly losing the empire he'd built with my mother at his side, he felt that my…*appreciation* for the ladies, shall we say, was something to do with my emotional needs *not being met*." Ciaran stretched his legs out on the coffee table.

"Did he reach that conclusion by himself? It sounds like something a therapist would say."

"I'm not sure. Either way, Fergal felt he'd cocked up. So, he decided to take matters into his own hands, and rather rashly embarked on finding me a mother figure."

"And did marrying Elsa help? Either of you?" I asked, nestling into the back of the sofa.

Ciaran took my feet, pulling them into the warmth of his hands. "Cold feet again," he said, rubbing them back to warmth. "Elsa worked wonders straightening him out. She whipped him into shape. He even lost a few pounds. He still enjoys his tipple, as you've seen, but not nearly as much."

"So she was good for him?" I asked, enjoying the sensation on my toes.

"I could see that she was good for him in some ways. Fergal, on the other hand, couldn't see any goodness in her at all." He laughed. "And then, it wasn't long until Fergie forgot the whole point of marrying her in the first place—to keep us on the straight and narrow—and began misbehaving himself." Ciaran shrugged.

"Which is where the lovely Penny comes into it, I take it? Whatever keeps you warm, I guess." Though I couldn't imagine how ice personified could keep anyone warm.

"In thirty years of marriage Fergal never strayed from my mother. But with Elsa, there was no love, nothing like what he'd had with Mum. He became lonelier than ever, and began to seek company in the arms of the women who would tell him what he wanted to hear."

"And that was?" I asked.

"That he's not an old man with a heart that can never be healed."

I thought about Fergal, and wondered how many people there must be in the world broken by love.

"The shoes were for Penny, weren't they? The shoes the cake was modelled on?"

Ciaran pulled the sage throw from the back of the sofa and laid it over my feet. "Fergal's no fool. He could have bought Penny those shoes from anywhere, but he chose to use Elsa's favourite boutique. Fergie wanted to be busted."

"But, Penny? I mean, I know she's stunning, and any man would want her on his arm, but…"

"But she's a bitch, too?"

"Isn't she? I've seen how she looks at you, Ciaran. She can't love your dad."

"He knows that." Ciaran smiled.

"But how can that be enough?"

"How do you think? Theirs is a mutually beneficial relationship. He knows she's a gold-digger, and only with him because he's the head of a big company with plenty of status…. He keeps her in trinkets and nice dresses—she makes him feel important. You know how it works. It's happening in households across the globe."

"But what happened to loving someone for the person they are? Instead of what you can get out of them?"

"Fergal will never love anyone like my mother. He's not open to that. And as boss of Argyll Inc., he knows every woman he meets sees his value in money before anything else," he said.

"Well, that's a real pity. He might find someone, somewhere. And Penny? Well, she should be looking for someone to love, too. It might cheer her up. How happy can a piece of jewellery make you at the end of the day?"

"Not everybody thinks like you, Holly."

All night we talked, like teenagers with all the time in the world. He'd never watched the sunrise, so just after seven, we took the throws from the sofa and went to watch the morning breaking over the waters of the reservoir. In those moments, before he would leave me again to think of him all day, Ciaran Argyll finally kissed me again. Long and gentle and true, as though the sun itself had reached right into me.

chapter 33

The cinema. I had not set foot in a cinema for *years*. Not since Charlie got us kicked out for snoring disruptively through a film. He had the affliction of movie-induced narcolepsy, and despite him being okay with missing the film after paying through the nose for a ticket, turned out the rest of the audience weren't.

But this week, I'd shared my first bucket of popcorn with Ciaran. He'd taken me to the cinema, and to the Mexican restaurant in Hunterstone that had made my mouth wet with hunger every evening as I'd left work, and the city theatre where he'd nearly fallen asleep watching the show; to the dog races of all places and then even to Atlas, where I had to admit, the food was incredible.

The last week spending time with him had been beyond wonderful. Something was happening, really happening. Something long forgotten.

When I asked Martha to help me find something for the charity ball, she'd burst into tears. Rob said it was her hormones, right before she'd punched him on the arm.

Hormones or not, the dress Martha had found was incredible. If there was a dress that could make a fashion-appreciative girl out of me, this was it. The colours shimmered from gunmetal to pewter, reminding me of frost on the hedgerows where the light caught. The V of the neck decoratively dipped towards what Martha told me was an empire line, where organza the colour of stormy skies fell all the way to the floor. I loved this dress. Not only did three-quarter-length lace sleeves mean Martha let me off with the fake tan, an undertaking that was only ever going to end in disaster, but the length of the dress meant a reprieve from heels. Once I'd seen myself in the mirror, and fell in love with how the dress made me look, I found myself hoping he would, too.

On Martha's insistence, and unusually little resistance from me, I'd spent all afternoon being preened and primped at her favourite salon.

Toby had come to pick me up while Ciaran welcomed guests, laughing at me when I scooped up my beautiful skirts and ran through the drizzle to the passenger seat.

"Hi, Toby!" I panted.

"You know, you're supposed to give me a chance to open the door for you, Holly. The back door, so you can arrive like a lady."

"Do you want me to get back out? Or climb over?" I offered.

"Just buckle up, or you'll get me into trouble." He grinned. "Nice dress, by the way."

The Grace Argyll Memorial Ball, affectionately dubbed Balls to Cancer by Fergal, was being held at Hawkeswood. The private road leading to the courtyard was filled with nondescript spotless cars, much like the one Toby had collected me in, all making their way in and out of the estate.

I wasn't the sweaty type but nervousness made me clammy. I wasn't there yet, but on seeing so many cars, the tides of my excitement had started to turn.

"Toby, do you have any deodorant?" I asked, as we waited in the pull-in for the car ahead to pass.

"I have deodorant for *men*."

"That's okay, Tobe. Better to be safe than sorry."

"In the glovebox," he said absently, nodding at the passing car.

"Wow, Toby. That's manly stuff!"

"Yeah, Ciaran'll be pleased you smell like a fourteen-stone driver.... He's always had a soft spot for me," he joked. "Right, now if I pull up here at the doors, you need to wait just one—"

I'd already opened the door. "Holly!" he called as I stepped from the car and straightened my dress.

"Yes?" I asked him, ducking to see him better.

"Have fun." He smiled.

I playfully sniffed near my arm and grimaced before breaking into a grin. "I will!"

Inside the lobby a waiter holding a tray of champagne flutes politely welcomed guests to the hall. I passed on the bubbly; that had been a lesson learnt.

"Are you familiar with the manor, madam?" another gentleman enquired.

"Not tonight." I smiled at him.

"Guests are currently enjoying canapés served in the drawing room, ma'am." Cool. I knew where that was.

"Would you happen to know the whereabouts of Mr Argyll?" I asked in my most ladylike voice.

"Why, am heer, darlin'!" boomed a thick Scottish accent above me. "By *God*, lass, you turn out well with ah bit ah

spit ahn polish." I'd seen enough of Fergal lately that I wasn't
unnerved by his kilt, despite my previous encounter with it.

He greeted me with an affectionate kiss on the cheek, bristling me with closely cropped whiskers.

"Hello, Fergie. You look handsome tonight."

Fergal held his arm out and led me through to the other
guests, swiping a glass of champagne on the way.

"Am glad yeh came, lass. The boy'll be pleased ta see yeh."

"Thanks, Fergal. I'll be glad to see him, too."

Fergal crossed the hallway with an air of regality, smiling the whole run until he brought us to a standstill just shy
of the drawing room. "My son's a good lad, Holly. People
dinnae realise, and they should. I'm glad he found yeh when
he did, lass."

I wasn't sure what to read in the lines of Fergal's face, but I
had to stop myself from falling into eyes that burned as deeply
brown as his son's. Sometimes, there weren't any words, and
only a kiss would suffice. I perched up and kissed him lightly
just where his beard broke under skin weathered by years of
hard living.

"Shall we?" he asked. And into the fray we went.

I knew Penny would be here somewhere, swanning around,
marking her territory. But I didn't care. The drawing room
opened out into the next room and under the stateliness of
the surroundings some two hundred guests in exquisite evening wear and dinner suits diluted the fascination of any one
person. You would have had to be a royal to stand out from
this crowd. Royal, or wearing the only other kilt in the room.

Through the crowd of trousers and gowns, I caught my first
glimpse of the finest pair of legs I'd see all night.

The tan of Ciaran's skin sat handsomely against the deepest
grey of his shirt collar, with waistcoat and jacket in matching

graphite tone. Argyll tartan was a subtle affair, predominantly a deep muted blue set almost indecipherably over more graphite. I'd wanted to take more of his outfit in, but I couldn't keep my eyes from finding his. He was talking animatedly to two senior ladies, dressed in enough finery to buy the average home, no doubt. He brought one of their hands to his mouth, and then her friend's. He was such a charmer. I was charmed from here.

"He gets that from me," Fergal growled into my ear, leaving me to Ciaran, now making his way towards me.

I watched him stride certainly all the way to where I waited for him.

"Wow," he said, placing his hand at my waist, grazing his thumb over the detailing of the sash there. I was going to kiss Martha again when I got home.

"I like your sporran." I grinned.

"I like your everything," he countered, leaning in to kiss my cheek. "You look beautiful, Holly."

And I was done for the night. I could spill food down myself, trip over, whatever. The look in Ciaran's eyes was what I'd most wanted from the evening, and I already had it. To tuck away and keep forever.

Ciaran introduced me to many of the women there, and they were all lovely, and when it came time for him to do his thing for Argyll Inc., he left me with Mary, who I was thrilled to see in evening wear, too. Mary sat with me at the table where place-names had us set either side to where Ciaran would be seated when he joined us.

"Will Fergal be on this table, too?" I asked, trying not to start grabbing at all the other little cards facing away from me.

"Oh, no, dear. Fergal will be up on the top table with the representatives from the charities. He takes Grace's fundraiser very seriously," she whispered.

"Shouldn't Ciaran be up there with them?" I asked. "I know how important tonight is to him, too."

Mary gave me a mother's smile. Not *my* mother's, but *a* mother's.

"Oh, it is, but he told me that there was something else very important he wanted to be sat next to on *this* table. You know, Holly, I shouldn't interfere but I've never seen him this way, not since…"

"Clara?" I interjected. I couldn't help it.

"Yes. Clara. Have you met her this evening?"

Suddenly, I felt as though I'd been plunged into an ice bucket.

"Clara's here? Now?" I asked, surveying the pockets of people around us.

"Don't worry, dear. That's all done with. But it was important that the Sawyers were here tonight. I heard Ciaran telling his father as much. And, James Sawyer is a swine, but he was very fond of Grace, of the care she showed for Clara when she was courting Ciaran. He'll give generously to the cause tonight and that's why we're all here, after all. He'll enjoy the free advertising it affords him, too, I expect," she said quietly.

"I didn't know that the Argylls were working with Sawyers. I thought they were rivals?"

"Oh, they are. That wound will never be healed. But there's definitely something going on. There have been a lot of heated phone calls of late between the offices. Whatever it is, it's all hush-hush. Look, there's James Sawyer now, just there…three tables from the podium, next to the gentleman with the medals on his jacket."

James Sawyer was as gaudy as his company sign. *Swine* suited him, a man who had clearly enjoyed the spoils of affluent living for a good while. Hair that couldn't possibly be still that dark by itself was slicked back from a pink shining head, thrown back with raucous laughter making sure we all knew he was in the room.

Next to him, a desert bloom by comparison, a young woman with perfectly sleek brunette hair, tumbling long over her strapless primrose gown, laughed along with him.

"Clara's lucky she's only inherited her father's dark hair," Mary said quietly, "and his money, of course. Not that she needs it. She married into a *fortune.*"

"A girl with everything, then," I said softly, trying not to admire the way she held herself. I felt my simple flat shoes curling underneath my dress under the table. I should have worn heels. *Tall is elegant*, Martha had said.

"Rumours are, things aren't going all that well for Clara. As much as I once liked the girl, as did we all, I can't bring myself to feel sorry for her."

Mary's candidness surprised me. It might have been her changed role tonight, but I hoped it was that she felt comfortable talking to me.

"Did Clara...spend much time here? When you all liked her, I mean," I asked furtively.

"Oh, yes. They were a couple for a long time. During Grace's illness, Clara supported Ciaran. Sawyer was one of Fergal's business associates back then, before things turned sour. The two families became good friends as Clara and Ciaran made their way through senior school together. To all intents and purposes Clara was Ciaran's first real girlfriend."

"So they were childhood sweethearts?" I asked. My feet were still fidgeting.

"Oh, yes. Not that Ciaran would tell you this. He doesn't like to speak about his feelings, that boy. I do worry about him," she mused. "Grace was a wonderful woman—we became good friends. I miss her terribly. Ciaran's more of a nephew to me than anything else. I've watched him go from nappies to sports cars, and I saw the change in him in those years. Everyone whispered that Ciaran started to go off track after his mother died, but it wasn't then. He was doing so well, a seventeen-year-old boy keeping watch over his father. I was so proud of the way he behaved. And then Clara abandoned him." Mary's eyes had glazed over. I'd have been compelled to comfort her had a tray of champagne not arrived next to us.

"Champagne, ladies?" I took two glasses to get rid of him before the conversation changed.

"Oh, no, I shouldn't." Mary smiled.

"No, neither should I, but I'll make a pact with you, Mary. I'll keep count of your drinks if you'll keep count of mine." I smiled at her, and she was bright and warm again.

"You're so different to girls like Clara and that horrendous Penny, Holly."

"Don't you believe it. I might have all sorts of dastardly plans up this dress."

"You're different. I see it. And so does Ciaran. I've been waiting a long time to see him like he is now. That sullenness of his lifted. Clara confused him, spoiled his view of love and affection. She was good for him—to begin with—but I always worried that Ciaran looked too much to Clara for the affection he missed from his mother. Their relationship had developed nicely and they did seem set to eventually settle down together."

"How long were they together, Mary?"

"Let me see. They were courting since around Ciaran's sixteenth birthday, and became engaged two, maybe three, years after that before Clara went off to university. Then, after Ciaran had waited faithfully for her—travelling to her at weekends and waiting for her return in each of the holidays—she finally completed her studies, came home one day and broke his heart."

I'd been stuck at university, pining for Charlie for three

years before we'd been able to move in together. I understood it wasn't the most fertile ground for a relationship to grow, but those that made it were stronger for it.

"Had she met someone else, at university?" I asked.

"Oh, yes, she'd met someone else. But not at university, the wicked girl. She dropped Ciaran like a hot rock for a boy they'd both known through school. Ciaran had waited all that time for her, to start their life together properly, keeping himself occupied earning his own money on his father's building sites while she was away. Ciaran was working his way up from all the mess of concrete and rubble, but Fergal was not well then. The company wasn't doing as it should. When Clara did return, her ideas didn't marry up with Ciaran's. While Ciaran was talking future plans, she was feeding her father inside information on Fergal's business worries. His vulnerabilities."

I looked over again at Clara, so elegant and statuesque. She was almost as beautiful as Ciaran; they must have looked incredible together.

"Could she have been trying to help them? To get her father to help Fergal, maybe?"

"James Sawyer took full advantage of information he shouldn't ever have been privy to, and made the most of business opportunities under Fergal's nose. His daughter saw Argyll Inc. as a sinking ship, and one that she was better off jumping sooner, rather than going down with later. She liked Ciaran— I'm sure of that—but not enough to sign up to a life of financial uncertainty. Not when her future husband cut a far more financially promising suitor who appealed more to her father than Ciaran did."

"That's terrible," I stammered. "How could she do that? She must have made him feel so…"

"I'll tell you how that girl made Ciaran feel. She made him feel worthless."

I wanted to find Ciaran. Not to say anything to him, but to just…hold him. Just for a minute, and then let him go on his way again. All of a sudden, I didn't feel so bad about my shoes. There were worse ones I could find myself in.

"So what did Ciaran do? When she broke the engagement?" I asked, beginning to look for him in the crowd.

"What *didn't* he do, that boy? Ciaran was a troubled young man, Holly. I think Clara had kept his grief for his mother at a manageable level. But her behaviour brought it all crashing down on him. He was so lost. Unreachable. His mum hadn't left him deliberately, of course, but Clara had. Whatever the ins and outs, on both counts love had cost him. Ciaran seemed incapable of any sort of love after that."

That wasn't the Ciaran I'd been with, watching the sunlight on the reservoir, helping me to plant an apple tree in the garden this week. But I knew now where his shadows came from, the ones that occasionally crept into his expression when he thought no one was watching.

"And now, Mary? Do you think he might be capable now?" I asked, hanging on her words.

Mary patted my hand on the table. "I hope so, Holly. He needs the right girl to teach him, though. That girl convinced him that his worth was something measurable only by his financial success. A notion that completely flew in the face of what Grace had taught him. But then, he doesn't have his mother's influence anymore, does he?"

"No. I suppose not." I knew I shouldn't ask. Mary had already told me things Ciaran had chosen not to, but learning that there was so much I hadn't known, I couldn't help but dig deeper. "Mary, I've seen things about Ciaran, in the press. He said that they rarely write anything good about him. Is that true?"

"Oh, completely!" Her voice was musical as she laughed.

"But he's only got himself to blame for most of it. Ciaran's been single for seven years, and in all that time the extent of his involvement with women has been purely sexual. I'm surprised it hasn't dropped off!" Mary's candor seemed to increase with her consumption of champagne. I felt like I'd plied her with alcohol for my own ends. "He has such a blinkered view of women now, not at all helped by the fact that he's incredibly rich and incredibly attractive, of course. He's had a steady stream of women flinging themselves at the foot of his bed for too long, which has only compounded his view of their obsession with all things material. He soon got bored with the hordes of girls following him around, and started pursuing more and more unattainable woman, much to the press's delight."

"And did he have much luck? With unattainable women?" I asked, already wishing I'd left it alone.

"Most of them have their price, Holly. That's one thing you'll see a lot of around Ciaran and his father. People with their prices. It's been so long since Ciaran's encountered a young woman with enough substance to stand up for her own ideals, I think he'd probably thought *you* were from another planet!"

"How very sad for him," I said, finding him in the far corner of the room talking to Toby, who was nibbling at a tray of canapés.

"Ciaran's a good boy, Holly. It's sad that he isn't the man he wants to be. Truly, he wants to be his mother's son again."

chapter 34

Mary's insight had both reassured and unsettled me. Reassured, because Clara could wear what the hell she liked, she'd still be a gold-digger, and unsettled because I felt bad that Ciaran had been treated so badly.

I'd left Mary after watching her drink a glass of fresh orange juice, to lessen the bubbles in her system, and had gone off in search of Ciaran. I found him on the grass outside the orangery, keeping Toby company while he smoked a cigarette. Penny was with them, too.

"Hi. I was just coming to find you," he said, turning to face me at the top of the stone steps.

"I've saved you a trip, then," I said, completely unfazed by our company. "Can I have a word?" I asked.

"Sure," he said. "I'll catch you after the speeches, Toby."

Toby nodded and sucked on his cigarette again.

"Hol, how are the armpits holding out?" Toby called after us.

"All good so far!" I grinned. My days of being awkward around Penny were over. She could scowl all she liked.

"So where are we going? Is something the matter?" Ciaran asked, following me through the gardens.

I kept on stalking over the grass, beyond where the lights from the party succumbed to the darkness of the estate, until we came to stand under the arbour. Had he have been wearing a white shirt, our position might have been given away, but there wasn't enough light here to illuminate the paleness of my forearms or any other skin on show.

"What's the matter, Holly?" he asked.

I could barely see him in the dark. I took his hands and put them over my hips. I let my own slip between the fabric of his waistcoat and the satin lining of his jacket, and stepped into him as closely as I could go. I couldn't say it. Not yet. But I could feel it, lingering there on my lips, waiting to be spoken. I pushed myself up onto tiptoes, and let him feel the words where they lay, ready to be released into the world when the time came. This kiss was my promise to him that I would never use him, or care where he bought his clothes, or leave him for a bigger number. And his promise to me? He didn't need one.

When we finally broke for air, I could just see the edge of the crooked smile I'd left there.

"That was…very agreeable." He laughed softly.

"Do we have to go back inside?" I asked, hoping for another kiss.

"Ah, I'm afraid we do. Fergal's giving his speech soon. You won't want to miss that. He's bound to offend somebody," he said drily.

"And then?" I asked, biting my lip. "Why don't we slip away? You can show me what's under that kilt." My forwardness surprised both of us. Since the bakery, we hadn't shared more than a kiss here and there, but I ached to feel his hands on me again, without the uncertainty and unexpectedness.

The uncertainty was gone. I knew how I felt about him and with everything I had I hoped he felt the same way.

"Are you trying to corrupt me, Mrs Jefferson?" he said, and it caught me off guard.

"*Holly*, I meant. I'm sorry. I should've said *Holly*." Ciaran had been caught, too.

"No, Ciaran. It's fine, really." I didn't want Ciaran to feel bad. After everything Mary had said, I didn't want him to feel bad about anything ever again. "So, slipping away? You could stay at mine, if you'd like?"

He pulled me into him again. "Why don't you stay here, with me? I haven't shown you my art collection yet."

"Come *on*...you do not collect art." I giggled.

He grabbed me under the backs of my legs and hoisted me into the air.

"Your feet are always either cold or wet. Allow me, madam," he said, carrying me back across the lawns.

Before we reached the garden off the back of the orangery, I claimed another kiss from him, just to remind him of how much I wanted us to spend the night together. Slowly he let me down to the floor.

"I'm glad you invited me here tonight, Ciaran," I said, savouring every last second of him before I had to share him again with the rest of the party.

"And I'm glad I'm wearing a sporran, or else I might have someone's eye out with what's stirring under this kilt." He grinned.

I was still cackling with laughter when we moved back through the house to sneak to our seats as the food was already starting to be served. Over the heads of people breaking into bread rolls and waiters dancing around their shoulders, Clara Sawyer watched Ciaran with interest while he held my chair out for me.

The food was better than Atlas even, and it was humbling to hear the incredible charity work so many forfeited their time and goodwill for. With unimaginable prizes, the auction alone had raised over thirty thousand pounds, which, along with the rest of the evening's proceeds, were going to be divided between Grace's three named charities, helping bereaved families, children living with cancer and medical research.

Everyone was in good spirits by the time it came to Fergal's final address of the night.

Ciaran leaned into me. "Each year, after he's said his thank-yous to everyone, Fergal nominates which of the board of directors has done the most over the year to keep him from being arrested." He smiled. "It's a bit of fun, his way of saying *thank you* and *sorry* all in one go, without getting sentimental about it."

"Sounds like a twenty-four-seven job." I smiled. "What does the nominated great one get for their trouble?"

"Nothing, just his appreciation. Which holds weight with any one of them."

The whole room listened attentively as Fergal brought us to the end of the night.

"Now then," he said assuredly, looking at his fingernails before grasping the back of his chair again. "As yeh know, each year it falls teh one person teh hold their hands up an' admit that ma ongoing freedoms—teh go about ma unconventional lifestyle with questionable integrity an' little regard—are in part, often largely, down teh them. Teh their unfaltering reliability an' steadfastness as not only ma colleague, but ma friend." I looked over to see James Sawyer, completely unperturbed at hearing all the qualities he lacked in a man. It made me cold to think of him turning the holly forest into money. "Over the years I have appointed a true gentleman, an' two not-so-gentle women, for this accolade, an' I'm glad teh see all of them present tonight."

Cordial laughter rippled across the audience. Ciaran leaned over to me and whispered, "I'll bet you eighty-two pence and a kiss that Bertie Randall gets it this year."

I shushed him and kept listening.

"But am afraid I havenae been honest with yeh, an' the time has come for me teh set the record straight." Ciaran shifted uneasily in the chair next to me. "Cancer is a wicked disease. It gets into the heart of a family, an' causes damage that cannot be cured by medicine or miracle. I couldn't help ma beloved Gracie in her fight, but shamefully I have shied away from ma own. Well. No longer."

Ciaran stood from his chair next to me, and looked across the room of attendees at his father. Clara, her father, Mary, Penny... Every face I knew had the same look of bemusement on it.

Fergal locked eyes on his son. "Sit down, boy. Let your old man finish, eh?"

Ciaran looked around himself awkwardly. Then, across the room a gentleman stood, looking over this way. Another gentleman behind the first did the same.

"Let your father speak, Ciaran," said the first, calmly. He didn't sit back down.

"Bertie's right, lad. Let him speak," echoed the second.

Behind us, a woman's voice much nearer. "Let him speak, Ciaran."

Mary leaned past me towards Ciaran's waist. "Ciaran, if the board aren't worried, you've no need to fuss," she whispered. "Sit down."

Ciaran slowly took his seat again. The jokiness in him was gone.

"My boy, everyone," Fergal said. "Who, despite my best efforts, has turned out not too badly at all."

I looked to Ciaran, the tension undulating from him, but he was fixated by his father as if Fergal were talking only to him.

"He turned thirty years of age a few weeks ago. Can you believe that? A know, a dinnae look old enough." Fergal laughed lightly to himself before the seriousness found him again. "For the last seven years, Ciaran, ma son, has shown the loyalty and tenacity of a man twice his years. As you all know, when Ciaran first made it through the builder's boot camp I inflicted on him, the company was not at its best." Like her father, Clara seemed unruffled by the reminiscence. "What yeh dinnae know, what none of you outside of ma unflinching board of directors know, is that since Ciaran was twenty-three years old, he has dedicated himself to cleaning up ma mess an' saving what we'd built up here. Ciaran, along with the directors, slowed the demise of Argyll Inc. an' grabbed it by the reins when I dinnae have it in me teh even get out of bed."

Flurries of whispers floated around us.

"It was not me who led the board in getting Argyll Inc. back on track, but ma boy."

Whispers grew into murmurs.

"He's come in for a lot of criticism, an' he's had a lot to prove. Had he have been like the rest of us, he'd have never sworn the board to secrecy to save belittling me to the rest of ma peers. He'd have enjoyed the praise he was worthy of, instead of allowing the rest of the world to regard him as some snot-nosed kid hanging on to his father's coat-tails."

Ciaran's hands were stiff against the table.

"But ma son is not *just* ma son. He's Gracie's, too…and his mother's influence still resonates inside him."

There were no whispers, no murmurs now, but Clara at least looked less comfortable.

"Ciaran, you are true of heart. You have galvanized Argyll Inc. Son, you've galvanized me. But it's time that you took your rightful place at the helm. Not standing in the shadows so that a can save face, but driving the family business. The business a started, and you're going teh continue pushing forward."

Mary was dabbing her eyes with one of the napkins. Ciaran had gone quite still next to me.

"Son, there isnee an award big enough fer what you've done fer me. So am giving you what you've earned. I'm giving you the company."

Mary's whimpers grew, and from behind me somewhere another woman began to sniffle.

"Would you all stand with me now an' raise a glass, in toasting the new CEO of Argyll Inc., ma son! Ciaran Argyll!"

I just caught sight of Penny, a furious pout on her face before the people between us stood, blocking her nicely from view. The room thundered in rapturous applause around us, and Ciaran, shell-shocked, weaved his way between handshakers and back-slappers as he tried to reach his father. My hands were aching I was clapping so hard, and on tiptoes I could just see Fergal embracing his son.

"Right then, let's get the bloody music started!" he roared over the crowd.

chapter 35

Ciaran returned to our table, eventually, where both Mary and I group-hugged him until he had to ask for us to put him down.

"I take it this means we won't be slipping away, then?" I whispered into his ear.

"Do you see all these women?" he asked, putting his head next to mine. The room did have a high proportion of older ladies. "They all want to dance with me now."

"I'll just bet they do. I mean, you have letters now and everything, Mr CEO."

"As soon as I've danced with them, we'll be slipping away, okay? I promise."

I was just so proud to be with him that I didn't mind losing Ciaran after that. Like a new bride, everybody wanted to talk to and congratulate him. He didn't need me slowing him down, so I left him to it, spending most of my time being flung around the dance floor by Fergal. That man had some energy; it was a mammoth task just to keep up. Even the flats couldn't save my feet, though. After he finally said he was going for breath, I decided to sit out in the hall in hiding before he came back.

The cool of the tiles felt good under one foot while I rubbed the ache from the other.

"So where's the golden boy?" Penny spat, waving an unlit cigarette in her fingers.

"I don't know, enjoying himself somewhere, I hope," I said, ignoring the glare peeping from beneath a sweeping platinum fringe. Black wasn't really Penny's colour. It made her look more tyrannical than usual.

"No doubt. You know, I'll bet I know where he is." She smiled, almost crossing her arms. "If you were interested?"

I wasn't going to bite.

"It's no surprise that *you* are interested, Penny. You backed the wrong horse."

Penny bit onto her bottom lip and smiled. "I've ridden both of those horses, Holly, and they're both the wrong ones."

"Save it, Penny. I'm not interested in anything you have to say. There isn't a good word in you, so go smoke your cigarette."

Toby walked in from the courtyard. "Evening, ladies. Anyone seen Ciaran? I want to know if I can knock off or not."

"You are so pathetic," Penny sneered at me. "One taste of the high life and you think you've made it."

"Made it? What do you think I'm trying to *make*, Penny? You shouldn't judge everybody by *your* standards."

"I don't." She grinned derisively. "I judge them by Clara's, and you haven't got a chance."

Penny may not have had any good words, but she always knew the words that would dig deepest.

"All right, Penny. That'll do," Toby said.

"Mind your own business, taxi driver," she hissed. "Are

you supposed to even be inside the house? You don't belong in here."

I was already standing. "You nasty piece of work, Penny—"

"And you don't belong here, either. Ciaran would have ditched you sooner if you hadn't played the poor-little-widow card." It was amazing how some people knew just what to say to make you feel physically sick right then and there. "And now Clara knows what he's worth, it won't be long before they're all loved up again. Now, where was it I saw Clara disappearing about twenty minutes ago? Ah, yes, up those stairs," she hissed, jabbing a black painted fingernail towards the landing above us. "Did you say you didn't know where Ciaran was?" she taunted. "Oh, dear, Holly, widowed again."

Penny pushed past Toby, blowing out through the doors like a storm.

"Ignore her, Holly. She's sick with jealously. She's been trying to bang Ciaran forever. He's not interested."

Toby left me to my thoughts.

I hadn't seen Ciaran for at least half an hour. *Don't bite, Holly. Don't take the bait.* I looked up through the staircase to the landing above.

I wasn't biting; I was simply going to use the upstairs bathroom. I'd been invited to stay, after all. I wasn't wandering around. I just wasn't using the same floor that the rest of the guests were using.

Okay, so I didn't actually need the bathroom, but once upstairs the bathroom I knew lay at the far end of the corridor seemed a good place to try to talk myself down. I clicked the door closed quietly, and went straight to the vanity unit to tell myself what an idiot I was being. An untrusting, ungrateful idiot who couldn't just let herself get on with it.

I looked at my reflection in the subtly tarnished mirror. I still looked pretty sharp. My hair had sagged a little, probably from Fergal's vigour, but otherwise my make-up still looked good.

Clara's glossy brunette hair had been perfect, all night hanging flawlessly over her primrose-yellow dress, until she'd disappeared, half an hour or so ago.

Don't poke holes in it, Hol. You like him. You really, really like him. Go back down to the party.

Yes, that was what I would do. Right after I'd freshened up a little.

The night was drawing to a close and, anytime soon, I was going to get Ciaran all to myself, and peel him out of that kilt. I was still smiling into the mirror when the first strained whimper came through the wall next to me. I froze over the taps, just stopping short of setting them to flow.

Another frantic whimper, then *thud, thud, thud.*

I knew it wasn't Penny.

The distinctive grunts and groans of sex became clearer with every cry she made, but he, whoever he was, was a quiet lover.

Silently, I let myself out of the bathroom and followed the wall around to the left, to the room I could hear for certain was where they were having sex. Just a few lamps on tables kept the first floor in subdued light, but I could see that the door was slightly ajar.

It smelled of flowers outside of these rooms. Mary must have had them all freshly dressed for the party, in case anyone was to stay over. I shuffled along the wall, and stumbled on the soft mound of fabric.

I thought it was a yellow blanket at first, but blankets didn't come in silk and chiffon, unzipped so that their wearer could slip effortlessly from them. My heart started to thud in my mouth.

"Yes, yes!" she cried. I held my breath. "Ooh, yes. That's it, there…"

I watched the floor now, in case I staggered on anything else, but at sight of Ciaran's kilt and jacket on the floor, my feet simply wouldn't go any further.

"Oh! That feels…so…good! Yes! Harder, harder…"

I felt dizzy. Her body, thudding against the wall, mimicked the pulse jumping in my neck. I was going to faint.

"Holly? Are you looking for Ciaran?" I spun my head around to see Mary at the end of the hall.

Panicked interruption in the room behind me and the door that had been ajar slammed shut on us. Mary's smile had dropped when I turned back to her, then she, too, saw Clara's and Ciaran's clothes strewn on the floor.

"Oh, dear," she said, her face gone ashen.

The tears were coming. *No, no tears!*

The corridor seemed to have grown in length when I ran past Mary for the head of the stairs. I skipped down them and yanked open the heavy wooden door.

The rain had started again outside; Penny was chain-smoking in the vestibule. I ran out past her.

"'Bye, Holly."

Out across the courtyard, towards the walled entrance.

"Holly?" Toby shouted. "Where are you going?"

I kept on running. I needed to get out of here *now*.

"Holly?"

I'd nearly made it across the courtyard when Toby backed the car all the way out until it sat between me and the wall pillars. He ran the window down. "Holly? What's happening? Where are you going?"

"Home." I shivered.

"Home?" I moved to walk around the car, and he jumped out then. "Hang on. What's happened?"

I started snivelling against the imminent explosion of cry-ing. "All right, Holly, all right. Do you want me to take you home?" he asked.

"Yes, please," I managed as the first tears began to fall.

"Holly?" Ciaran crowed from the steps where Penny now stood, risking the rain for a better view. He'd managed to get his kilt back on but he hadn't had time for the jacket and waistcoat.

I scurried into the back of Toby's car, and tried to hold myself together as he pulled forward again to swing the car around.

Ciaran dashed out in front of us and Toby stopped for him. Through Toby's open window Ciaran called to me. "Holly, where are you going?"

"Go away, Ciaran! Leave me alone!"

"What? *Holly?*"

"Toby, drive!" I said.

"Holly? Have you gone mad?"

"Toby, if you don't drive, I'll walk, damn it!" Although I didn't sound so convincing snivelling between words.

"Look, mate, let me run her home, then you can call her, okay? I'm just going to take her," Toby said, pulling the car away.

"Holly!" Ciaran shouted.

"*Drive*, Toby!"

"I'm driving! I'm driving! Blimey."

Toby flicked the wipers on and their rhythmical *schlumping* sound masked my fitful sobs in the back.

You stupid girl. You stupid, stupid girl.

We'd been travelling in thick silence for nearly ten minutes when Toby broke the quiet.

"I hope you're ready to kiss and make up, 'cos those look like Aston Martin headlights behind us."

Ciaran was on the hill behind, closing the distance.

"Ignore him, Toby. Once we're through the forest, he'll get bored," I said.

"Then you don't know *Ciaran* very well," he muttered.

"Isn't he drunk? He shouldn't even be driving," I snapped.

"Ciaran never drinks more than a glass. Haven't you noticed that?" he said.

I hadn't noticed that, no.

It was no darker under the canopy of fir trees as we cruised into the forest. Everything was just black everywhere. Black and wet.

I ignored Ciaran, who was now hanging back several car lengths behind.

"He'll wait now until I drop you at the cottage, in case he distracts my driving," Toby said.

He put his main beam on, lighting up the entrance to the forestry commission.

The speed monitor flashed. We were doing the forty limit. I wanted Toby to go faster, but didn't ask.

"Did you see that?" he said, shifting the lights from full beam to half and back again.

"See what?"

I looked up through the motion of the wipers in time to see a doe, just standing there in the middle of the headlights, right ahead in the road.

"*Shit!*" Toby slammed the brakes on, sending the car skidding over to the right of the deer as she bolted for the trees. We came to a halt just in time to see the silhouette of three or four more deer leaping from the embankment across the road behind us, their forms lit brightly by Ciaran's growing headlights.

A second screech of wet wheels and, in the shining beams

of Ciaran's car, I saw the explosion of his windscreen, splintering into a thousand twinkling fragments across the road.

The last thing I heard was screaming.

chapter 36

Follow the red arrows, they said.

Not green, the colour of new babies. Or white, the colour of loved ones gone before they'd arrived.

Red. Like the colour that glistened on Ciaran's roof as the stag suffered its last there.

Follow the red arrows when they finally came to tell us that he was badly concussed, but had been very, very lucky.

Mary had already visited with Fergal. Toby had got through to her while she was tearing a strip off Fergal after catching him at it with Clara in one of the bedrooms. While Ciaran slept, his father told him he'd found her wandering around near the bedrooms, probably looking for someone else, and had taken that as a direct invitation to thank James Sawyer once again for attending. To show he had no *hard* feelings to-wards them.

He was shameless, but I couldn't bring myself to frown on anything that had killed two gold-diggers with one stone. Besides, I was hardly whiter than white.

And what would my comeuppance be? I was an imposter here. I had no right.

But I couldn't leave.

I'd been here all night, watching him, waiting for him to at least groan, or wake up even and tell me to leave. But there were only the sounds of monitors, bleeping away the hours. There were none of these sounds when I'd been at the hospital with Charlie.

Just nothingness.

I moved around the bed to look at his face again. The airbag had taken most of the force from the front, but the deer had impacted the roof just over Ciaran's head. He'd had only one gash, two inches long, up into his hairline. It had bled so much, I'd thought he'd been killed. The glass everywhere, the blood…all over again.

Toby said I'd started to have a panic attack, which was when the paramedic had given me oxygen at the side of the road.

All that blood from a single cut. It had been stitched, but he'd have a good headache when he finally woke up.

I traced the line of his eyebrow where the last cut I'd caused him still shined a little pink.

"I'm sorry," I whispered. But it was so inadequate. I'd messed up. I'd poked my finger in it until it popped. He would wake up, and it all would be over.

I slipped my fingers around his.

"But first you have to wake up, Ciaran," I said in a tiny voice. "Wake up and tell me to go, back to my life with Dave. Where there's never any laughter, or fighting or fun. Where your crazy father doesn't rub me with his beard and Mary doesn't warm me with her kindness. And you. Where you don't give me butterflies in my stomach, and make me feel as though I could fall all the way to the bottom of your eyes. Tell me to go back to all that, Ciaran," I whispered, "and I will. I'll go because I know how extraordinarily lucky I was to have found you, and that I can't expect to get to keep you as well. Wake up, Ciaran. Wake up and tell me to go back to that life...where I didn't love you."

The night sky was beginning to soften through the blinds. It would be morning soon. I'd leave before he had any visitors, probably for the last time. I kicked off my ballerina pumps and tucked myself into the chair beside Ciaran's bed, drifting off for a few hours' sleep before the dawn.

There was more commotion out on the ward when I woke up again. It took me a few seconds to place where I was. I turned my head to check on him and was met by those beautiful brown eyes. I watched him for a few seconds, not sure that he was okay, then the eyes began to smile at me.

"Cold feet?" he asked, looking at my shoes discarded on the floor.

"Never."

chapter 37

Ciaran and I haven't moved in together. Not yet, anyway. Although now the shop has really taken off, thanks no end to Jesse's new girlfriend, Nat, Ciaran seems to be at the cottage more than I am. He likes to watch the sun on the reservoir. It brings him peace between the chaos of his work commitments, which in the last few months have gone through the roof since work started on the new super-development.

Argyll Inc.'s successful bid on the Lux Foundation land was granted on Ciaran's proposals to include a state-of-the-art cancer-research facility as part of the land development there, in Grace's name of course, with all construction work to be, most generously, funded by the company. This was understandably welcomed by the trustees, and once Ciaran had made the proposal there was no way James Sawyer could compete with a counter-offer. By his own admission the man isn't in the market to make money just so that he can give it all away again.

Ciaran's still deciding what to do with the smaller pocket of land the trust sold him. He said the site isn't so great but there's still money to be made so close to the intended infrastructure.

Rumour has it that James Sawyer has been hoping to get in on that action, but Ciaran's playing it all close to his chest.

When he's not giving the Sawyers the brush-off, he's running around after Fergal, who, despite the occasional slip, finally appears to be calming down. He's been spending more time with Mary now that he's not at the offices, pretending to work. She has a sobering effect on him and, let's face it, his behaviour can't surprise her. Between the Argyll boys, Mary's already seen it all.

Ciaran's formed a new friendship, too. He and Mrs Hedley seem to both benefit from each other's company. I think she has a little crush on him, but so long as he doesn't disappear around there for too many meals, I'm letting them get on with their love affair in peace. Mrs Hedley keeps him in eggs and soldiers, and Ciaran keeps her in tulips, and like most unconventional relationships, it works.

She's suggested he rig Daisy a swing in the garden. Ciaran's planning on tying it in the apple tree we planted for Charlie, although I think Daisy will be dating by the time the tree's grown enough. Rob says that Daisy won't be dating until she's forty, though, at least, so we'll see.

We'll measure her up when we get back there later. Ciaran's dragged us all out for a walk over the forest. I drove, of course, seeing as of the two of us, I'm the only one who *hasn't* driven into an animal the size of an armchair.

Ciaran also insisted that at least one of us has a flashy sports car to show off in, and we couldn't all fit in that. He has the sports car, obviously. I have whatever people carrier it is that I've got...something shiny, and *very* comfortable to drive. But he's on a ban now—no more unauthorized spending. I do miss my little burgundy van, but it has its own parking permit now, and lives outside the front of the shop. It's cute advertising and catches attention, just as Charlie said it would.

Nothing, however, catches quite so much attention as our troop, battling for order in the visitor centre car park.

"Martha, are we taking the full pushchair, or just clipping the car seat on top?" Rob called as Martha trudged for the ticket machine.

"Daisy's car seat, Rob! So Dave can't slobber all over her outfit again!"

"No slobbering on Daisy's outfit, Dave." Ciaran laughed, holding steadily on to Dave's lead. It was easy to steal a kiss when Dave was anchoring him to the spot.

"You taste of egg and soldiers!" I laughed, snuggling under his free arm.

"What can I say? My other girl treats me like a king."

"Fergal! That's someone else's car bonnet you're sitting on! Stand up!" Mary scolded, pulling Fergal up by his jacket collar.

"You're not cold, are you, Fergie?" I asked. "It's a lovely April morning!"

Fergal stood scowling at Mary next to him. "Aye, but am getting frostbite from Mary's cruelty. She's a cold woman," he said, before cuddling her into him affectionately.

"Right then," Ciaran said, locking the car, "are we all set? Has someone got the cake?"

"Check!" called Rob, feeding the white box into the bottom of the pram. There was something weird about making your own birthday cake, so Ciaran had got Jess to do it. I'd already peeked—it was a simple cake, star on top with my name and twenty-eight. So no big upset if Dave got at it before we did. I wasn't sure where that was going to be, though—we were walking away from the picnic tables. It was a balmy day, but it wasn't warm enough to pitch on the floor of the forest, even for chocolate cake. But, Ciaran was adamant that we go for a walk on my birthday, together, as a family.

We hadn't been here for almost six months. It had upset me

the last time, seeing all those fence panels claiming the woods as their own. I wasn't looking forward to seeing them again today, or worse, the eyesores Ciaran said Sawyers' would have built here by now. I was trying not to think about it, but when we rounded the path there was nowhere else to look than at the hideous teal panels.

"Why don't we go on up through the birch forest?" I asked hopefully.

"Because there's nowhere to eat cake up there," Ciaran said, drawing us all to a standstill. "And I have something to give you, and it's too big to carry all the way over there," he said, grinning.

"Come on, boy, get on with it. A want some of that cake!" Fergal scoffed.

"Yeah, thanks, Dad. That really sets the mood, cheers."

"Get on with what?" I asked him, recognising the shiftiness in his eyes. I looked behind me at Martha.

"Don't ask me—he wouldn't tell us anything. You're so guarded, Ciaran." She scowled.

"Right. Can I have everyone, bar Holly over there, by the bracken, please?" As was often the case, everyone did as he asked. Ciaran, content with our merry men's position, turned back to me.

"Holly…I've brought you here today, with our family, to ask you something…."

I felt my eyes widen.

I can't believe it! Not yet—it's too soon! I never thought that he would do this, here. But then, why not here? Here would be perfect, in a way…but not under the Sold sign on the holly forest, surely, and—

"No!" Ciaran said abruptly. "I can see your brain ticking, Holly. It's not that! Not *yet*, anyway."

I took a deep breath of relief and let it out slowly. *Not yet, anyway* sounded about perfect to me.

"What I wanted to ask you was if you'd like to come to Hollywood with me? I know we spoke about it once, and you said you wouldn't be impressed by all that. That you weren't even sure it existed, remember? That *Hollywood* would have to come to you?"

Fergal raised his eyebrows at that.

"In my defence, I was drunk at the time of that particular conversation. But *Hollywood*? Wow, Ciaran, that's quite a gift."

"Well? Will you come, then?"

"Er…when?" I asked, stunned.

"Now," he said, smiling at me. "Right now."

"Right now? As in *now* now? I can't, Ciaran…. I have work, and Dave and—"

Ciaran stood grinning at me. "Holly, I want you to close your eyes."

What was he up to? It was going to be a helicopter, or something equally outrageous swinging in to take us to the airport. I did as I was told and closed my eyes tightly.

"Take it away, boys!" he called, and from behind the fence I heard machinery thrum to life. Something tall and loud began to bleep over our heads, then the juddering of timber on metal, and dragging through the earth. A minute or so later and the machine engines all died away.

Martha whispered to herself, "Oh, Holly."

"Right, Holly, before you open your eyes, I want you to know that technically this is a birthday present, and not unauthorized spending." Eyes still tight shut, Ciaran planted a soft kiss on my mouth and whispered to me, "I know how much this meant to him, Holly. And now you can rest easy that it came to be. Happy birthday, darlin'. Open your eyes."

Beyond the missing fence panel in front of me was a mini-utopia, nestled in between the holly trees, still in there, untouched by Sawyers. A long cabinlike structure with a play area and greenhouses, a rope bridge, a firepit, a totem pole, chunky timber tables and benches. It was unbelievable. It looked like a holiday resort, but of the forest. Clean and natural and wholesome.

"The classrooms can take forty children if it rains. There's a second cabin through the trees. Toilets and kitchen facilities are around there, too."

I couldn't believe what I was seeing.

"But? But how? How has this happened?" I asked, staggering into the transformed woodland.

"Sawyer wanted some of the Lux site. I wanted this. I took him and Clara to lunch at Atlas the day after we'd won the Lux bid. I knew it was best to get in with Sawyer before he had too much time to think of terms."

I couldn't take it all in. "I don't know what to say, Ciaran. It's incredible, what you've done here."

"I did the easy bit, Holly. Charlie did all the negotiating. This couldn't have gone ahead without his vision."

"Thank you, Ciaran. *So much*," I said, holding back the deluge I could feel rising in my chest.

"Never mind that. You can thank me later," he said mischievously. "Now, what do you think of that sign up there?"

I looked up into the trees, at the great big star seemingly held suspended in the air. I recognised the depiction immediately.

"I love it, Ciaran. It's perfect. Everything is perfect."

And it was perfect.

"Let's eat cake!" Fergal cried, dancing in through the entrance with Daisy in his arms. Mary kissed Ciaran and followed Fergal in, Rob wheeled past with the pram in one hand, trying to keep Dave out of the cake with the other, and Martha walked by us, squeezing my arm on the way.

"Are you coming in?" Ciaran asked. "Fergie won't save you any just because it's your birthday." He smiled.

"I'm coming. I just want to look at the sign for a minute," I said, shooing him in.

I watched Ciaran go to join the others in the cabin and read the words to myself again.

Holly Wood Forest School—Where Futures Grow

★ ★ ★ ★ ★